Rosemary

ROSETTA SMITH

BOOK PUBLISHERS NETWORK
Changing the World One Book at a Time

Book Publishers Network
P.O. Box 2256
Bothell • WA • 98041
PH • 425-483-3040
www.bookpublishersnetwork.com

10 9 8 7 6 5 4 3 2 1

Printed in the United States of America

LCCN 2018958108
ISBN   978-1-948963-14-5

Editor: Julie Scandora
Cover designer: Laura Zugzda
Typographer: Melissa Vail Coffman

To my loving partner, Maine.

Prologue

ROSEMARY GAVE CARTER a quick hug, and finally faced Mary Lou, dreading their farewell. They grasped each other in a loving hug.

"Take care of yourself and keep in touch. We'll miss you so much," her friend said to her with static emotion.

"I will. Thanks! Thanks for everything!" There were no more words to be said. With tears filling her eyes, she quickly picked up her carry-on and turned away from the couple. Turning one last time to glance over her shoulder, she lifted her hand in a farewell wave as she entered the enclosed walkway to her plane. Tears swam in her eyes as she left her friends, the McCoys, behind. Rosemary would always owe them for her sanity and for allowing her to stay with them when she was desperately in need. It had been an ugly time of terrible sorrow and agony in her life, and she did not know what she would have done without the two of them.

Rosemary found her seat by the window, stowing her carry-on above the seat in front of her and settled in for the trip back to Washington State. She did not know what she would find. Her life had already been changed so much, and now it was about to change again. Would she ever find peace?

A white-haired gentleman claimed the seat next to hers after placing his baggage in the compartment above them. He smiled as he took his place, saying a warm hello. She murmured a greeting in response but quickly turned her head to look out the window. Rosemary was in no mood to talk. She just needed to meditate and think about her next steps. In Seattle, she would have to stay over and buy a car before driving to the coast. She hoped the weather was nice when she arrived.

When the plane began to taxi slowly on to the runway, she was deep in thought about the things that had happened to her in the past year or so. Like it or not, Rosemary was on her way.

⬗

Sometimes our riches are not what they seem. Many times, what we wish for lies beneath our very noses. Life can hand out enormous sorrows, seemingly more to one person than another. Such is the life of Rosemary Reegan. Her life is but one struggle after another. She must meet each one head on and finally decide what is most important to her.

Chapter One

ROSEMARY STEPPED OUT on to the old, deteriorating back porch that faced west towards the bay and took a deep breath of fresh, ocean air. On the other side of the house, the sun was rising behind the old weather-washed cabin, its rays just beginning to reach the ground fog that almost hid the shallow water ahead of her. The fog swirled around slowly, creating denseness in one spot and then thinning in another. It was a hazy dream world of odd shapes of nothingness, a world of fluff and haze appearing like a mirage, or like looking out on a landscape of some foreign planet. As she stood gazing out at the surreal scene, she took in another gulping lung full of the clean, moist, ocean air, sighed, and then stepped down the few stairs to the ground and headed into the fog on the sandy beach.

It was her first morning back, and as she walked, she experienced a deep pleasure at looking back to yesteryear. Rosemary felt the stress leaving her body as if it was peeling away layer by layer. How had she forgotten the peaceful and calming sounds of the big ocean? She could hear the roar of the incoming waves out beyond the little inlet, maybe a half a mile away. It was where one could dig clams when the tide was low, but if you waited too long and high tide came in, you might be stuck out there for a while or have to swim back through the low places where the ocean water had accumulated. That had happened to her several times. Why had she wanted to leave this in the first place? It was a haven, a healing place! Truly, she had forgotten.

Although she hadn't lived in this particular spot, her parents had always resided somewhere near the beach area. She had grown up not far away in the little town of Grayland.

Her feet sank into the loose, soft sand, and she swung her arms as she picked up momentum. In a few minutes as she warmed up her joints, she turned her walk into an easy jog along the water's edge. It felt wonderful to be back.

The fog had nearly dissipated, and the sun was up and warming enough on her return trip that she stripped off her sweatshirt and tied it around her waist. Perspiration began forming under her arms and along her forehead. She tingled with a new sensation of being alive for the first time in a long while. Maybe she would finally be able to see a definite tomorrow and some kind of a future for herself.

Her almost seventy-six-year-old father was eating his regular breakfast of Bran Buds cereal and his allotted one-cup-a-day morning coffee when she returned. His health had slipped over the winter, but spring had come early with a gentle mildness to make up for the long winter weather of gloomy clouds and rainy days, and he had perked up a little. Some rather warm, sunny days had preceded this early, beautiful day in June. The days were beginning to move forward to a long-awaited summer and some good weather. Now that his much-loved and only daughter was home, he was in the best of spirits and feeling much better. Her presence was a medicine not to be found in any pharmacy.

She had arrived just the day before, and her father had an inkling she just might stay around for a while. Matt Reegan was happy his daughter's divorce from pretty boy Jeffrey Archer was final at last after seventeen years of turmoil. He didn't know that much about it because she kept it all locked inside, but he did know it had been painful and was glad that chapter of her life was over.

He'd always worried about his little girl, knowing things were happening in her life that he couldn't help her with, but now maybe, he would be able to do that. There had not been much chance yet to talk about her plans, but what a delight it was to have her home!

"Hi, Pop! Up and at 'em already?" She leaned over and kissed him on his rough, rosy cheek. "What you got planned for your day?"

"Not a damn thing 'cept maybe take my favorite daughter to lunch. That okay with you?"

"Sure! I'd love it."

Matt grinned as he watched her pour herself a cup of coffee from his old percolator on the counter. He still thought of her as his baby girl, although she was thirty-seven. What a beautiful woman she'd grown up to be. She seemed a lot thinner now than when he'd seen her the last time. She looked healthy but a little pale, perhaps from lack of being out in the sunlight. That would change if she stayed with him awhile. He knew how much she used to enjoy the beach and being outside.

She looked so much like her mother with her heart-shaped face and her tawny-colored hair, its blond strands standing out like sun-kissed wheat. However, she was taller than her mother had been by a few inches. He remembered how she had grown another couple of inches after she'd finished high school. Her height was somewhere in between his six feet and Louise's short five-foot-three-inch frame. Something like five foot seven inches, a nice height for a woman.

And like her mother, Rosemary's childhood dimples were still prominent when she smiled. She also looked much younger now with her contacts and no longer wearing eyeglasses. She was beginning to look a lot more like David. He was also fair-skinned with light hair, just the opposite of Matt and his second son. Both Matt and Daniel had gotten their darker coloring from Matt's mother's side of the family.

Rosemary sat down in the chair across from her father, and as he finished his breakfast, she studied his face. It was lined and weathered from years of working outdoors, but he was still quite a handsome man, and his leathered, old face gave him character, a character everyone respected and loved. His once dark hair had turned almost snow-white, actually adding to his good looks and making him appear younger, rather than aging him. The whiteness had not extended to his dark mustache, except for only a few noticeable strands. She'd always loved the way his mustache tickled her face when she was a kid. He'd kiss her and then tease her with it. He'd been such a dear person in her life. She'd let too many years slip by for all the wrong reasons. And he did look tired.

She and her father had been as close as any father and daughter could be. Rosemary got on well with both of her parents, but her father was special, perhaps because he'd spoiled her a little after raising two rowdy sons and because she'd come along so late in their lives. He and Louise were already in their late thirties when she was conceived. She turned out to be their pride and joy from the very beginning of her arrival. As she grew, her father was always praising her for something, and because of it, she had a high self-esteem of herself as a child. She lost much of that confidence in herself after she'd married Jeffrey.

Even though Rosemary was an unplanned baby, Matt absolutely cherished her. He doted on her and took her with him almost every-place he went. She was used to him saying, "You're Poppa's princess" or "You're going to grow up, Princess, and do your poppa proud." He was especially pleased and praising when she brought home good grades from school.

Rosemary was a writer at an early age. She loved to do essays and write short stories beginning way back in elementary school. Throughout her school days and on into high school, her father was her biggest fan and supported her in her writing endeavors. He would read her work and critique it for her. Matt talked about her going to college from the time she could remember. Financially, he wasn't able to send his boys, but he was going to make sure his daughter got the chance to further her education. Rosemary never doubted that she would go on to college. She had a deep desire to earn her degree and go on with her writing endeavors. However, she wanted it for her parents as much as for herself. They were giving her an unattainable opportunity.

She must have been a terrible disappointment for him, she couldn't help thinking as she sat across from him at the table. *I really let him down.* However, he'd never complained, and she knew he loved her no less than always. What a wonderful man he was.

⤬

Matt lived most of his life in nearby towns or somewhere in the vicinity of the ocean on the coast of Washington State. His early life was spent in the small town of Aberdeen, some thirty-five to forty miles north of the Tokeland-Grayland area. Even then, he and his father would often travel to nearby Westport, a few miles north of Grayland, to fish.

In Aberdeen, he grew up, the only child of Edgar and Mabel Reegan. His father worked in one of several lumber companies, the prevailing industry in the area during that period. He worked hard and provided a fairly good life for his small family. They had a comfortable house and nice furnishings.

Matt's mother was a great cook, a practical one with her well-tended garden and all her canning and preserving of food. Matt's pals were always welcomed to the Reegan home and loved going there. It wasn't unusual to see a bunch of boys stuffing themselves full of his mother's homemade breads and tasty desserts such as apple crisps, cherry cobblers, and chocolate chip cookies by the dozens or a boy or two joining the family for a dinner of wonderful, homemade spaghetti.

Sometimes Matt was allowed to take along a friend when he and his father went on one of their fishing forays, and the lucky friend, whoever it was at the time, came home feeling great excitement about the fun he'd had with the Reegans. Matt grew to love the sport, and he would only ask those pals who, like himself, had a serious interest in fishing.

Surrounded by love and good friends, Matt grew up a happy young man. That changed shortly after his fifteenth birthday when, unexpectedly, Mabel Reegan died of pneumonia. His life was immensely transformed. It was a terrible shock to Matt and his father. Mabel contracted a virus Matt brought home from school, and while her son recuperated from his siege, she did not. The secondary infection that came with the virus took her life quickly without much warning.

Matt's father seemed to shrink from life after that. Suddenly, it was up to Matt to make sure his dad ate properly because he would often forget if not reminded. He'd go to work and put in his time, but at home, he would escape into a self-inflicted silence, usually in the privacy of his bedroom, the door closed behind him, shutting out Matt and the rest of the world.

It was difficult, but Matt managed to finish high school and receive his diploma. After graduation, he talked his father into selling the house in Aberdeen and moving to Grayland. He thought a change of environment would help snap his father back to life. There, in the tiny settlement just off the Pacific coast, they rented a small motel-like cabin, and Matt was able to get himself hired on a fishing boat.

It didn't feel like work to Matt, as he enjoyed fishing so much. The captain of the boat, Chris Toma, liked young Matt. He always made sure Matt had enough fish to take home for him and his dad to eat, and if the boats netted an overabundance of fish, Matt would be allowed to take the extra fish to the restaurants in the area. The owners would reciprocate with free meals for him and his dad and the other fisherman from the boat. It was a common and accepted practice at the time for the fishermen and restaurants to exchange fish for meals, and it worked well for both.

A new spark did seem to ignite Edgar Reegan as his son was hoping, and Matt saw that his father was beginning to enjoy the beach and its surroundings. He even went out on some of the fishing expeditions with Matt and the crew. Matt and Edgar enjoyed a renewed bonding, becoming close to each again as they'd once been.

Edgar developed a friendship with an older man his age, and on most days, they shared a walk on the beach. Matt had a couple of fishing buddies, whom he had a beer with once in a while, too. Life was good to them.

A nasty cold prevented Edgar from joining his son for dinner in Westport, as they were fond of doing a couple of times each week. He said he'd warm up some soup and Matt should call a friend and go enjoy himself. Matt tried calling a couple of his close buddies, but neither was home, so he went by himself. This was the night Matt met Louise.

She was a waitress at the Copper Kettle restaurant in Westport. With his happy-go-lucky personality and outgoing manner, Matt kidded around with her as she served him that first time. He was quite taken with her. Looking back, he'd known it was love at first sight for him.

Louise was a little thing, very petite and fair skinned with a clean and scrubbed look about her. Even with her hair pulled severely back into the hair net she was required to wear, she was very pretty. She had deep dimples on both sides of her face, heavily accentuated when she smiled, and she smiled a lot. Over the years, he would tell her many times how he fell in love with those endearing dimples before he fell in love with the rest of her.

After that night, Matt could hardly wait to see her once more. It was only a week later when he visited the restaurant again. Edgar was still recuperating, and so Matt went by himself once again. Happy his dad was feeling better but secretly glad to be going alone, Matt went to dinner at about the same time and on the same day of the week to be certain Louise would be working that evening. She was! He was nervous, to say the least, but very determined to ask her for a date.

Louise had been attracted to him also, and her eyes lit up when she saw him sit in a corner booth at the far end of the restaurant. It wasn't her table, but Louise asked the other waitress if she could take it for her. Her co-worker, Sally, gave her a knowing grin and nodded her head.

"Hi, Mr. Reegan. What'll it be tonight?"

"Please! It's Matt. Mr. Reegan sounds so old." He grinned at her and then stuttered, "Tonight, I'd like . . . tonight, I'd like . . . a date."

It startled her. She thought he was being awfully forward. To catch her breath, she asked, "What did you say?" although, of course, she'd heard him clearly.

"I'm asking for a date. How about it?"

"Well, I don't know. I don't know you. I'm not sure—"

"Louise," he interrupted, "ask anyone here on the beach. I'm an okay guy. I don't bite, and we can do something like go to my house for dinner. My dad will be there to chaperone us if it will make you feel better. You'll like him!" Then he grinned at her again. "But really, I'd prefer not to have old Dad a part of my dates."

The remark brought the barriers down; she was being silly, and she laughed out loud. "Me neither."

Louise and Matt dated for a year before he had enough money put aside to buy her a ring when he asked her to marry him. Even though she said yes, it would still be some time before they could plan a wedding.

His beloved had quit school early and taken her current job to support her mother and a younger brother when she was just sixteen. Louise had worked a variety of jobs even before then, starting when she was about twelve, like babysitting, cleaning houses, picking berries, and selling them. Whatever she could find. She had grown up very early through necessity and seemed older than she was.

Matt's hope was to be able to support her so she could stay home and not have to work any longer. Another year or so would go by before they could see their way clear to get married. By that time, her brother had graduated from high school and was going into the service. Her mom had moved in with a close friend to share expenses, so Louise's obligation to her family had lessened.

He was twenty-two and Louise was barely nineteen when their small church wedding took place in February of 1945 with her mother and his father standing in as their witnesses, a nice touch for the young couple to have the support of their single parents.

Louise and Matt lived in several places in and around Westport and Grayland until 1983 when he retired from fishing. Rosemary had quit college to get married the year before, and although her parents were greatly disappointed, they welcomed not having that crushing expense anymore. It was then that they sold their small modest home in Grayland and moved a little further south to the small village of Tokeland, just on the other side of the Shoalwater Bay Indian Reservation.

Matt continued to work at the fish canneries in both Westport and Tokeland during good fishing seasons, sometimes just to fill in, but he and Louise decided to take it easier and maybe travel a bit. In Tokeland, they purchased the small beach cabin he now lived in. Plans were made to remodel it, add on to the structure, and enjoy their retirement days. However, shortly after their move, Louise became ill, and their nest egg of money disappeared with massive medical bills, much of them not covered by insurance. After a year of dealing with her stomach cancer, Louise succumbed to the disease. Like his dad before him, Matt lost the only woman he'd ever loved, and it was so difficult to go on without her.

❧

Many deep lines of loneliness were etched in her father's face Rosemary noticed. It had been a terrible blow for him to lose her mother. They were one of the few genuine loving couples known to her. She'd never heard them argue or get angry at each other. It didn't seem fair that her mom had to die so early.

Her dad had worked so hard to give her mother and his family everything. Rosemary truly realized for the first time that she'd never fully appreciated what it must have taken to raise her brothers and her, how difficult it must have been to save the money he'd spent to send her to college almost eighteen years before. She'd wasted it, hadn't she, and for what? For a long unhealthy marriage, dead before it had begun. That's what! How could she have done that to him? Her two older brothers hadn't been able to even think about college. There just wasn't enough money then. But they gave her that opportunity, and she had squandered the chance by not finishing college and not earning her degree. She felt so sorry for the grief she'd caused them and would always carry that guilt. Why had she not come home more often? If only she could do it all over again.

While she sat at the table drinking the last dregs of her coffee and with these thoughts rushing through her mind, Rosemary coupled her thoughts with that of her brothers whom she really didn't know very well. She was so young when they left home.

David, the Reegans' firstborn, was nearly fifteen years Rosemary's senior, born a couple of years after their parents married. He'd gone on to make a career out of the air force after high school. Now after thirty-plus years, he was retiring as a lieutenant colonel. This event was to occur in another month or so. He was stationed in Alabama, and she hadn't seen him since 1984 when they had all been home for their mother's funeral service. Rosemary would like to take her father to the retirement party her sister-in-law would, no doubt, have for David, but Rosemary feared that her father wasn't strong enough to handle the plane trip and decided not to bring up the subject.

Her youngest brother, Danny, had come home from Memphis for their mom's funeral, too. It certainly hadn't been a very pleasant time. When she thought about it at all, it brought tears to her eyes. Her now ex-husband, Jeffrey, had unwillingly come home with her. She was sure he thought her family was beneath him. How she wished afterwards that she hadn't talked him into accompanying her. After the funeral and during their short stay, Jeffrey had been at his worst; in fact, he had acted like a child. He had Rosemary jumping through hoops the entire time. *Get me this! Get me that! Rosemary, do this! Rosemary, do that!* She knew he was just showing off, but it embarrassed her in front of her family. He wasn't the greatest person in the world to live with, but he didn't act quite that badly at home. Maybe it was because he was gone so much of the time that she hadn't noticed how demeaning he could be.

He pursued his childish behavior with a vengeance towards her, while literally ignoring her family. Although Rosemary was thoroughly humiliated, she refused to start any arguments with him for her family to witness. She desperately tried smoothing things over and attempted to keep her cool. It was a very stressful time for her. But her family clearly saw what Jeffrey was doing, and her placating him did nothing to ease the situation in the family's eyes.

❧

Danny, who was ten years older than Rosemary, couldn't stand his brother-in-law and, after the funeral, finally had had enough. He shouted at Jeffrey, "Why don't you do some things for yourself, man? The woman has just lost her mother, for God's sake."

The two men proceeded to get into a terrible argument, and if David hadn't pulled them away from each other, it is very likely they would have had a physical encounter right then and there. Jeffrey became very agitated; he turned around and yelled at Rosemary to get her things packed. Before she realized it, they were leaving. Her father put his arm around her as she tearfully moved towards the door to follow her husband.

"Why don't you stay, Rosemary, and go home later?"

Wiping away the beginning of tears and trying not to cry, she shook her head.

"Are you sure, honey?" Quietly, he asked her the question that had been on his mind for some time. "Does he mistreat you at home?"

She shook her head, then kissed him, and turned away.

He grabbed her arm and whispered in her ear, "Come home if things get out of hand, and let me know how you are. I'll be worrying about you."

"I'll be okay, Pop. I love you," she said, not looking at him, as she once again headed to the door. She held back her tears of anguish. She didn't want to leave, but she had to go home and see if she could straighten out some of her marriage issues.

David had already said goodbye to Rosemary and remained in the kitchen.

Danny, who was standing by the door, reached out, caught her by the shoulder, turned her around to him, and hugged her tightly. "Why do you let that man treat you like shit, Rosemary? He's such a complete ass. You deserve better."

She couldn't hold back. The tears began flowing down her face, and she swiped at them again as she tried to explain, "It's not easy, Danny. After you've been married awhile you . . . I . . . I'm just sorry my family had to be part of this. I . . . I have to go." Rosemary pulled away from her dear brother, continued on to the car, and heard his last words without acknowledging them.

"Well, don't bring him around me again. I don't care if I ever see the damn jerk again." Then Danny turned and walked back into the house.

Her father stood on the porch long after the car had disappeared around the corner. His heart ached for his only daughter. His baby! He felt such sadness, both for his profound grief at the loss of his beloved Louise and for his daughter's pain.

❧

Rosemary, deep in thought for a few minutes as she relived the past, suddenly jerked and quickly came back to the present when her father asked her, "Feel like talking, honey?"

"Sure, Pop. It's so good to be with you again. Will you let me stay for a while?" She paused briefly, her father's head already nodding yes, and then she said, "Maybe longer than a while!"

"It's not much of a place, Princess. Never did get it fixed up like I wanted. After your mom passed away, I didn't see much sense in spending the money. But you're welcome to stay for as long as you like. I'm sure you know that."

She smiled at him, reached over, and patted his rough hand, callused from a lifetime of honest, hard work. "I'm not sure about anything, but for now I need to land some place and get my head on straight before I make any decisions for the rest of my life. My choices for the first part weren't so wonderful."

Matt opened his mouth to dispute her statement.

But before he could say anything she changed the subject. "The air smells so sweet and clean here, and I feel relaxed and at home."

"That's good, Rosemary! That's good! So happy to hear you were on your way when you called last Monday. Had no chance to buy groceries. Don't do much driving with these old eyes anymore. Have friends close by who pick up things for me now and then."

"Oh, Pop, not to worry! We'll pick up some things when YOU take ME to lunch." She got up, collected the few dishes, and carried them to the sink to wash. "By the way, I noticed some nice new homes down towards the dock." On her way in the day before, she'd just wanted to see how it all still looked, and so she had driven past her father's cabin and on down to the point to make a U-turn. She was so surprised to see the big new homes along the way, most of them situated along the waterside of the highway where the view was spectacular.

"When did you see them?"

"When I came in yesterday. I drove right down to the dock before coming here. Had to have myself a good look. Things are quite different. 'Course, it's been a long time since I was here last, but it looks like you have neighbors who might be on the prosperous side of things by the appearances of those big places."

"Yes, things tend to change when you're gone for so many years," Matt said, subtly making his point.

Rosemary looked away so her father couldn't see her making a sour face at herself and the rolling of her eyes.

It had been a long, long time, way too long, and time had a way of making many changes.

Matt went on, "And yep, those new homes are something, aren't they? They make this little place look like a shack." He laughed heartily. "Come to think of it, it is a shack." Then his voice turned sad. "Sure did want to get this place redone for your mom." Matt was quiet for a moment, and Rosemary knew he was recollecting memories of her mom. Then he spoke again with a lift to his voice this time as he remembered something. "By the way," he told her, "one of them good-looking homes belongs to someone you know."

"Oh, is that right? And who is that, pray tell?" She couldn't imagine anyone she might know who would possibly still live in this area.

Tokeland was the size of a small village, not even a town, with only an old vintage hotel that housed a homey little restaurant and a fish cannery nearby, which employed a handful of people. At one time, there had been a post office and a café at the point by the marina. The post office had been moved up towards the reservation near the main highway, so people had to drive a couple of miles to pick up their mail now, and the café went out of business. There were also a campground, the marina, and a number of fishermen around during fishing season or crabbers going out to check their crab pots.

"Remember Margie Hansen and Thomas Henderson? You used to run around with those two in school." He watched Rosemary's mouth form a little *O* as she remembered her two best friends from long ago.

Thinking about those wonderful school years, she spoke her thoughts out loud. "The three of us—Margie, Thomas, and me! Yes, we rode the school bus together every day until Thomas got his license and started driving that old beat-up car of his." She giggled as she remembered. "I didn't think that car was going to make it half the time, but it usually got us there. He was always repairing it. And the three of us in band together. Old Thomas could really beat those drums. Do you remember, Pop, the time he brought those drums over and we had a concert outside—me and my clarinet and Margie with her horn? Did we drive you and Mom crazy or what?"

"No, you made a lot of noise all right, but it didn't bother us. We called it happy noise. We never complained. You were having a good time, and we were so happy that you had good friends."

Rosemary continued to pull out her memories. "We were best friends early on, and in high school, we went to all the games together; there were so many other things we did as a threesome. And the prom!" She laughed some more. "Poor old Thomas got stuck taking me because I was stood up by my date. What a good friend he was. God, we had such good times." *They went so fast,* she thought.

She didn't know why she hadn't made more of an effort to keep in touch with either of them. Although they crossed her mind briefly from time to time, she hadn't given too much thought to her old high school days in a long while. She'd been too caught up in the ugliness of her marriage. It seemed like another lifetime. Suddenly, she yearned to see them both again. It was a refreshing thought. Were they happily married? Did they have children? Where did they live? And who had the new house at the beach that her dad was talking about?

Just then her father spoke, "Guess which one of the two owns one of them castles?" Her father grinned devilishly as he teased her.

She smiled and said she couldn't imagine.

"Ah, Margie and her husband! Would you believe it's their summer place? Can't remember her husband's name. He's some big land developer up in the Seattle area."

"Margie! You're kidding. A summer home!" She wondered what their real home looked like. "Well, good for her! Happy she's done so well. Have you seen her? How did you discover all this?"

Matt enjoyed the way his daughter's eyes lit up when she was excited about something. "She was walking past here one day a month or so ago. Recognized me first. Asked about you. But, of course, I didn't know you were coming home then. She's much slimmer than she used to be. Pretty girl."

"That is so great, Pop! I do hope I get to see her. It's been a long time. And how about Thomas Henderson? Know anything about him?"

"Oh, he's around. Got a little place over between North Cove and Grayland."

"Gosh, I'm surprised. I remember when you wrote and told me he moved away years ago and had gotten married."

Matt slowly nodded his head. "He did. Don't know what happened. He came back, maybe ten, eleven years ago. No wife with him! Never did hear whether he was divorced or what. I even fished with him a little and worked beside him at the cannery a bit, back when I was still helping them out some. Always been a nice guy."

"Yes, he was," Rosemary agreed.

"See him around occasionally. He and another guy up the line here have a business in the other guy's garage—repair engines for boats, cars, lawn mowers, that kind of stuff. Think he periodically still works at the cannery when fishing's good and they need extra help. Hasn't changed much. He's as lean as a beanpole. Always has been. Just like his Dad was, as I recall. I expect you'll see him sooner or later."

"Gosh. I can't believe he lives here. At one time he loved living in this area, loved the fishing, but as he got older, he changed his mind and became anxious to move away from the beach. Said it never really had anything to offer him." Rosemary suddenly had a great desire to see her friends again. She would make a point of looking them up. Yes, it was good to be home.

CHAPTER TWO

As ROSEMARY CAME UP THE WALK, she admired the pretty flowers planted both in the flowerbeds and in the large pots grouped together on the wide steps leading to the porch, which ran the length of house front and around the corner. Nervously, Rosemary wiped her sweaty hands on the sides of her jeans before knocking softly on the beautiful oak door. Why was she so jumpy? She guessed it was because it had been so many years. Would their friendship be the same? They had taken different paths, and there would be so many changes in both of them since last they met. She heard footsteps, and the door opened before Rosemary felt ready.

The woman standing in front of her wore a navy-blue tank top and white shorts, showing off her trim and nicely tanned legs. She was as slim as Rosemary's father indicated. Her hair was short, cut in a chic pixie formed around her head, which accentuated her small features and still beautiful skin. And while she had been a longhaired brunette as a girl, it was now cosmetically frosted, streaked with blond highlights. Although it was very becoming on her, Rosemary was stunned and felt like she was looking at a stranger. Margie looked simply wonderful, but she just didn't appear to look much like the Margie Hansen Rosemary had known during their earlier years. She stared in awe of the changes she saw in her old friend.

Rosemary's voice was shaking as she said, "Ah, Margie?" She questioned whether it was really her.

"Yes! Who? My God, Rosemary! I can't believe it's you!" In just seconds, she had her arms outstretched, and they were both crying and laughing at the same time while hugging each other for all they were worth. Nothing had changed, Rosemary realized. Nothing! She was so relieved. It was still her best friend, Margie, who embraced her ever so warmly.

"Oh, you look absolutely great. How did you get so skinny?"

Margie's lusty laugh, the same one she had in high school, thrilled Rosemary. "Finally lost my baby fat. You look great yourself, kid."

"No, I don't, Margie, but it is nice for you to say so. I was a mess when I got here a couple of weeks ago. I'm being slowly resuscitated, though. This air is so fresh, not like Cincinnati in the least. I really am beginning to feel like a new person."

"That means you're going to stay awhile, I hope. We have a lot of catching up to do." Without waiting for an answer, Margie took her friend's arm and pulled her inside. "Come on in. Let's have a drink, girl. Celebrate a reunion!"

Rosemary followed her friend down a long hallway, bypassing a big kitchen on her left and had a glimpse of a huge, lovely living room on the right. When they got to the end of the hall, she stepped into a cozy sunroom facing the water. The room was done up in country prints and white rattan furniture, with candles and flowers everywhere, all of which invited guests to make themselves at home.

"Sit!" Margie ordered. "What'll it be? Wine, soft drink, or other?"

"White wine would be good," Rosemary answered. She sat down, trying one of the rattan chairs. They had very firm and comfortable seat cushions. Nice furniture, she could tell. Expensive!

Margie turned, saying as she left the room, "I'll be right back with two glasses and white wine. One *momento!*"

While she was gone, Rosemary got up and walked to the huge windows, which were dressed with slatted wood blinds, and gazed at the pretty view of the bay. What a lovely room. *Guess it only takes money,* she thought, but she was happy for her friend who apparently had married well.

Soon Margie returned, carrying the drinks on a tray, along with slices of cheese and snack crackers. "Okay, you didn't say! Going to stick around for a while?"

Rosemary nodded her head but didn't explain further as she lifted her glass in the air and declared, "Cheers, my friend. It is so good to see you again. " They tapped their glasses together and took a sip. Then Rosemary commented, "Yes, I'm home for a while, maybe a long while. Guess you must know, I'm freshly divorced."

"Gosh no," Margie stammered, "I didn't. Your father never said anything when I saw him recently. I'm sorry! I was just going to ask about your husband."

"Well, don't be sorry! In actuality, we've been divorced emotionally for a good many years, only it wasn't legal, and I didn't do anything about it until now. I don't know how we got through all those years. It's over and I'm so glad. Oh, Margie, it feels so good to be away from it all and that big city. I hated it. The beach feels so right. Besides, my dad needs me here."

Margie nodded her head. "It's a strain when they get older, isn't it? Lost my mother in 1983. It was so hard. I had to make so many trips with her to the Virginia Mason Hospital in Seattle, and she died in spite of it all. The only good thing was I met Frank there. He's such a gem! We don't get away from Seattle often, but he knows how much I love the beach, so he built this place. For me really! I'm here much more than he can be."

"I am surprised. My mom died in '84. I didn't know you lost your mother before I did. I feel so guilty about not keeping in touch."

Margie shook her head. "It's a two-way street, you know. I let my communication skills get rusty, too. Can't believe all these years have gone by."

"Me neither. Tell me more about Frank," Rosemary inquired.

"Well, Frank Donahan is my terrific counterpart, my better half, let's say." She grinned. "I love that man so much. He's a great guy. He's rather serious most of the time, but he still knows how to have a good time. Works too hard, but his business is doing so well. That's the trade-off, you know. You run a business, you make money, but you can't always enjoy life like you want. There simply is not enough time. I hope you'll meet him soon. You'll like him." Margie took a sip of her drink, and so did Rosemary.

"Frank tries to come here as often as he can, and he doesn't mind if I come here by myself. I love the peace and quiet." As she reached for a slice of cheese and a cracker, she remarked, "You remember I was the only one of the three of us in high school who didn't want to leave the coast."

Then to clarify what she meant by the three of them, she asked Rosemary if she remembered Thomas. Rosemary nodded and opened her mouth to ask about him, but before she could, Margie changed the subject. She had so much to say.

"I'm hoping when Frank retires someday, we'll come and live here permanently or at least for half of the year. There's absolutely nothing I'd like more." Margie barely took a breath before continuing. "I met Frank at the hospital as I said. He was visiting a friend who had been in an accident at the same time Mom was having one of her treatments. We were both sitting in the waiting room, and we casually started talking to each other. I could tell right away that he was a very nice man. He told me to call him when I came to Seattle again. Said he would show me around if I had time on my hands waiting for Mom at one of her treatments. At the end when Mom was admitted to the hospital and I knew she was going to die, I did phone him. I had no one, and I remembered what he'd said. I dug through my purse and found his number. Wasn't even sure I still had it. He came right over."

Rosemary murmured, "Bless him."

"We couldn't get away from the hospital, but he came there and sat with me. It was so nice to have his support. He was with me when she died, and that meant so much to me."

"What a nice person he must be. Did you start dating right after that?"

"I went back to Seattle a couple of times, and we went out. What a time we had. I fell like a ton of bricks. He made a lot of trips down here to see me after that, too. In fact, he pursued me like a fiend. 'Course I loved it! Finally, he got so tired of driving down here he asked me to marry him. Of course, I had decided to do that the first time I met him, I think." Margie laughed with her usual gusto. "He's really super. Wait until you meet him! I consider myself quite lucky, and we're very happy. The only problems we have are his having to work all the time and the fact that we'd like to have a baby but haven't been able to get pregnant."

"I'm sorry, Margie. You'd make the best m-m-mother!" Rosemary was almost unable to get the words out. A great ball of fire started to burn deep in her stomach, and it suddenly became a giant, searing pain. It almost made her bend over. No, she couldn't talk about it yet. She just couldn't! It was best that her story waited for another time.

Noticing a grimace on Rosemary's face, Margie asked if she was okay.

"Yes, oh yes, I'm fine." Rosemary caught her breath, somewhat diminishing her pain, and quickly changed the subject. "Your house is so beautiful. No wonder you love coming here."

"Thank you, Rosemary. It may be a little sophisticated for this community, but I absolutely love it, and as I told you, I am hoping that eventually one day we will be able to spend much more of our time here."

"I hope you and Frank will get that chance. I am sure it will happen for you. By the way, Margie, you mentioned Thomas. Dad tells me he's back here in this area, too."

"Yep! Been back for quite a while now. See him a lot. He nearly always comes over for drinks when Frank's here. They get on well. And Thomas and I have dinner together frequently when I'm down here by myself and lonely for company. He's almost always available. I call him my cheap date. "

Rosemary grinned at the label her friend used for Thomas and asked, "Has he changed much?"

"Not a whole lot. He's still Mr. Nice. Always was a gentleman, don't you think? Guys like him are like dinosaurs, very rare. Not many of them around anymore."

Rosemary agreed. "That's for sure." She wondered if she should ask any more questions about Thomas. She felt a little nosey, but her curiosity got the best of her. "Dad said he was probably married at one time but came home with no wife and no explanation and—"

"If you ask Thomas that," Margie interrupted, "he'll just say, 'Marriage? What marriage?' Whatever it was, he ain't talking. Not even to me, and we talk about everything else."

"Okay, I'll remember not to ask in case I run into him."

"Run into him, hell! I'm calling him, and we're going out to dinner tomorrow night, the three of us."

Rosemary stuttered, "Well, I-I don't—"

Margie put out both hands, palms up, and shoved them in Rosemary's direction. "No! No excuses! We're going and that's that!" She was so emphatic that Rosemary didn't know what to say. Margie headed for the phone in the corner of the room, and as she dialed the phone, she casually remarked, "Did you know Thomas was head over heels in love with you years ago?"

Rosemary was stupefied. "He was what? No, we were just good . . ."

But her friend was already speaking into the phone. "Thomas! Hi! Looking for a cheap date for tomorrow night? Sure! Let's go down to the hotel in Westport. Five-thirty sound okay?" She paused a minute, listening to Thomas, and then said, "Okay, I'll meet you there. Bye."

"Margie," Rosemary exclaimed after her friend hung up the phone, "what do you mean, he was in love with me? We were always just close friends, the same as you and me. And how come you didn't tell him I was coming along with you?"

Like a Cheshire cat, Margie grinned. "I want to surprise the hell out of him, and no, he wasn't just your friend, Rosemary. He really was in love with you. He told me so, many years ago." She looked puzzled. "You really didn't know, did you?"

Rosemary's face flushed a pale red. "No! You're kidding me! Oh my God! I don't believe it. Well, I hope he's gotten over that."

"I really don't know. He's asked about you, of course, but he hasn't mentioned his feelings about you in years. Anyway, five o'clock tomorrow! Be ready and I'll pick you up. We'll shock the man silly."

❦

The two friends were a bit late getting away from Tokeland the next evening, so they hurried from the parking lot into the restaurant. Margie spotted Thomas by the window as they came in the door. He didn't see them, as he was looking out at the boats in the marina beside the hotel. Margie was in front and led the way, Rosemary right behind her.

Again Rosemary found herself nervous about the meeting, especially after what she had been told.

They reached the table, and Thomas, spotting Margie out of the corner of his eye, turned with a smile. "It's about time you got here. I was beginning to think you stood me . . ." Then he saw that she had someone else with her.

Margie leaned over and quickly planted a sisterly kiss on the side of his open mouth to distract him momentarily before stepping aside and remarking, "Brought a guest with me, Thomas."

There was that hint of recognition, but his brain did not immediately register that it was Rosemary standing in front of him. When it did, he couldn't believe his eyes. There was a shocked silence. After all, Rosemary had changed. She had grown a couple of inches after leaving school and was quite a bit slimmer than he remembered. In the ensuing years, she'd also had a crooked front tooth straightened and now was wearing contact lenses, instead of her eyeglasses. But to Thomas, she was still Rosemary with her long sandy-colored hair and beautiful blue eyes. His heart fluttered. In his eyes, she was the most beautiful woman he'd ever known. His feelings about her hadn't changed one iota.

He was tongue-tied, and Rosemary didn't quite know what to say either and could only stare at her old high school friend. She noted the early streaks of gray in his reddish-blond hair, mostly in his sideburns, and now he wore the eyeglasses she'd been able to shed. But the glasses looked very dignified on him.

Finally, Margie broke the heavy silence by prompting them with her next comment. "Well do you remember our third musketeer, Thomas?" She laughed heartily. "Close your mouth and say hello."

After swallowing, his Adam's apple sliding up and down a couple of times, and staring for a few more seconds while Margie laughed some more in amusement, Thomas managed to say, "Rosemary, is that really you? Oh, my God! What a sight for sore eyes!"

Rosemary nodded with a smile and held out her hand to shake his, "Hi, Thomas. How are you?"

But Thomas ignored her hand, quickly pulling himself up from the table. He leaned over, putting his arms gently around her and kissing her briefly on the mouth. It was a chaste kiss, but he felt his blood warm at her touch. He couldn't believe she was here. And the feelings he'd always felt for her, which he thought he'd contained, now bloomed once again. He'd never felt such joy.

All those years and he'd never kissed her before. He'd always been like her brother and best friend as far as she was concerned. Never anything else! He'd certainly wanted it to be, but he'd lacked the courage to step over that line, and then she was gone off to college. She never came back, and he never had the opportunity to tell her how he felt. "This is the most wonderful surprise," he said with his hands still holding her shoulders.

Rosemary laughed nervously as she drew back. "Well, it's nice to see you, too. Been a long time, hasn't it?" She finally expelled a big sigh. She thought he looked great and hadn't changed that much. As her father had told her, he was still tall and lanky, although his upper torso was more muscled than she remembered and he wore his hair longer than before.

"It certainly has been. Come on, ladies! Sit down. Let's have a drink before we order dinner. We need to talk!"

The three of them went on to have a wonderful evening of celebration, reliving their lives of years ago and enjoying each other's questions and stories. Inside himself, Thomas's soul glowed. He could not stop looking at Rosemary. She was gorgeous, even more so than he remembered. He watched her closely, noticed a little hesitation when they moved their conversation to present times. Margie did most of the talking then. Rosemary commented on her divorce but changed the subject quickly. Thomas understood. He didn't talk about his either. She talked about her dad, and his ears perked up when he heard her say she was probably staying on with her father, with no further plans at the present. His heart pounded. She was going to be living here again. What good fortune and another chance for him, he hoped.

Rosemary felt Thomas's eyes on her throughout the evening, and once or twice their eyes met head-on, but she always looked away, embarrassed at having heard about his romantic feelings for her in the past. How strange she'd never guessed. She really hoped he didn't still feel that way. She certainly did not want to get into any kind of relationship now and maybe ever again after what she had been through.

Margie returned to Seattle a couple of days later, promising to come back for a few weeks in August. Rosemary settled into a routine with her father, jogging out on the beach every morning, driving to the post office and picking up groceries in Westport. She enjoyed cooking their meals and keeping house for her father.

Occasionally the two of them would go out to an early dinner if Matt felt up to it. And on most Sundays, if Matt was feeling fit enough, they would attend services at the Presbyterian church, where she had attended Sunday school throughout her childhood. The pastor, who had led the church for all those years, was as old as her father and had long since retired. However, there were a few of Matt's peers still in attendance, and it was good for him to partake. She was enjoying being with her father and doing those things that made life a little easier for him. Rosemary knew he loved having her with him; it made him very joyous.

A couple of weeks after the dinner she'd shared with her two friends, Thomas called her. "Hi. Rosemary, it's me. Thomas."

"Oh, hello, Thomas. How're you doing?" She was surprised and yet not surprised to hear his voice. She admitted to herself that she was happy to hear from him.

"I'm doing super. Wanted to tell you how much I enjoyed dinner with you and Margie. Sure was fun talking about old times, huh?"

She nodded her head and agreed it was nice. "Yes, it was," she said. I enjoyed myself very much."

"Care to have dinner with me this weekend, Friday or Saturday night? Your choice."

For a moment, Rosemary didn't know what to say. She had been so delighted to see her two best friends and to have them in her life again. However, Margie's disclosure about Thomas's feelings for her and remembering how he looked at her the other night bothered her a little. She hoped he didn't still feel that way. She didn't want to start something she wasn't ready for, and she certainly didn't want to hurt his feelings. She was terribly afraid of getting hurt. She had told herself that she would never get involved again. Her marriage had done her in. She just didn't feel she could ever trust another man again. But this was Thomas, her old friend. Why couldn't they still be friends? She could keep it cool, couldn't she?

After a moment of silence, Rosemary surprised herself and said, "Okay, Saturday would be fine."

When she hung up and told her father who the caller was, he was delighted. "Go and have a good time, honey. You need to get out and enjoy yourself. And Thomas is a good man."

On Saturday evening, they drove to the outskirts of Aberdeen and ate at the Nordic Inn Restaurant located right off the highway near the Grays Harbor Community College. They enjoyed a steak and salad dinner and nursed one beer apiece, whiling away several hours of talking before returning to the beach area.

As they neared the small town of Grayland on their return drive, Rosemary asked Thomas, "Do you live on the beach side or on the east side of the highway?"

"Fortunately, on the beach side. I can only see the ocean from the bedroom upstairs, but it's enough for me to know I can jog down to the water in a only a few minutes and enjoy it."

"I always thought you were so anxious to leave this area and make your life someplace else."

"Well, I changed my mind about that as you can see. I might ask you the same question, Rosemary. You've come back, too."

Rosemary smiled and nodded her head and said, "Looks like I have, doesn't it?

He laughed at her. "I've had enough of the big cities myself. I like the peace and quiet that the ocean offers, and I like having a house instead of a condo or an apartment. Lived in those and don't want any more. My house is small, but it has everything I need." He paused and then said, "Hey, let's stop, and I'll show you around. I even did my dishes this morning and picked up my dirty socks."

She laughed at him. "Prepared for everything, are you?"

"Yep, you never know who you're going to bring . . . ah, who is going to show up at your door."

He brought his speed down as they entered the little beach town, and then three-quarters of a mile on the other side of town, Thomas turned right towards the water and, after a block or so, turned right again. There were quite a few small homes and cabins that were screened from the highway by a thick greenbelt, and anyone passing through would never have guessed they were there. The neighborhood had a quiet, sedate feeling. They passed the first house on the right and pulled into the driveway of the second one.

Thomas's home was a small A-frame beach cottage. What she could see in the dark with the car headlights on looked neat and well kept. There was a freshly mowed lawn and a flowerbed blooming in a variety of colors along the front walkway. Some kind of light in the backyard behind the house allowed just enough illumination for her to see that the yard was backed up against the greenbelt, creating a very private space.

He turned off the engine, shut off the headlights, and then ran around to open the passenger door. "Looks like my porch light is burned out. Um! Didn't realize that," he said, as he dug out his penlight and assisted Rosemary to the front door. He unlocked it, flipped on the inside light switch, and allowed her to step into a small but cozy living space, brightly lit and neatly arranged around a big stone fireplace with the kitchen towards the rear of the house. Although the quarters were small, everything was in its place, certainly not an image of most bachelor pads and a man living alone.

Thomas carried on a running conversation regarding the purchase of the place and how he had modernized the kitchen with new cabinets and appliances as he fixed them cups of hot apple cider. They sat on bar stools at the kitchen counter, sipping the hot liquid. He was a little nervous. And he couldn't keep his eyes off Rosemary. He couldn't believe she was here with him after all these years. Thomas had never forgotten her. Now, he wondered if he would get a second opportunity to tell her how he felt. He'd certainly missed that chance before because of his shyness. How could he tell her that he'd loved her before and that, upon seeing her again, knew he still did? He wanted to reach over and hug her, but she seemed a bit fragile somehow and appeared to be nervous with him, too. Something had happened to her along the way to make her so distrusting. Thomas realized he would have to walk a fine line for a while, being careful not to scare her away.

"Your place is very nice, Thomas. I can see why you like it. It's very warm and cozy, especially with that lovely fireplace in the center. And I noticed that you have a very private backyard, which I could see a little bit of when we drove up. I like privacy. Everyone needs a get-away or a corner to tuck themselves into sometimes."

"Yeah, I've worked on the place, trying to put my signature on it. It feels right for me anyway. Come on over and take a better look outside." Thomas was already up, and so Rosemary followed him to the sliding door facing the backyard. He flipped on a switch, and a floodlight lit up the backyard almost as bright as day. It was very private with the green-belt behind and hedges along both sides, closing it almost entirely off from the rest of the neighborhood. As in the front, there were more flowers along the edge of the yard and in big planters along one side of the patio slab. Two reclining deck chairs sat waiting for occupants. A large cement birdbath stood in the very center of the yard. It was very inviting.

"What a great place for you to relax, especially during the summer. It's beautiful," Rosemary exclaimed, as Thomas slid the door back into place and they returned to their drinks.

"I found a spot on the beach not far from Dad's cabin. It's in amongst some driftwood. I've been going out there lately to do some writing. It's the perfect spot when the weather is nice."

"Still writing, are you?"

"Yes, I'm still attempting to write that novel I've always talked about. I tucked it away for quite a while, so I'm having a tough time getting started again. I've worked on it for years, but there have been a lot of distractions, and I hope to really get involved in it now."

Rosemary looked at her watch. It was nearly midnight. "I think maybe I'd better get home. Thank you for such a nice evening, Thomas." It had been a fun night, she admitted to herself as they got up to leave. She was glad she'd decided to spend the evening with him. Truthfully, she'd been just a little on edge. She didn't know for sure, but it did seem like Thomas wanted something more than friendship, and if that was true, she needed to put the brakes on right away. She wasn't ready for anything resembling a relationship. However, he hadn't come on to her during the entire evening, so she was a little more relaxed and felt quite safe. They were just two good friends enjoying an evening together again, she told herself.

At the front door, Thomas had his penlight ready as he switched off the house lights. "I'll fix that light tomorrow," he said aloud as a reminder. The penlight lent a small streak of light, but it was still quite dark. As he closed the door, he reached for her arm to keep her from falling down the few steps. Then, without thinking about it, he caught her shoulders with his hands and turned her around to face him, gathering her tenderly into his arms. Thomas hadn't planned this, but he couldn't help himself. He tried to say something, but the words stuck in his throat. He brought his face closer, slanting his mouth towards hers, overwhelmed by the burning love he felt. Poised in mid-air for a split second he finally did give into his need to touch her, and their lips met. It all happened so fast it caught Rosemary totally off guard; she didn't have a chance to resist. In fact, if she'd been able to admit it to herself, she found it quite pleasant. Thomas smelled of soap and cleanliness, and his lips were soft and pliable. When she didn't pull away, he deepened the kiss, and their bodies warmed to each other.

But suddenly Rosemary came to her senses, pulled away and stuttered, "Thomas, I-I c-c-can't d-do this now. Please understand."

Softly he asked her, "What is it you can't do, Rosemary? Explain it to me."

"I'm . . . recovering from a very bad . . . relationship . . . a really bad marriage! I'm not ready for any commitments. I may never be." Tears came to her eyes as she told him this.

The tears melted him, and as he took her hand and led her to the car, he said compassionately, "Don't ever say never. Never is a long time, Rosemary." To tone things down, he explained, "You know, I've not asked for any commitment from you. It was a great evening we had tonight. I can't remember when I've enjoyed one so much. The kiss? Well, it was wonderful! It was a culmination of a perfect evening, don't you agree? I'm sorry if I overstepped the boundaries you've set. I wouldn't want to harm our friendship in any way. Come on. I'll take you home now."

What had he done? He'd moved too quickly, not giving her enough time. What a dumb thing for him to do! Thomas knew she was troubled. He didn't want to lose her now that he had found her again.

"I think you're special, too, Thomas, only . . . I . . ." Rosemary didn't know what else to say, so she entered the car as he held the door open for her. He was quiet as he got into the driver's seat and backed the car out of the driveway.

She began to feel like such a fool, and a few tears slid down her cheeks in the darkness of the car as he drove her home. Neither of them spoke a word until they arrived at her father's house. There was a tense silence. Suddenly Rosemary spoke. "I'm so sorry, Thomas. I really had a wonderful time tonight. Thank you so much."

"No need to be sorry," but his voice broke as he spoke. "I had a nice time, too." He walked her to the door and abruptly bade her good night.

Rosemary was sure he was angry with her.

She almost called Thomas the next morning to apologize again. Certainly, she had hurt his feelings. She really needed to let him know how much she treasured his friendship, but she kept putting the call off and finally let it go.

Rosemary half expected him to call but was grateful when he did not. She didn't want to deal with his feelings for her. She had to admit he was as much fun to be with as he used to be. Why couldn't their friendship remain as it had always been? She kept recalling what Margie had told her. Perhaps their friendship wasn't the way she remembered it to be. "Damn," she swore to herself as she made her morning trek along the beach. She sputtered aloud to herself, "No commitments, Rosemary. Do you hear me?" At the same time, she knew she was lucky to have both her friends back in her life, and she really wanted to keep Thomas as her friend. The whole thing depressed her. She would just try to keep things as cool as she could and hope they could still enjoy each other's company. Was that possible?

Three weeks later in mid-August, Margie showed up with her husband, Frank, in two cars. He was spending the weekend, and then Margie would stay on for a few weeks after he returned to Seattle. The women looked forward to this time and made plans to visit, have dinner, and walk the beach together whenever they could.

On the phone, Margie declared, "I've called Thomas to come to dinner tonight. Cocktails at six thirty. Have to run. See you tonight." Her friend had given Rosemary no chance to say no. She hadn't heard from Thomas in the three weeks since their dinner, and she was a little stressed about seeing him again that evening.

Her father was becoming more fragile, and Rosemary thought maybe she could use him as an excuse for not showing up, but when she explained the call to him, he urged her to go. Matt always went to bed early and was usually asleep by seven or so. "You go and have a good time, honey. I can call you if I need you for anything."

The four of them had cocktails first, followed by a tasty dinner of barbecued chicken on the grill, with corn on the cob, green salad, and rolls. Then they played cards and laughed together over old times. Rosemary had liked Frank immediately. He was warm and friendly and very much in love with his wife. He seemed to take no offense at being left out when the conversation got around to recalling memories of earlier years by the other three. Of course, Frank had some good stories of his own childhood to tell, as he recalled growing up on a farm. It was a different kind of childhood from the one the three of them had experienced. He and Thomas seemed to get along quite well. It was obvious to Rosemary they each had a high regard for the other. A mutual respect.

Thomas was very much the gentleman with Rosemary, and he kept everything very low-key, as did she, never mentioning their dinner date or the kiss she had pulled away from. Rosemary was sorry when the evening had to end. It was very nice to be with people her age. She thoroughly enjoyed herself.

Rosemary had walked to the Donahans' that evening. It was such a short distance, less than a half mile, and she was used to walking and enjoyed it. But, of course, Thomas had to go in that direction anyway to go home, so when the evening ended, he offered to give her a ride. How could she refuse without being rude?

When he pulled his car into the Reegans' driveway, he turned to her and said, "Then you aren't angry with me anymore?"

She quickly answered him, "Thomas, I was never angry, though I was sure you were with me." She couldn't quite meet his eyes and turned towards the windshield, staring out into the night. "I just have to take one step at a time."

"I understand, Rosemary," he responded. "Life has its little twists and turns, and we all have problems, but I want so much to keep our friendship. I've missed you all these years. A lot!"

"I value your friendship, as well. You know that. There's . . . just no room . . . for a stressful relationship right now." Rosemary turned back to face Thomas. "No, I don't mean stressful. I mean I'm scared to become involved with anyone again." And then she blurted out, "My husband was the most terrible me-centered person you can imagine. He never cared about anyone except himself. I never realized until I got rid of the bastard how terrible things really were. I've done a lot of healing, believe me, but I need more time. So many things have happened to me, and I feel like I've found some peace again. Coming back to this place is helping me so much." Rosemary turned, facing the windshield again.

Thomas listened without saying anything. He wanted to keep her talking, help her get rid of the anger and resentment that seemed to fill her. He loved her so much. Had always loved her. Although he wanted something more than her friendship, he knew he couldn't fight something if he didn't know what he was fighting. He could see that she was very vulnerable right now, and he was fearful that he would be the one to hurt her. Patience. That's what he'd have to have if he intended to get close to her in any way. He had to be careful not to frighten her away. Thomas realized he would have to tear down the protective wall she'd built, one brick at a time, and it wasn't going to be easy.

Rosemary sat very still. She was silent for so long Thomas finally spoke, hoping he could prompt her to continue. "Where did you meet him? Your husband?"

"At college," she said and didn't say anything further.

When she didn't, Thomas was prompted to speak again because he didn't want her to leave. He wanted to keep her there with him for as long as possible. "The last couple of times I saw you were when Margie, you, and I got together that summer after graduation. I remember clearly the last Labor Day weekend when we had a picnic together in North Cove on the beach. That spot is no longer there. Due to major erosion, the ocean has swallowed it up."

Rosemary nodded, remembering.

"But remember that huge tree where we spread out our picnic lunch? It rained shortly after we got there, and that beautiful tree pretty much protected us from getting wet. Do you remember?"

Her head was nodding again as she recalled their picnic.

"We knew it was a last time for the three of us to be together. None of us wanted to leave, and it was dark when we started back. We got soaked to the skin by the time we walked up the path to the car, but I remember we were laughing and giggling." Thomas could visualize with perfect clarity that entire day so long ago. He could feel the words they spoke, the emotions, some with laughter, others with the tears the three of them shed as they said their goodbyes. It had been so painful for him to see Rosemary leave, not to tell her how he felt, not to know when she would be back. He had tried once in high school to tell her how he felt, but she hadn't received the message. She had her own dreams then, and they didn't seem to include him. "Rosemary, it was a sad time when you told us both goodbye and prepared to leave. I will never forget it. It was time for you to leave for college in California. Your dad had scraped and saved for years to send you. And you said, 'I owe it to him.'"

"And I did . . . but—"

"Yes, but at the same time, I knew it wasn't just for your parents' sake. You were very excited about moving away and getting on with your life."

"Yes, I admit I was," she said quietly.

Thomas went on. "I was talking about going to Seattle, too, even though I didn't actually go for a couple of years. After you left us that last night, I remember how Margie fell apart. She cried so hard because she thought she was the only one staying behind. The three musketeers were to be no more. It was depressing. Something was really missing, I have to tell you." If only she knew how much she was missed. His life had been meaningless for quite a while after that.

His talking made Rosemary remember those memories she'd tucked away, although she didn't want to think about them right then. She stayed quiet and didn't say any more as she listened to Thomas talk away.

"Margie went to work at the doctor's office in Westport. I went to work on the boat full-time that summer, and it wasn't the same anymore. We—" Abruptly, Thomas stopped and then said sheepishly,

"Oops, looks like I got carried away reminiscing. I asked you about your ex and then startled babbling away."

A soft laugh bubbled out of Rosemary, and a tiny smile touched her lips. Thomas enjoyed seeing her smile, although this was a brief and sad one. He had always liked the sound of her voice and her laughter.

She touched his arm and said, "It's nice to reminisce when the memories are of such good friends." Then her voice sobered, "I don't particularly want to talk about my ex, but since you asked, I'll tell you a little. I met Jeffrey at college. In my second year. He was a senior. I, a lowly sophomore. Jeffrey was on the football team and the soccer team, in this club, in that club. He wasn't just a well-muscled, athletic jock but an intelligent jock at that. He was handsome, suave, and sugar coated. At first, I didn't want anything to do with him. But eventually, I fell for him, hook, line, and sinker."

Thomas heard the sorrow and anger in her voice as she discussed her ex-husband, knowing she'd been hurt badly. However, he had her talking now, and he listened intently while she spoke about her former life.

CHAPTER THREE

AS ROSEMARY RECITED HER STORY to Thomas, she remembered how excited she was to go off to school in California. She'd gotten a small scholarship from the Westport Kiwanis Club upon graduation, and her dad had drawn the rest of what she needed from his savings account. She and her dad had already taken one trip right after graduation to check out her acceptance to Stanford before she made her final decision. So in September, she flew off to California, happy and excited about a new adventure in her life. She felt grown up and ready for the world, although she keenly felt the loss of her friends. She had to make a concentrated effort on the plane to push that particular emotion to the back of her mind and set her thoughts to the journey ahead of her.

Rosemary managed to find a taxi at the airport to transport her and her luggage to the college campus. With the help of her driver and a campus directory, she had no trouble finding her dormitory. She arrived a couple of days before her roommate, allowing time to get her things organized and to explore the campus further. She was so certain she was prepared for everything, but she was soon to find out not all things are as they seem.

There were only a few other girls in the dorm with her when she arrived, but as the others moved in, she felt lost in their midst. Many of them were sophomores or older and beyond being the new kid on the block. None of them paid much attention to her except to say a quick "hello" in passing, and no one really befriended her in any way. They had already established their own little groups, it appeared, and she felt totally ignored. It deflated her ego and gave way to a lack of confidence. Suddenly, Rosemary experienced an overwhelming case of homesickness, missing all that was familiar to her—her home, her parents, and her friends. She felt lonely and unsure of herself. However, her anxiety was short-lived.

Her roommate arrived on the scene, and things were suddenly quite different. Upon first introductions, Julia gave Rosemary a big hug and said, "We're going to have a grand year, you and me!" And they did, becoming the closest of friends. If it hadn't been for Julia, Rosemary might have packed up and gone home.

Julia, a tiny spitfire from central Texas, was a very outgoing and kind person who accepted everyone as her friend. No one could resist her charm and her friendly demeanor. It was Julia's first year, too, but no one would have guessed that for she vigorously jumped into every situation with both feet. Her laughter, her gaiety, and her grand Texas warmth towards others spread throughout the dorm. Soon everyone knew who Julia was, and as she included her new roommate in most of her plans, Rosemary finally found herself a part of this unique group also. The attitude of the other girls was noticeably different, changing things significantly for her. She had been accepted and once again looked forward to her first school year.

It was to be a memorable one. Rosemary made many friends and enjoyed the camaraderie of those friendships. Although she flew home for Christmas that December and was delighted to see her parents again, she decided to stay in California when the school year ended. She found a job in the school library, took a summer writing class, and enjoyed the partially emptied campus.

She dated a couple of nice guys during that time. One of them, Michael Feinstein, was a fellow who worked at the library with her. He was studying law. Michael had little extra time but managed to share dinner with her on occasion, and they jogged together through the campus on many Saturday mornings or once in a while in the early evening. Michael might give her a friendly goodnight kiss when he brought her home, but that's all it was. It was a very nice and uncluttered friendship.

Another fellow student, Archie Anderson, had been in a couple of classes with Rosemary over the winter, and they sometimes studied together. She teasingly called him Archibald, even though it wasn't his name. "Archie" was it, his given name. He was like a brother to her, and during the school year, they had gone to a couple of student dances and joined in on other college activities like football games. They might have been called dates. Archie was a warm individual and a gentleman. She enjoyed his company.

His parents lived only a half-hour's drive from the campus, so even during that summer when he went home to live and work at a part-time job there, he called her a couple of times to keep in touch. They managed to take in a couple of movies and several trips to the beach. Rosemary enjoyed that summer of 1981 very much—she was adapted to college life, liked her friends, and felt independent and in control of her life.

At the end of August, Rosemary and Archie found a table in Marc's Restaurant after a movie and discovered Jeffrey Archer eating at the table next to them. Archie knew Jeffrey well. The two men were in the same frat building during the school year. Jeffrey waved to them and came over to their table. Rosemary was introduced, and so as not to be rude, Archie invited Jeffrey to share their table.

Rosemary had seen Jeffrey around. He was a popular guy on campus; she knew that for sure, and you would have had to be a dunce not to know he was one of the big jock football players. Everyone knew him, especially the girls. There was always a group of people around him, except for that evening, which was very unusual. She was surprised he was alone for a change. Even though she had to admit he was very handsome and quite a charmer, he was totally out of her league. She couldn't ever compete with that ego of his.

"Haven't seen you around campus, Rosie. You must have been hiding because I certainly wouldn't have missed you if you were there," he said with a smile.

"Ah, Jeff, she doesn't like to be called Rosie." Archie raised his eyebrows as he warned the other man.

"Oops, sorry. Rosemary. Okay, little Rosemary, you starting your first year?"

"No, I was here last year," she said indignantly. *He is so condescending and really thinks he is something*, she thought to herself.

"A sophomore, then. What you majoring in?"

"Well, I have an English major as my goal. Someday maybe I'll teach, so I'm taking a lot of English courses and languages, and I like to write." She didn't tell him she wanted someday to author a novel, which she was attempting to write whenever she could find the time.

Jeffrey sounded interested all of a sudden. "Hm! Well, they have a great advanced writing course next semester you might want to try. Ms. Jackson is a great professor in the arts. The best I hear." Suddenly he looked at his watch. "Well, guys, I have a date. Gotta go! Very nice meeting you, *Rose-mar-y!*" He enunciated her name very carefully and winked at her as he got up. "See you around!"

She watched him walk away. His stride was long and full of confidence. He was so very sure of himself. Well, he was not for her and turned her attention back to Archie, who was in the midst of telling her a funny story. Having had her attention distracted because of Jeffrey, she didn't hear the first part of the story, so she really didn't get the punch line but laughed anyway.

Archie knew that she was only partially listening and wondered what was wrong. Then he realized. Of course, he'd just introduced her to the big man of the campus, and she seemed to have been mesmerized by him. *My God, what have I done?* he berated himself. That wolf will eat her for breakfast. He didn't want her to have anything to do with Archer.

"Rosemary, I don't know what you think of that guy, but beware; he's not what he seems. He enjoys breaking all the ladies' hearts."

Faking surprise that her thoughts were on Jeffrey, she said quickly, "What? What guy?"

"You know who I mean. Jeffrey Archer, the Romeo, who just left here. He's okay, except where women are concerned. He loves them and leaves them faster than you can count them. Believe me. Don't ever get involved with that schmuck." Then he muttered, "Why in the hell did I introduce you?"

"What are you talking about?"

"Nothing, nothing," he said as he focused on the coffee and dessert that the waitress set down in front of him.

Rosemary's face turned a little pink when she said with a huff, "Archie, I have no interest in the charming Mr. Archer. We don't run in the same circles." Then her voice softened as she smiled at him, "But thanks for acting like my big brother." She patted his hand and received a grin from him.

As far as she was concerned, she would never end up running around with any of Jeffrey's crowd. But Rosemary attended a couple of football games with Archie and couldn't help watching the man in action on the field. She also caught glimpses of him with groups of people in the student lounge occasionally, mostly adoring women, who were all competing for his attention. They seemed to hang on to every word he spoke. Well, she wasn't planning on becoming one of his adoring fans, so she tried to pay as little attention to him as possible.

One evening in the lounge, she spotted Jeffrey across the room, catching him looking in her direction at the same time. He gave her a nod and little wink, probably to let her know that he remembered meeting her. *How kind of him to give me his undivided attention for a couple of seconds*, she thought. Rosemary couldn't care less. She smiled and nodded back and then turned away. She didn't want him to think that her response was anything more than a friendly gesture. Actually, she didn't want to think of him at all. Yet, subconsciously she knew she felt an attraction to him, and she fought against it.

In December just before Christmas break and before she left for Washington for the holidays, Rosemary signed up for the writing course that was to begin in January, the one Jeffrey had mentioned to her. She had her classes all set for the following quarter when she left.

Her parents had surprised her with another plane ticket to come home as they had done the year before. She felt guilty, knowing they didn't really have the money, but she had stayed on campus during the summer quarter so it had been a year since she'd been home. You had to be with family during the Christmas holidays. How could you not?

It turned out to be a very relaxing Christmas for her. It was just the three of them for the better part of that week. They talked on the phone with her brothers and their wives and enjoyed the company of a couple of her parents' friends for Christmas dinner. They played some table games, ate, and laughed a lot. Rosemary was so happy to be with her parents again. She had really missed them. She tried to reach Margie at her mother's home but couldn't get anyone, and she was sure Thomas had gone on to Seattle so she didn't bother calling him.

Rosemary enjoyed listening to her folks talk about their plans for retirement but knew they were waiting until she finished school, another two and half years away. She was aware of their sacrifice, only they didn't think of it as such. They told her of their plans to move on down the road to Tokeland where it was even more tranquil and not as touristy. The three enjoyed their quiet times and their privacy.

It was quiet at the beach, and by the end of the week, Rosemary felt thoroughly refreshed. Even though she loved her folks, she missed her college friends and her classes and was ready to get back at the end of the week.

Julia took Rosemary with her to a New Year's party off campus where she met some new friends, including a nice young man named Danny James from Iowa. He was attending Stanford, too. After chatting with him for a while, she discovered they had a lot in common. He was going to take the same writing class she was registered for and eventually wanted a career in broadcasting or anything to do with the media, perhaps anchor a newscast on a TV station someday. It was a hard career to break into, but one he thought he might like to pursue. They talked and danced a couple of times, enjoying each other, and when he asked her to go out later in the week, she said yes. He was a cheerful guy and fun to be with, and she even wondered if maybe she could become serious about him.

Danny had corn-colored blond hair, as only an Iowan could, lightened by those hot Midwest summer days and the deepest blue eyes she had ever seen. She compared them to Paul Newman's blue eyes, one time her favorite actor. Danny had wide football shoulders and a muscular build, only he didn't care much for sports. He had the look of a farmer's son, but he was no hayseed and surprised people with his intelligence.

Having done plenty of hard work on his father's farm, Danny was definitely ready to move into a world beyond the farm life of his parents. He had a soft Iowan accent and a very outgoing personality, liked by everyone he met on campus. Rosemary thought he was handsome, and she liked him, mostly because he treated her with such respect.

After the meeting at the dance, they spent a lot of time together; that is, as much as they could spare from their studies. There were times when other couples would join them for different college activities, sometimes just a Friday night get-together for pizza or hamburgers at a fast-food place.

Rosemary's classes were going well; she was dating a great guy and having a good time, happy and contented with her life while working towards her degree. The only thing disturbing her was Jeffrey; her attraction to him still bothered her, no matter how she tried to push it away.

In January, she started her new writing class. Rosemary was completely taken back when she discovered Jeffrey Archer in the class. He didn't strike her as an English major student, but she would find out that he was, indeed, very suited to the group. She had to admit he was smart and a great asset to the class. Almost immediately, he began to flirt with her. He managed to get a seat right behind her the first day and completely disarmed her with his attention. She was determined not to pay any attention to him and leaned heavily on her new relationship with Danny, who sat on one side of her. She would arrive at class with Danny and leave with him, her arm linked in his, as an announcement to Jeffrey that she was already taken.

It didn't seem to sway him. He would lean forward and whisper in her ear, "How about dinner tonight?" She would shake her head and notice that Danny was watching them with a frown on his face. When he wouldn't stop, she would shush him with a "Shh!" It was difficult to focus on her class work when he hassled her.

Halfway through the evening at a campus dance with Danny one Saturday night, Rosemary observed Jeffrey coming in the door with a couple of his sidekicks, two other football players from the team. He was his old charming self, making conversations with everyone he passed, hugs for the ladies, a handshake or a pat on the shoulder for the guys. Everyone's attention riveted on the mighty man as he strolled into the room. Rosemary turned away so he wouldn't think she'd noticed him. But this time when Jeffrey saw her, he came right over to say hello, bringing his brilliant smile with him.

She thought he was very artificial and promised herself not to let him work his charm on her. He was just about to ask her to dance when she jumped up and said, "Come on, Danny. Didn't you ask me for this one?"

When Danny smiled in agreement and the two of them clasped hands and started towards the dance floor, Jeffrey said with a big grin, "See you in class, Rosie. Save me one of those dances next time around." *In your dreams, Jeffrey Archer,* she told herself. Shortly after the incident, Jeffrey and his friends disappeared. She didn't know she was so tense until he'd gone. Finally, she relaxed and enjoyed the rest of the evening with Danny.

Rosemary tried to make a big deal of showing her interest in Danny whenever Jeffrey happened to be around. She gave Danny her undivided attention. When Jeffrey wouldn't give up, she finally told him she was going steady with Danny, thinking that would dissuade him. Of course, they weren't really going steady. Danny squired her around, and they had even come close to going to bed together one night, but he'd made it clear he wasn't going to get serious about any-one until he'd met his goals.

Danny was protective of Rosemary, though. He knew Jeffrey was always harassing her and finally asked her if it was bothering her. Could he help her by demanding that Jeffrey leave her alone? If she'd said the word, Danny would gladly have taken steps to get him out of the way. However, she assured Danny she wasn't the least bit interested in the man and that he would eventually get tired and go away.

"Thanks, but no thanks, Danny. It's okay. I can handle him and that big ego of his just fine." That's what she thought.

After the episode at the dance, Rosemary redoubled her efforts to let others know that she and Danny were an item and that she wasn't interested in anyone else. For a little while after that, Jeffrey stopped annoying her; he left her alone, and Rosemary thought he had finally given up. Then one day she found a note in one of her books.

If you are going steady with Danny, how come I saw him with another girl at lunchtime yesterday? Are you holding me at arm's length, my darling? Look, I promise not to bite! Go out to dinner with me. Just try me out. You might like me, at least a little bit. And if you still don't, no harm done. We'll each go our merry way and I'll leave you alone. Come on Rosie. Take a chance!

Yours,
Jeffrey

"Yours," my foot, Rosemary muttered. She did wonder about Danny and the other girl Jeffrey had mentioned, but the fact was she and Danny didn't have an exclusive relationship. They had promised each other nothing. He was free to do what he wanted. It really wasn't any of her business. Furthermore, it was probably just some girl sitting with him. Jeffrey was just trying everything in his little bucket of tricks. The jerk!

In the coming weeks, Danny started asking her out less and less, and except for their one shared class, she didn't see him much. He maintained his studies were keeping him too busy and he had little free time. It was a fact that he had taken some difficult classes that semester, and she understood. But she had also seen him once with another girl some distance away and was finally convinced that it was probably over between them. She missed him. He was a nice guy and had been a good friend. Losing Danny, however, didn't end her life. She buried herself in her writing and her class courses and began spending any spare time she had with her girlfriends again. She and Julia always had a good time together. Rosemary was fine with the way her life was going. She didn't need Danny or Jeffrey.

That didn't mean Jeffrey gave up. He continued to press Rosemary whenever he saw her in class or in passing.

"Hey, sweetie," he would say with a smile on his face, "I'm still waiting for that date. When you going to say okay? Tonight, tomorrow night?"

"I am busy, Jeffrey. Have a heavy class load this semester. Can't do it," she would tell him over and over again. He just wouldn't give up.

Back in Thomas's car, Rosemary bowed her head at the memories pouring from her. She'd stopped talking for a bit and then finally spoke again with a sob breaking through her voice. Thomas's heart ached for her, and he fought the urge to pull her into his arms to comfort her.

"I-I really was overcome when he paid so much attention to me . . . TO ME . . . little Rosemary No-Nothing Reegan from Nowhere Pacific Coast, Washington. Jeffrey Archer, this well-known, popular football star, pursuing me! He sat next to me in our writing class and flirted with me all the time. He was always smiling at me, his beautiful white teeth flashing in that California tanned face. I found it . . . I found it very hard to concentrate on anything. It was so disconcerting. He was so insistent, and he wouldn't give up. My attention to my classes and my passion for writing seemed swallowed up with the tenseness I felt. My grades were suffering. In fact, I don't know how I managed to get a passing grade that year. I tried to hold him off, but it didn't work. I WAS attracted to him. I finally admitted it to myself. My downfall!"

Rosemary took a breath. She was quiet for another moment, but it seemed once she'd gotten started, she couldn't stop. She was getting it all out, and Thomas gladly listened, wanting very much to find out what had happened to them.

"Finally, I allowed myself to accept a dinner invitation with him. I couldn't say no again. *Just this once*, I told myself. *I'll go out with him one time and that will be it. He'll stop then.* But, of course, it wasn't the last time. He was so attentive and loving towards me, and he had me eating out of his hand. I was completely bowled over by his attention." Rosemary laid her head back on the car seat. "It was the first of many dates with him. Before the quarter was over, we were an exclusive item, dating no one else. I was the envy of all the girls. And I have to admit I was so proud. It felt good to be so popular and have all the girls jealous of me. I was certainly blind-sided."

Once more Rosemary stopped talking. It was very quiet in the car again. Thomas froze. He didn't utter a sound. The silence became heavier. Finally, turning his head, he studied Rosemary's profile, watching a tiny tear roll from her left eye down her cheek. He wanted to reach out and wipe it away, but he didn't dare move. Suddenly she seemed to come to her senses. Her head came up, and she looked at him, "Oh, I'm so sorry, Thomas. How stupid of me. What a bore I am!"

"No, it's okay, Rosemary. Please go on," he encouraged her. "Get it out of your system. I'm here to listen. Really, I am a good listener."

"Yes, you are," she murmured and looked down at her lap. Then she closed her eyes. Why she was telling him all these things, she didn't know. But it helped so much to say them out loud and to have someone care.

Rosemary spoke again. "It didn't take much for him . . . for him to convince . . . to talk me into his . . . bed. He was so good at convincing you about anything." A sob caught in her throat, but she managed to go on. "We took precautions, but it didn't work. Just before Jeffrey's graduation, I found out I was pregnant."

Thomas shivered. He was stunned. There had been no mention of a child, so something must have happened to the pregnancy. He sensed this would be a bad story, but perhaps worse than he had thought. Still, he didn't say anything, and as Rosemary opened up to the rest of her tale, the present faded away for her again. She was vividly recalling the day she told Jeffrey on the phone.

❧

"Rosie, honey."

That was what Jeffrey called her. She always hated it. How come she never told him just how much she hated that nickname?

"Sorry, I can't make it over tonight. There's a dinner for the senior football players that I have to attend."

"Jeffrey, no, not tonight. I have to see you! I need to talk to you! It's . . . it's very important!"

"Save it for tomorrow, honey. They're expecting me. I have to be there," he insisted. "Look, Rosie, I have to go. Call you in the morning."

Yeah, take two aspirin and go to bed, she thought sarcastically. "Jeffrey, wait . . . don't hang up! We have a problem . . . I saw the doctor today." There was a heavy silence. Then she said it aloud, "I'm pregnant." She never wanted to tell him on the phone, but she couldn't wait. She was so worried. A longer silence ensued between them. Her heart stopped. She waited for him to say something. Anything! After a few more seconds, she asked quietly, "Jeffrey?"

"Rosemary!"

Ah now, we have the name right!

"How in the hell did this happen? I don't believe this." He took a deep breath, and tears spilled down her cheeks as his harsh voice came across the phone line. "I can't deal with this now! Damn it! I'll talk to you later!" The phone went dead as he hung up.

Rosemary never heard from him the next day or the day after that. His graduation took place three days later. She didn't go because she guessed it was over for them. However, that afternoon following the ceremony, she was surprised when he appeared at her door. She looked ghastly. She hadn't slept and had spent several nights crying, her eyes puffy, her energy spent.

"Okay, I'm here. Now what do we do about this, Rosemary?"

She looked him straight in the eyes and asked him blandly, "Do you love me?" *If he says no*, Rosemary thought, *I'll slam the door in his face, and it will all be over within a couple of minutes.* But he didn't.

"Yes . . . yes, of course I do. Look, can we talk about an abortion? I'll find the money."

"No! Absolutely not," she shouted out at him. "No!"

"Okay, okay, calm down," Jeffrey said. "I didn't think so. Look, Rosie, I have to leave for Cincinnati tomorrow as planned. The folks are expecting me. You knew all along how my dad expected me to step into the family business once I graduated. Let me meet with him, and I'll come back in a few weeks. You'll be okay until then, won't you?" He put his arms around her, but Rosemary stiffened, feeling it was only his latest tactic to keep her calm. She really didn't believe him. She didn't believe he would come back.

"Yeah, I guess so," she muttered. She had no argument to pursue with him. Wasn't this her own damn fault? Her own damn problem! It was his escape, and she wouldn't see his face again ever! Now what would she do? Her family planned on having her come home for the summer since she hadn't gone home the summer before. Instead, she would have to tell them she had another job. Then she would have to find one and work as long as she was able. She'd have to get a cheaper place and save as much as she could. Could she survive this situation all by herself? She guessed she would have to.

As soon as her classes ended the following week, Rosemary studied the help wanted ads, calling on a number of them. Nothing turned up. Finally after several weeks, she called about a listing for a position in the administration office of a local hotel chain, located not far from the campus and her apartment. She was told to bring in the application they would forward to her in the mail. In just a few days after submitting the application, she was given an interview, which went quite well. She didn't tell them she was pregnant. It really didn't matter; they knew she was a student and subject to change. In only a few days she was informed that she had been accepted for the job and was to start immediately the next day. She was so relieved, even knowing it would be just a temporary fix to her problems. At least it was a start.

The next day, Jeffrey shocked her as he let himself in with his own key. She was in the bathroom just finishing her makeup and hair in preparation for her first day on the new job. When she heard the sound of the key in the door and came into the other room, she was astonished to see Jeffrey standing there. She had been so certain he wouldn't return.

He walked over to her, gave her a peck on the cheek, and presented her with two plane tickets to Reno, where he said they would get married and then fly on to Cincinnati. He had a few days before getting back to his job at his father's company, and they would use it for a quick honeymoon, he explained.

Rosemary should have been grateful for his unexpected return, and she tried to be happy about it, but something seemed wrong, and doubt nibbled at her insides. She was no longer sure this is what she wanted, but she needed to do it for the baby's sake.

She felt a great sense of loss at leaving school and a lot of guilt for wasting her parents' money and dashing their hopes for her college degree. Leaving home and going to college had been her biggest dream and theirs, too. She was always going to be a writer, wasn't she? She thought about all the honors she had received for her essays and stories in her high school classes and how she had wanted to pursue a writing career ever since she could remember. Until she met Jeffrey, it was her only goal in life. Now what was going to happen? Maybe it would still work out. Nothing said she couldn't take some writing classes wherever they lived, even if she was married. Maybe even some day, she could still earn her degree. It would just take a little longer. She was going to miss the college life and her friend, Julia. How difficult it was going to be to leave everything.

In the end, she didn't feel she had a choice. A baby was on the way. And although, it was going to be a big disappointment to her parents, she could at least save face with them about her pregnancy by being married.

On the plane the next day, Jeffrey drank a lot of booze. He chattered during the entire flight. He said to her, "I told Father we were already married secretly. He wasn't very happy about it, but he told me to come and get you. My mother won't speak to me now." He laughed drunkenly, "Oh, well, it's the old man I have to please." How insulting he was, Rosemary thought to herself, and shrank unhappily into her seat, while he ordered still another drink. She didn't want to listen to him talk that way.

"Hey, Rosie, how come you're so quiet? I'm doing the right thing here, aren't I?" He turned glaring at her and stumbling over his words. "Didn't have to come back and get you, you know. How's about some credit for that, huh?"

"Jeffrey, stop it. We don't have to do this. I don't want you to marry me just because it seems like the right thing to do or because you feel sorry for me. We'll only make ourselves unhappy, if that's the case. And, I don't want to be the cause of any family strife."

"Hey," he said testily, "did I say I was unhappy? Come on! It'll all work out." He kissed her sloppily on the cheek and took another drink. His words were becoming more slurred, and shortly, his head lobbed over onto her shoulder, as he snored softly in her ear. She gained no comfort from his words or his head snuggled into her shoulder. She felt burdened.

The plane landed on the tarmac at the Reno airfield about 11:00 a.m., and the courtesy van was waiting to take them to the hotel. They checked in and then took a taxi to the courthouse for the marriage license. They already had the blood tests with them. It was twelve thirty when they returned to their room.

They hadn't eaten much on the plane, so Jeffrey called for a meal to be delivered to their room. She heard him order a drink for himself as she lay down on the bed. She didn't feel much like eating. Her stomach was upset. Was it something she ate on the plane? Or was she just doubtful and nervous? She felt drained emotionally from all that had taken place over the last couple of days. It had happened too fast, and she was exhausted.

Their wedding appointment was for three o'clock so she hoped if she could have an hour's rest, maybe she would feel better. She managed to get herself together when Jeffrey woke her up about fifty minutes later. She felt very groggy. At the last minute just before they left their room, Jeffrey shoved some papers into her hand. "Here I forgot. You have to sign these. Here and right here!" She signed her name hastily without looking at them. He folded them, went to the closet for her coat, and thrust it at her as he looked at his watch. "We have to go." She was so tired and cranky, and her stomach still hurt. She stumbled through the door just wanting to get it over with. Some way to start a marriage!

Right after their short ceremony, Jeffrey brought his new bride back to their hotel room. She hardly had her coat off before he had his hands all over her, reaching for her zipper at the back of her dress and nudging her towards the bed. He wanted to make love to her. She pulled away.

"No, Jeffrey! Not now," she pleaded.

But he paid no attention, kissing her roughly, and not so gently, pushing her down on the bed, yanking on her dress.

"Jeffrey, please! Not now," she cried out again.

"Oh, come on, Rosemary! We're legal now," he said coarsely. "Let's celebrate the real stuff." Not having gotten her dress down, he began to raise it up to her waist and lowered himself on top of her, trying to kiss her. She pushed at him, sobbing and crying out again, "Jeffrey, please! I'm really not feeling well. Let me get some rest first."

He rolled over and off the bed on to his feet. "Have it your way. You're a real live wire today," he said as he zipped up his pants. "Well, go ahead, then. Take your nap. I'm going out and try my luck at the tables and enjoy myself." He put on his jacket, sarcastically snapping his heels together and mockingly giving her a military salute. Then with an angry scowl on his face, he quickly disappeared out the door.

Rosemary lay on the bed in the darkened room, tears seeping out of her eyes, as she wondered what she had done to herself. What a way to start a life together. Was this how it was going to be? *Maybe it will be different once we get settled.*

In ten minutes, she was asleep, worn out completely. She slept fitfully, waking up several times with a cramping sensation in the lower part of her abdomen.

She woke from a deep sleep just after 9:00 p.m. The hotel room was quiet, except for the whirring sound of the air conditioner. Jeffrey was still gone. She slept again until about eleven thirty when she woke up once again, this time with sharp stabbing pains. Her dress was soaked with perspiration. When she got up, it hurt to move, and when she managed to turn on the lamp by the bed, she saw the blood-drenched sheets. It wasn't perspiration; it was her blood. She was hemorrhaging. Somehow, she managed to make it to the bathroom, half-walking, half-crawling. The pain was almost unbearable. Rosemary was very frightened and so alone.

At approximately eleven-fifty, Jeffrey came in the door and found her unconscious on the bathroom floor. The next time she woke up was at a Reno hospital.

"Mrs. Archer," a female voice asked, "are you awake?"

Rosemary lay with her eyes closed, not recognizing her new last name or caring. Then someone gently nudged her on the shoulder. The voice repeated itself, "Are you awake now, Mrs. Archer?"

Rosemary opened her eyes and saw a woman all in white. It took a few seconds to realize the woman was a nurse and she was in a hospital.

"Now, that's a good girl. How are you doing honey? Ready to see your husband now? The poor guy's been waiting here all night. Been pretty worried about you, he has." She walked to the windows and drew back the drapes and sunlight cascaded into the room. Rosemary closed her eyes against the light. The nurse was back at her bedside in a flash. "There, that's better. Let's have a look at you." The heavy-set and gray-haired nurse took her patient's temperature and checked her other vital signs. Then she said, "Well now, you're doing very well. Everything seems pretty normal. I'll go down the hall and tell Mr. Archer he can come in now. Okay?" The woman didn't wait for an answer, and as soon as she left, Rosemary looked slowly and carefully around the room. She was afraid to ask what had happened. Why was she here? Her body felt bruised and sore. She couldn't remember a thing, but somehow she knew why as she placed her hands over her stomach.

Jeffrey appeared, rumpled and unshaven, bearded stubble beginning to show on the lower part of his face. "Hey there! Hi! You look so much better, Rosie. How you feeling?" He solicitously reached over to smooth her hair back from her face. Then he bent over and lightly brushed his lips across her forehead.

"What am I doing here?" Her voice came out weak and croaking as if she had a cold. She swallowed and then cleared her throat. She needed confirmation, even though she'd already guessed what had taken place.

Jeffrey took her hand, rubbing it with his. "Honey, there's no other way to tell you than just to say it. You've had a miscarriage, I'm afraid."

Yes, she had sensed it. She closed her eyes, sighed deeply, and let the tears roll.

He rubbed her hand comfortingly. "It's okay, Rosie. You're going to be fine. We'll have other children later, when we're ready."

Released later that afternoon, she was told to rest for a couple of days and not to do anything too strenuous for a couple of weeks. Although she hadn't begun to bond with her pregnancy yet, Rosemary realized a deep sense of loss and was quite despondent over it. Jeffrey was gentle with her, and for that she was appreciative. Perhaps they could make a go of this marriage after all. She was certainly going to try. And, as her husband said, they would have another baby later.

During her time in the hospital, Jeffrey phoned his parents to inform them that he and Rosemary were delayed for a couple of days but didn't tell them why. He didn't think it was necessary for them to know. Rosemary regained a little of her strength back, was resigning herself to her loss and determined to carry on by the time they were back on the plane.

Rosemary thought perhaps her new in-laws would be at the airport to meet them, but there was no one there when they arrived in Cincinnati. She didn't want to ask Jeffrey why. She saw him glance quickly around the airport area, but when he didn't spot anyone, he called for taxi service without saying anything to her.

She was still in somewhat of a fog and had given absolutely no thought to where they might be going until they left the airport and the city itself. All of a sudden, it came to her, and she looked around to see where they were. She saw a very nice residential area of old, but fairly large homes. It was only then that she asked Jeffrey, "Where are we going?"

"Mom and Dad purchased us a home. We're just about there. A couple more blocks." The area was one of Cincinnati's upper-middle-class sections. The houses were neat and well kept. Most of the properties were fenced in around nicely manicured lawns, long driveways, and lovely gardens and trees throughout.

So this is what it is like to have money. She couldn't believe that the Archers would just up and buy them a house. When she asked more questions about it, Jeffrey just laughed and shrugged his shoulders, "The old man has plenty of money. It was part of the deal if I came back and learned the business from the bottom up so I could take over some day. My destiny, I guess. It's always been a given that I would take over the company one day."

The cab stopped, and she peered around Jeffrey's shoulders and through the window.

He said, "Not bad, huh, wife?" He stepped out to help the cab driver get their bags from the trunk, while Rosemary stood and gazed at the house's gigantic double front doors and the roses surrounding the tiled, court-like entry leading to them. It was a stately old house and quite beautiful. It took her breath away and made her feel a little uncomfortable. She had never lived like this or even dreamed of the money it would take to live with this kind of environment. How was she going to fit into this life style? She took a deep breath and stepped away from the car.

Jeffrey went to work the next day and immediately settled into his entry-level job at the Archer Manufacturing Company in preparation for an eventual job with a title, leaving Rosemary to fend for herself in the big, old house. Oh yes, there was also the gift of a housekeeper, who came in once a week. Marina Menchez was a quiet woman with limited English, so even without the language barrier, making friends with her was not possible. It was quickly noted that the woman preferred to do her work with as little conversation as possible. Rosemary learned to go into another part of the house and leave Marina to her cleaning.

The house had a well-designed and efficient kitchen with a win-dowed nook that housed a narrow table and padded benches, the per-fect spot for a cup of coffee. Off to one side was a huge walk-in pantry. In between, sliding glass doors led to a large deck. It overlooked a beautiful rose garden just beyond. Combined with the roses near the front entry, Rosemary couldn't help but think of it as a great testimonial to the for-mer occupants' love of roses. Another door led to a small, still-empty room next to the kitchen. She didn't know what they would use it for yet.

The front of the house had a huge entry, leading from the grand double doors, and just inside at the very center of the house, there was an exceptionally wide and grand staircase, branching off both to the left and right on the upper floor, which contained four bedrooms, each with its own bathroom.

A large living room with a gigantic fireplace was on the left side of the staircase and several ceiling-to-floor windows, providing lots of nat-ural light. A library/office area took up the space on the right side with a powder room fitted in under the high point of the staircase. A formal dining room was situated behind the library room, around the corner from the kitchen. It had beautifully built-in china cupboards, taking up an entire inside wall, with four enormous French doors completing the outside wall. Those beautiful glass doors opened directly out to a corner of the decking. The deck itself wrapped across the back and along one side of the house.

There was not yet much furniture, and the house seemed hollow and cavernous in its emptiness. The living room and dining rooms were bare. Jeffrey purchased and set up a desk in the library/office area, stock-ing it with his books and files. Later, Rosemary planned to share some of those shelves after she asked her family to ship her collection of stored and beloved books.

In the master bedroom, a king-sized bed filled a quarter of the room; Rosemary would eventually make a nice sitting area at one end with plenty of space left over. At the moment, the only other furniture in the room was one end table with a lamp.

Drawers were built right into the closet areas, and the closets were so big they were a joke. Rosemary giggled every time she saw them. Hers was so big her measly wardrobe took up only a tenth of the area, and that was just her closet. Jeffrey had his own.

Since Jeffrey worked from dawn to dark, the long days were rather lonely for Rosemary, but she discovered her enjoyment in working in the rose gardens. She made it clear to the gardeners who maintained the mammoth yard that the roses were to be left for her as it helped to fill in the time. She made certain she remembered to bring freshly cut roses inside every other day or so to be placed strategically around the house. She loved the scent of the blossoms as it filled the rooms.

Rosemary certainly missed her college life, her friends, and especially her roommate, Julia. Julia, like her childhood friend Margie, had become much like a sister to her. Rosemary had constantly teased her friend about her Texan accent during their short time together, but she actually loved listening to the charming drawl. Julia had been such an enjoyment, so easy-going and full of life. The absence of their close friendship created a deep hole in her heart. She wrote one letter to Julia and received a quick, jovial response, but she felt more sadness than joy at the letter. It only reminded her of what she had given up. She tried to write another letter to her friend but didn't have much to say and finally discarded the attempt. There was nothing in common for them to share anymore. How things had changed.

Rosemary also missed her English and writing classes, tied to her greatest passion of writing. At least it had been until Jeffrey arrived on the scene. And strangely, it was only now that she truly began to feel the loss of the baby she had miscarried.

It wasn't long before Jeffrey began to pull in a larger salary, and he told Rosemary to purchase a new wardrobe and to go ahead and furnish the house, giving her free rein to do whatever she wanted. The project kept her busy for months, but when everything was done, the elation she expected wasn't there. She had done a beautiful job of pulling everything together. She had created rooms of warmth and color and, at the same time, kept a simple coziness to the old house. However, there was no one there to enjoy it with her. She was still very lonely and confused about her relationship with Jeffrey.

The first time Rosemary met her in-laws, things didn't go very well, and the times that followed weren't much better. In the beginning from the way Jeffrey had talked about his mother, Rosemary had already conjured up a picture of an overbearing woman with money and influence, one who could make life miserable for her new daughter-in-law if she desired. There was a certainty that she would never measure up to the high expectations Mrs. Archer expected of a wife to her only son.

Mary Ellen Archer didn't like Rosemary and hardly bothered to cover up her dislike. As a matter of fact, she had little to say to her new daughter-in-law. Actually it wasn't Rosemary, herself, that Mary Ellen disliked so much; it was Rosemary's holding the position of wife of Jeffrey, one no woman would have been able to fill.

The few times they'd been together, Mary Ellen had directed most of her conversation to her son, pretty much ignoring Rosemary. Rosemary hated the visits, and on that issue, her husband seemingly agreed with her. His mother irritated him, too. His conversations were directed basically to his father. Rosemary felt somewhat more comfortable with her new father-in-law, as Edward Archer seemed to be a decent man and included Rosemary in all the conversations as best he could. Rosemary didn't know what she would have done if it hadn't been for that bit of kindness. She realized she might have a chance to get to know him better, and perhaps they might even become good friends in time.

Of course, Mary Ellen was no dummy. She knew her son was being groomed to take over the business someday and she was obligated to include her daughter-in-law in her inner social circle, much to her distaste. And although Rosemary meant to refuse the invitations sent to her, in the end, she realized she needed to attend some of these functions to support her husband and the advancements that were to come. However, it was a chore to be with the upper echelons of the well-to-do, to keep herself poised and smiling, not to mention put up with their extreme boredom. It was such a different life style from anything she had ever known, and at times, it was very disconcerting. As far as Rosemary was concerned, Mary Ellen and her circle of friends were all nothing but social snobs. But she tried to be the good wife and socialize with them.

At one of their city charity events, Rosemary met a new friend, and this woman would literally save her life. Rosemary was getting her coat from the coat check counter near the door, preparing to leave the fashion show and luncheon, just ending. A tall, slim woman with a head full of very curly, long, auburn hair came to stand near her.

Looking straight ahead, the woman quietly whispered out the side of her mouth. "I saw you sitting over at the table near mine looking quite bored, and I said to myself, *Ah, there's a woman who agrees with my sentiment. These are the most boring, time-wasting affairs in the world. How will I survive another?*"

Rosemary was startled. She didn't know what to say.

As the woman saw the strange and quizzical look on Rosemary's face, she turned to face her and began to laugh. She looked over her shoulder to make sure no one was listening and whispered again. "I pegged you right, didn't I? You're not enjoying yourself whatsoever. Am I right?" She was grinning and Rosemary put a hand over her mouth to suppress a schoolgirl giggle.

"Does it show that much?"

"Uh huh! Yes, madam, it does!" The woman smiled and put out her hand. "Hi! My name's Mary Lou McCoy, and you are the boss's new daughter-in-law, aren't you? Everyone's been a-buzz since Jeffrey returned married and to someone none of them knows. They can't stand it. They're all so nosy." Again, the laughter bubbled out of the woman's mouth. There was no doubt she was enjoying herself.

Rosemary grasped the hand offered to her and shook it, not quite sure how she should take this woman but liking her all the same. She answered carefully. "Yes, that's me. Rosemary, the invader!"

"Ha, ha! I like that," Mary Lou grinned. "And I'm not going to ask any more questions either."

"Good." Rosemary returned her smile. "You don't want to hear all my deep, dark secrets anyway. Do you work for the company then?"

"Nope, but my husband does. Carter works in the Marketing Department. He's been there for fifteen years."

Rosemary assumed her husband was older because this gal looked to be not much older than Rosemary, herself. "Are you obligated to join these little . . . ah, social gatherings?"

"Yes, I guess I am, more or less. I don't come to them all. I dread most of them, but some of them are for really good causes, I must add. I like the ones that pertain to helping kids." She whispered again. "The worst part is I can't stand some of these people." Then Mary Lou said louder, "Hey, but now that I think I've met someone who shares my values, perhaps they won't be so dry and inhospitable. And I say inhospitable because most of these women don't like me very well. I say what I think, and you mustn't do that in this group of people." She looked over Rosemary's shoulder and saw a group of women leaving the dining area and coming towards them. "Rosemary, I have the company roster with your name on it. I'll give you a call. We'll have our own private lunch somewhere. That okay with you?"

"I would love it," Rosemary smiled at her new friend as they said their goodbyes.

Mary Lou was a wonderful change in Rosemary's life. They did see each other often after that and became very close friends. She finally had a confidante, something that had been missing in her life.

Mary Lou was a couple of years older and had come from a good family but not quite as well off as the Archers were. Like Rosemary, she came from a simple family in a small town. She had been raised in a tiny fishing town tucked away on the Atlantic Coast quite similar to Rosemary's growing up at the beach on the Pacific Coast, except that Mary Lou's father was the small town's only attorney.

As Jeffrey moved up into middle management of the family business, he found himself working beside Mary Lou's husband, Carter McCoy, in the Marketing Department. This pleased Rosemary so much because she felt free to invite them to their home. She felt comfortable with both of them. For a while, they did things as a foursome—dinner back and forth between them and a couple of weekend trips with the other couple. It was just perfect for Rosemary, and she was grateful for that time . . . while it lasted.

At first she didn't notice it, but in a while she began to see that Jeffrey had a way of setting himself apart from the group with a sense of superiority. Carter never said anything. He was very easy going, but Rosemary perceived that the other couple was very much aware of her husband's standoffish manner, and she no longer felt quite so comfortable when they were all together.

Being intelligent and a fast learner, Jeffrey soon made his way to the top of the ladder at the company, doing just what his father had planned for him. At the upper-management level now, Jeffrey was put in charge of production. Jeffrey suddenly became unavailable for any more social commitments with the McCoys. He maintained he was too busy, and it was necessary to work late most days to get an edge on his newfound duties. One thing was for certain—now that Jeffrey had moved up to top management, he looked down on Carter for making no advancements within the company. Carter liked the job he had with no ambition to make any moves upwards or sideways. Although the women continued to be the best of friends, the four of them no longer spent time together.

Chapter Four

In August of 1984, Rosemary made a short trip back to Washington. Sadly, her mother was ill with stomach cancer and had been for some time. Her parents had not told her. Now she was undergoing a third round of chemotherapy in Seattle, and it didn't look very promising, so they had no choice but to let their daughter know. By the time Rosemary arrived and after her mother's fifth treatment, Louise began to feel stronger, and the prognosis seemed much better. She was released from the hospital, and Rosemary spent a few more days with them before returning to Cincinnati. Her father looked strong and healthy, and she was certain he would take special care of her mother. She left them with a hopeful feeling. However, a few months later, the cancer suddenly began to progress rapidly, and in one short month, her mother passed away after her difficult struggle with the disease.

Rosemary pleaded with her husband to attend the funeral with her. He had never met her family, and she thought it was only proper that he join her at this solemn occasion. He balked at the idea, not being the least bit interested in flying out to Washington State, but he finally gave in to her pleadings. She was greatly relieved for she was pregnant again, even though she hadn't announced the news to anyone yet, including Jeffrey. She'd been too taken up with worry for her mother. Because of her previous miscarriage, she had been nervous about travelling alone.

They arrived in Seattle the day before the funeral, rented a car, and drove to the coast. Too late, she discovered what a mistake it was to have taken Jeffrey with her. He acted like a spoiled child the whole time they were there, without bothering to hide the fact that it seemed an immense imposition for him to have come at all. Her brothers, whom she hadn't seen for so long, were thoroughly disgusted, and they didn't hide that fact either. She was so embarrassed at Jeffrey's behavior. It wasn't enough that she was mourning the death of her mother and trying her best to support her devastated father, but she had to concern herself about her husband, as well.

A couple of days after the funeral and several days of putting up with Jeffrey's antics, found Rosemary and her husband heading back to Cincinnati a day earlier than planned. During the return trip home, it took everything Rosemary had to hold back her tears, which threatened to burst at any moment. She was so humiliated. How had she gotten herself into this predicament anyway? There certainly wasn't anything between the two of them anymore. Jeffrey seemed to have his own agenda, and she certainly wasn't a part of it. And the baby! The baby, who should have been such a blessing to both of them, was going to be a blessing only to her, it appeared. She wanted the baby more than anything and was very impatient for its birth. Rosemary was certain her husband's involvement in their child's life would be almost nil. The questions lingered in her mind. What on earth should she do for the future? What recourse did she have? All she knew for the present time was she would be the best mother she could be, and in the meantime, she would take life one day at a time.

At least before the trip, they were able to converse with each other during those infrequent times when Jeffrey was at home, and even occasionally, they shared an intimate evening together. Well, maybe it wasn't exactly intimate. She tried—a nice candle-lit dinner or two and some mechanical lovemaking here and there. Each time she hoped things would get better, but they never did. Actually, because of this rarity, she was very surprised that she had gotten pregnant. Now, they hardly spoke to each other, and she hadn't shared her pregnancy with him yet. He was absent even more than before. Oh, his excuses were always work related, but truthfully, she found them hard to believe. There was no understanding of how anyone could work as many hours as he proposed to be doing.

Rosemary tried to keep herself occupied and took up her pen and paper again, attempting to focus on her almost forgotten novel, to accomplish her dream of being an author of published works. She had a great start with many ideas floating around in her head and some research to do yet. She began again by dedicating several hours to her writing efforts every morning after she'd finished jogging her regular two miles. The doctor had told her she could jog since she was used to doing it before her pregnancy but not to overdo it.

It wasn't long before her pregnancy began to show, and she finally divulged her secret, although she was reluctant to share it with Jeffrey. As suspected, he didn't seem very interested, but then she could never tell what his true feelings were about anything. He asked her when it was due but little more about it, which wasn't surprising due to their circumstances at the time.

Jeffrey continued to stretch his workday, coming home very late every night. Usually Rosemary didn't hear him arriving in the wee hours of the morning. She was usually asleep when he left the house and asleep when he returned. And he'd moved into another bedroom, saying he didn't want to disturb her. She became accustomed to eating and living alone, with the exception of occasionally having lunch with her friend, Mary Lou.

A big expansion was going on at the company, and Edward Archer felt his son was ready for the responsibility of heading up this project. He relieved Jeffrey of his current job and put him temporarily in charge of the new in-depth assignment.

"You're going to get your feet wet on this one, son. Think you can handle it?"

"Just let me at it. I'll show you how it's done," he grinned.

His father thought perhaps his son was a little overconfident, yet Jeffrey had displayed creativeness in all the departments Edward had placed him. He couldn't have been happier with the result of his son's work to this point. He would let Jeffrey go for it. "Just keep me informed as you go along. The architect's design on the new building is over there." Edward pointed to his desk. "Take a look at it and let me know what you think. In my opinion, and I'm sure you might agree, some of those conference rooms are too small, and I would like to see a bigger parking lot for the employees. We may need to go after that property west of here; see if those people are willing to sell at a reasonable price."

"Okay, Dad. Will do. I'll take them with me and give them a good study." Jeffrey was anxious to get going on it; he wanted to show his father and everyone else just what he was capable of doing.

After endless weeks of late hours, Jeffrey arrived home early on the afternoon of December 23. He was to help his father host the company's annual Christmas party this year. It was scheduled for that evening, and he'd come home to change into more formal attire for the event.

As the CEO, Edward expressed a fervent wish each year that all employees, titled or untitled, attend this function. And, of course, Jeffrey desired to make an impression on everyone so he was very anxious to be part of celebration. He wanted all the employees to know who he was, as if they didn't already.

Rosemary was expected to go, of course, and at first, she balked at the idea. She didn't care anymore that her husband was never around and certainly didn't concern herself much about what was going on at the Archer Company. She was just satisfied to be planning the nursery for her baby and spending time working on her novel.

But she decided she had a duty to attend the party. Mary Lou and Carter would be there, along with some friends of the McCoys and a few other nice couples she'd met. And as the time grew nearer, she actually began to look forward to the evening. It was Christmas, after all, and a night out would be good for her.

She purchased a new maternity dress in navy blue, which when accessorized with the beautiful sapphire earrings she'd received recently from the Archers for her twenty-second birthday, looked rather chic. She was sure her father-in-law had been the instigator of that wonderful gift, but regardless of who was responsible, she had been overwhelmed and touched by the gesture. She put on her new low-heeled pumps that, fortunately, she had been able to find in almost the same color as the dress. She felt cheerful as she admired the image she studied in the full-length mirror of her dressing room.

It was quite a surprise when Jeffrey came out of the bathroom and saw her all dressed and made up and said to her, "You look very nice, Rosemary." He had stopped calling her Rosie. "I really like the new dress. You'll be the hit of the ball." There was some satisfaction in hearing him compliment her, but was he saying it only to make her feel good? Or was it because she was presentable as his wife and good enough for the assistant vice president of the company? She didn't know the reason, but she thanked him sweetly.

Not long after their entrance to the ballroom at the King's Palace Hotel, Jeffrey nonchalantly moved away from her to shake hands and to greet people he knew well. Then as she said hello to the few she knew, he casually drifted away from her. Well, that was perfectly fine with her. She had expected no less. Rosemary scanned the room quickly until she located Carter and Mary Lou across the floor near the bar. She headed in that direction but was stopped a couple of times by women she had met at those dutiful social engagements. She spoke briefly with each one and finally reached the McCoys.

"Hi! My, don't you two look nice all dressed up."

"Yep, Carter and I clean up pretty good." Mary Lou laughed.

"Mary Lou, red is very, very becoming on you. Why don't you wear that color more often?"

"Cause it makes me feel like a Jezebel."

Carter put his arm around his wife. "She is a Jezebel, but I love her anyway."

Mary Lou gave him a little punch but grinned at him before turning back to her friend. Rosemary envied them their relationship with each other. "Look who's talking. That's a stunning dress! Hey, you're beginning to show a little bit there, mother-to-be." She reached over and patted Rosemary's stomach.

Rosemary smiled at Mary Lou. "Only a few months to go. The baby is due around March 30. The nursery is ready and I am, too."

The days were flying past so quickly; the time was going to be there before Rosemary knew it. She couldn't wait. She was going to smother her child with love, and it was going to love her back. How she needed that.

Bob Ager, one of Carter's former partners in the Marketing Department, and his wife, Ida, stopped to chat for a few minutes with the three of them. While Rosemary was talking to Ida, she heard Carter tell his wife he wanted her to meet someone.

Mary Lou wiggled her fingers at Rosemary and said, "Be right back. Jeffrey will be at the podium with his dad tonight, I imagine. Be sure to sit with us when they get ready to make their speeches." Rosemary nodded. Yes, that's where Jeffrey would be, in the spotlight of course, and she was grateful she didn't have to sit by herself or with strangers.

After the Agers left, she wondered where her in-laws were, as she hadn't seen them come into the room yet. As her eyes searched the large room, now rapidly filling with people, she spotted Jeffrey huddled with his father and mother behind one of the four, large marble pillars in the room, not far away from where Rosemary stood.

They weren't aware of her, and Rosemary didn't want to interrupt them so she turned to the barman and asked for a small glass of 7 Up. Never one to drink much alcohol, she was especially careful while carrying this baby. She wasn't taking any chances.

When the drink was poured, she turned around and saw that the elder Archers had moved on, and Jeffrey was now animatedly talking to a woman at his side. Rosemary eased her way over towards them. She could see only the woman's back and didn't recognize who it was, but she noticed how close the two of them had their heads together.

As she moved closer and the woman changed her position, Rosemary saw that it was none other than Gaile Moyan. She was one of Mary Ellen Archer's cohorts. Although Gaile was a woman a dozen years younger than Rosemary's mother-in-law, she was definitely a woman fashioned from the same mold as Mary Ellen in that she had the same giant superiority complex.

Gaile was standing very close to Jeffrey, whispering something into his ear. Jeffrey threw his head back and roared, and the woman laughed with him. Instead of approaching any further, Rosemary stopped to listen to what Gaile was saying.

"So, my darlin', you're dealing with the big boys now. Yes? Carol tells me she joins you over at the Derby Club sometimes in the evenings for drinks now. Very, very nice! You're working yourself up to the big time, boy. It's not easy to get a membership in that club, you know." And just in case he wasn't aware of it, she added, "Don's been a member for years now."

She was referring to her husband, whom Rosemary had never seen and neither had many of the others at the company. Word was Gaile and Don didn't get along and were rarely seen together, just like her and Jeffrey. Rosemary couldn't help but compare their situations.

She wondered if Gaile's husband was at the club tonight. She was sure he probably preferred it to the Archer shindig and being with his snooty wife.

Gaile continued, "Drinks are cheap there. Entertainment is good. No one tells tales out of school, do they? Everyone keeps quiet. You get the works, huh?"

Jeffrey rolled his eyes, insolently shrugging his shoulders and smiled smugly, while slyly sharing the secret of the club's activities with her. He glanced around the room, briefly scanning the ballroom for his wife. He didn't see her standing near them, as there was an elderly couple blocking his line of vision. "Ah, yeah it's . . . nice. Get a lot of business done there, you understand." He laughed again.

Big joke, Rosemary thought. She understood the implications of the conversation the two were having, and her stomached recoiled. *Has he no shame?* She wondered.

Jeffrey still didn't see her, but Rosemary realized the very moment Gaile spotted her because the woman's acidy voice grew an octave louder. "How is Carol by the way? She's a sweet gal, isn't she?"

"Well, Carol and I are only—." He stopped when he saw Rosemary. "Oh, hi, darling," Jeffrey said in surprise. He called her endearing names only in public. There was a slight but deeper color in his cheeks. "I didn't see you. Have you been floating around meeting some new people? Gaile, you've met my wife, Rosemary, haven't you?"

"No, but 'tis a great pleasure, darlin'," she drawled. Gaile didn't offer her hand nor did Rosemary make the effort to offer hers. "My, I do hope I didn't let the cat out of the bag with the company's after-hour stories. Your royal master here gets around some, if you know what I mean." It was a deliberate ploy to embarrass Rosemary or perhaps both her and Jeffrey.

"Oh, not at all, Gaile." Rosemary lathered on the sweetness. "Not at all! Jeffrey always lets me know where he's going to be and what's going on, don't you, darlin'? She tucked her arm under his.

Jeffrey didn't say anything but looked at her with his mouth hanging open. Her response had gotten his attention.

Rosemary continued, "I am just . . . well, you can see, pregnant and tired a lot so I . . . haven't been able to go out with him much." She wanted to smash her fist into the woman's nose and his, too.

Jeffrey stood stiffly beside her, as he heard the sarcasm drip from his wife's icy voice, and for once, he didn't know how to respond. He could feel her body vibrate with anger. How much had she heard, he was wondering. Caught off guard and somewhat embarrassed, he tried to smile as if it was a joke, but Gaile gave him a knowing and pitiful smile in return.

Saved by the bell. Just then someone picked up the microphone and announced that dinner was being served. People began to move to their tables, and Gaile used that as an excuse to make her escape.

Jeffrey quickly pulled away from his wife's arm, which was still linked to his. "You were rude, Rosemary!"

"Was I, Jeffrey? Well, perhaps, darling. Does it matter?" Rosemary was steaming but she wasn't about to lose her cool.

"We'll talk later. Excuse me. I have to join Dad." He hastily left her side. Rosemary angrily stalked off. She was tempted to leave and find her own way home. Then she saw that the McCoys were looking for her. They waved, and Rosemary walked towards them and dropped heavily into a chair.

"Are you okay, Rosemary? You look white as a ghost."

"I am fine! Thanks." Someone at the table started talking about what was on the menu, a discussion ensued, and Rosemary picked up her menu, not to read it but to hide behind it, as she tried to swallow her bitterness.

After dinner, Edward gave a little talk about the company and praised his employees for the job they had done for the company, informing them how that resulted in great profits for the year and ample bonuses would be handed out on December 30. There was a big applause after that announcement.

Then it was Jeffrey's turn. He talked about the expansion that was almost complete, the changes that were to be made in the infrastructure of offices, the warehouse, who would be in the new building after the first of the year, and who would remain where they were.

"As your vice president for next year, I envision our production will be almost double. While we will be hiring some new people, we will be depending on all of you to give us 100 percent as, of course, you have in the past. I hope you will work with me to make all this production happen, and perhaps the bonuses will be even more next year."

Rosemary was caught off guard. Jeffrey hadn't bothered to tell her of his latest promotion from assistant vice president to the vice presidency itself. She wondered where Oliver Hansen, vice president until now, was going or if he was retiring. *Well, well, congratulations, my dear husband,* she said silently. *I wish I could be happy for you,* she thought sadly. The good feelings she had earlier in the day had disappeared with the episode she'd just been through. She was left feeling deflated and depressed, an emotion that was becoming a major part of her life. How could she continue this charade, keep living with this man, and still save her sanity? Right now, her focus was on her baby and the only reason she could muddle through this mess.

After the speeches, a three-piece combo came in to play, and there was dancing. Out of obligation, she realized, Jeffrey asked her to dance the first dance with him. Everyone was watching, and she could hardly refuse, although that's exactly what she wanted to do. He smiled gaily at her for the benefit of his audience but said little to Rosemary as they made their way around the room. She was relieved when other couples began to crowd the dance floor. He was stiff and formal; so was she. She did not enjoy being in his arms any more than he liked having her there. When the music stopped, she excused herself to go to the ladies room. After ten minutes or so of fussing with her makeup and hair, which she did only for the purpose of postponing a return to the party, she forced herself to go back to the ballroom.

Immediately, she spotted Jeffrey dancing with a very beautiful young lady. Was that Carol, she wondered. She watched him pick one pretty woman and then another to dance with him. *Ah, maybe that was Carol, the one with the short red hair.* Yes, he was dancing a second and then a third dance with that one. That must be Carol. They were dancing quite close, improperly so, and the woman was very focused on her charming partner. Jeffrey wasn't being very discreet, was he? Then she saw the Archers at a table on the other side of the floor. Mary Ellen's voice was being exercised as usual, talking nonstop to another woman at her table, but Edward was watching the dance floor intensely. Rosemary could tell that his attention was riveted towards his son and his dancing partner. She wondered what her father-in-law thought about this little scenario.

Rosemary felt the evening would never end. She didn't want to make a scene, but she was ready to go and made that fact known to Jeffrey. She made some light conversation with the McCoys but hardly remembered what they talked about. Finally, the band quit playing and people began to leave.

On the way home, neither Jeffrey nor Rosemary spoke until they were only blocks from the house. Quietly, Rosemary asked him, "Is that where you spend your late hours every night? At . . . the club? With Carol? I have to admit she's quite pretty."

Jeffrey stammered, as he waved his hand, "Carol! Carol! She's no one. She's just the executive assistant for Carter McCoy. She . . . she was temporarily involved in the expansion project with me, that's all."

There was another electric silence between them for a moment, and then he spoke, "Don't listen to big mouth Gaile Moyan. She's like my mother. Likes to hear herself talk."

Yeah, right! Rosemary shook her head back and forth in the darkened car, not believing a word he said. She really was tired of this whole business, and it wasn't worth fighting about now. She didn't care what he did.

After that evening, Jeffrey began to come home earlier on most days, at least for a while. She believed he was only cooling his heels because people were talking about him and Carol. And, yes, there was gossip. Mary Lou had told Rosemary as much. She didn't know if Jeffrey was seeing the woman at the present but guessed he might be due to the many nights he wasn't around. It was difficult, but Rosemary would wait until the baby's birth before making any permanent decisions about her life and that of her child; however, a decision would definitely have to be made.

Christmas quickly led to New Year's Eve. The new year of 1985 began with a bang. A snowstorm arrived late in the evening, dumping several feet of the fluffy, white stuff, keeping Rosemary and Jeffrey locked inside for three or four days. Trapped at home, Jeffrey stayed in his office, and Rosemary spent her time in the kitchen nook where she did her writing. There were momentary glimpses of each other as they carried on with their own agendas. Rosemary fixed light meals for herself and took them to her room. She didn't know what he did about his meals and didn't care. Rosemary was glad when the weather cleared and her husband was out of the house again. She felt the release of tension leave her body as soon as he was gone.

At the end of January, Rosemary invited Mary Lou to lunch. She hadn't seen her friend since the company's Christmas party. The two women were having a nice little chat and enjoying the tasty, green salad Rosemary had prepared. All of a sudden, Rosemary excused herself to go the bathroom. To her surprise and great panic, she discovered she was bleeding. Letting out a scream, Mary Lou came quickly to help her and then drove her to the doctor's office, where he examined her with great concern. He didn't want to take any chances of a miscarriage, so he sent her home to be confined to her bed for the rest of her pregnancy. After losing her first child, Rosemary was more than willing to listen to his advice to be very careful. She would do anything to save this baby. It was all she lived for.

Jeffrey hired a private nurse to be with Rosemary during the day, and again for a while, he was home every evening to help her. He seemed gentle with her, and although they didn't have much to say to each other, he willingly tended to her needs in the evenings. Just when she started to put some trust in him again, things seemed to backfire.

Two weeks into her confinement, after taking care of her dinner and assisting her with preparations for bed, Jeffrey informed her that it was necessary to go back to the office and finish some reports. Then began a series of his having to go back to the office every other night or so. Rosemary knew he was lying. There was nothing to do about it, at least not at the present time. But she would. She was only concentrating on saving her baby now; it was her only priority.

The weeks passed slowly. On the evening of February 27, 1985, still more than three weeks before her due date, Rosemary's water broke. Jeffrey, who happened to be at home for once, rushed her to the hospital. After a very difficult twelve hours of labor, their son entered the world.

My son, she thought selfishly to herself. *He's all mine.* Rosemary was ecstatic with joy. Her beautiful baby was small but in perfect health with all his fingers and toes and a cute button nose. She was ready to love him with all her might. The void in her marriage really didn't matter anymore.

Jeffrey didn't show very much interest in his new son, which was par for the course; in fact, that was all the better for Rosemary. She named her son Mathew Edward, Mathew after her father, Edward after Jeffrey's. The baby was her life now.

Rosemary welcomed the business of each day with her new son. She put her writing aside and pushed other details of her life into the background as she delved into the state of motherhood with complete abandonment. Rosemary joyfully observed Mathew's alertness and the bubbly smiles he gave her as he began to interact with his mother and react to his surroundings. He was a happy baby with a loving mother leading the way. As he grew from an infant to a small child, he accumulated a definite little personality all his own. He was the love of Rosemary's life.

From the beginning, little Mathew's grandmother Mary Ellen would coo and talk to him, seemingly showing her love in her own little way, but she never asked to hold him. It wasn't that she was afraid to hold him; she just didn't want to muss up her hair or wrinkle her dress. Of course, that was the way Jeffrey grew up. There was always a nurse or a babysitter taking care of him when he was a child.

However, Mary Ellen thought her grandson not only looked just like his father but also would be as smart as him. She constantly bragged about her grandson to others. Edward Archer took to his grandson like a duck to water, making up for his son's absence and his wife's lack of a loving touch. He would hold Mathew and coo and talk to him for long periods. Mathew soon grew to recognize his Bopa whenever he came to the house.

Mary Lou McCoy dropped in often to see Rosemary and Mathew, and to Rosemary's surprise, so did several of the other women she had become acquainted with during all those stuffy obligatory programs she had attended. Of course, Rosemary now had an excuse for not attending "have-to" meetings and boring lunches. She was contented in her new role as a mother.

Jeffrey usually saw Mathew on Saturday mornings but didn't spend much time with the baby before locking himself in the library or going back to the office for "a few hours." Rosemary didn't think he really knew how to interact with someone so small, and he seemed satisfied to let Rosemary do the parenting. That was okay with her.

As Mathew grew, his mother took him for walks and to the park to play. He loved exploring for bugs and things crawling on the ground and was delighted when a stray dog befriended him or the friendly neighborhood cat brushed around his fat, little toddler legs.

Later when he was three, Rosemary introduced him to a play school not far from home, so he could meet other children his age. A year later, it was followed by four mornings a week in a preschool that he dearly loved.

The older the boy became, the more his grandfather adored him. Edward would often stop by unannounced to see his grandson. Generally, he carried some small gift in his pocket for the boy. Rosemary welcomed the visits, realizing the bond being created was a very special thing for them both. Watching her father-in-law, she thought it was perhaps the happiest moments of his life, certainly since she had known him anyway.

Rosemary had determined there would not be another child so Mathew became that much more precious. She wanted to take Mathew to see his other grandfather and was thinking about it but hadn't yet approached Jeffrey with the idea. If she did go, she might not come back, she realized. She thought many times she would walk out on her marriage, but there were several reasons why she hadn't moved in that direction. Although she hated to admit it, the Archer money was one of the things that kept her in Cincinnati. Financially, it would help her to raise her son, providing him with the very best education he'd need for his future, and she wasn't sure she had the heart to separate Mathew from his beloved Bopa.

After the incident with Jeffrey following her mother's funeral, Rosemary tried to convince her father everything was okay with her, that things had been straightened out. If she left Jeffrey, she would have no place to go but to Washington.

Every week Rosemary wrote letters to her father, filling him in on all the things his little namesake was doing, how rapidly he seemed to be growing, and what a great little guy he was.

She missed her family desperately and longed to see them. As luck would have it, in the spring of 1989, she had the opportunity to see her brother Daniel. He was making a business trip from his home in Memphis to Springfield, Ohio. She received a phone call from him, hoping she would drive to Springfield for a couple of days. He didn't feel he could come to her due to the never-resolved bad feelings between him and her husband. It wasn't that long of a drive; she decided to do it.

Mathew was about four years old then, and of course, Rosemary took him along with her, making the trip an overnight stay. She lied to Jeffrey, telling him her former roommate, Julia, was there, and she was making a quick trip to meet up with her friend. It made little difference to Jeffrey that she was going, but it might have had she told him it was her brother she was seeing. Ever since the trip to Washington, Jeffrey wanted absolutely nothing to do with her family.

Rosemary and Daniel had a wonderful time together, only regretful that their time was so limited and passed so quickly. Jeffrey's name was never mentioned by either of them during their short visit.

Mathew was well behaved and loved his doting uncle almost from the beginning. Daniel and his wife had not been able to have children of their own. After two miscarriages and Mimi almost losing her life, they'd decided not to try again due to her health. Daniel had always wanted children; Rosemary could tell he would have been a great father from the way he related to his nephew.

Her brother filled her in on David, who had two boys—Jacob, fourteen, and Jesse, nine. The brothers had been together recently, and Daniel couldn't help but brag about his two other nephews. It made Rosemary sad for she'd never had the chance to meet them. She hoped to see them one day not too far in the future.

Letters from her brothers had been rare. Neither was good at corresponding. She didn't write to her sisters-in-law either because she didn't really know them. Rosemary and her parents had gone to David and Jean's wedding in Seattle in June 1967, where he lived for a short time after graduating from high school. Rosemary had been just five years old at the time. And although she had talked to Daniel's wife, Mimi, on the phone, Rosemary had met her only once. That was at their wedding in Las Vegas when Rosemary was around eleven. She and her parents had spent four days there. It had been her first jet plane ride and her mother's, too. They were both thrilled. David and Jean had attended the wedding, and they all had enjoyed the event and their time together as a family. It was a fond memory for Rosemary, albeit a fading one.

So this meeting with Daniel was the first she'd seen any of her family since her mother's death. Her thirst for getting reacquainted with her brother kept them up into the wee hours of the morning. She didn't want to give up a second with him. It was, in many ways, a healing visit for Rosemary, but at the same time, she felt sadness and regret for missing all those years without knowing her brothers and their families. They were very nice men. And she was sorry, too, that she hadn't seen her beloved father in such a long time. It made her determined that one way or another she would see him soon.

It was difficult to say goodbye when they parted, and she felt the great bear hug Daniel gave her long afterwards on her drive back home. She wanted to cry but held her tears, so Mathew wouldn't see them and ask questions. She would save them for later.

Somehow the promise she made to see her father never came to fruition so it was with great surprise and much happiness that in May of 1990, almost a year after visiting with her brother, she received wonderful news in a letter from her father. Deciding that his daughter was never going to bring his grandson home for a visit, he made plans to come to them instead. Rosemary was excited about the news until she remembered Jeffrey. How would Jeffrey treat his father-in-law? He had no use for her family, so would he be discourteous and rude? Would he embarrass both her and her father?

She should have had no concerns. She and her father saw little of Jeffrey while he was there. Matt was an early riser and briefly crossed paths with his son-in-law as he left the house for his office on a couple of mornings. Obligatory greetings were said, and that was that! And Jeffrey was there for only one weekend meal during Matt's five-day stay. During those times, Jeffrey was courteous, if not formal in his demeanor, but he didn't interfere with the two of them or their plans or say anything out of line. Rosemary was very grateful for that.

At five years old, Mathew was still a small boy but one with long legs and the energy of an older child, it seemed to his mother. There were no dull moments, and by the time his grandpa Matt was ready to leave for home, they had become best buddies. Of course, Matt thought his grandson was the world's greatest grandchild. He was so proud of him and Rosemary, relieved to know that the two of them were fine and that Jeffrey, for all his indifference, wasn't abusing them. That had been his greatest fear. Oh, he could tell things weren't as they seemed, and he knew just how good his daughter was at pretending everything was fine, all for his benefit. She didn't share much of her life with him. Rosemary was good at keeping her personal problems to herself. But her son was her greatest joy, and Matt was thankful she had the boy in her life.

The time flew past quickly, as it always seemed to do, and soon it was time for Matt to leave. It was very difficult for them to say their farewells. This time Rosemary couldn't hide her tears.

"Dad, I can't tell you how much your visit has meant to me. I hope you'll come again."

He hugged her, "I've enjoyed myself, too, princess. Maybe you and Mathew can come and visit me next. Only let's not let so much time go by. I love you, sweetie!"

Rosemary couldn't let him go. She squeezed harder. "I love you, too, Dad. I'll miss you so much. Yes, we'll see about a visit." She pulled away, wiping away her tears. "Have a good trip. I'll pray for your safe return."

And then he was going, walking towards the airport gate, turning and waving to them one last time before he disappeared through the door.

Mathew had been interested in and distracted by the large crowd of people around him in the airport, but when he suddenly realized his grandfather was gone, he began to cry. "I want my Grandpo." The two of them, both crying now, turned towards the airport garage to get the car.

Soon enough, it was time for Rosemary to enroll young Mathew in kindergarten; however, she would remain an active part of her son's school day. The school she'd selected was a private co-op, which encouraged parental participation. She volunteered for anything the school needed, from cookies for a party and driving for field trips to helping out in the classroom when the teacher needed assistance.

Rosemary was very pleased with the progress she saw in her son that year and in the years to come. As he matured, she went to all her son's soccer games, programs, and special events and enjoyed every minute of them. She was a doer. Everyone, from the teachers on down to the parents, grew to respect Rosemary, and they liked her well-behaved son, too. He was happy, good mannered, and every bit a credit to Rosemary's child rearing.

She tried very hard not to dote on her son, but her enjoyment in him made her want to be with him all the time. She made herself available wherever she was needed. The two of them were very close, and she liked the way he was growing up. He was a kind and considerate little person and very loving towards her, his teachers, and his young friends. He was even kind to his father in their rare moments when they were together, but Jeffrey was blinded to that fact; he didn't even seem to notice.

By the time Mathew was in the third grade, Rosemary had become well known at the little Crest Haven Elementary School. One of the parents approached her and asked her if she would consider running for president of the PTA. She was hesitant at first, saying she would consider it, and when many other parents pressured her to do so, she finally agreed. She was elected and served for several years in that capacity. The parents just kept voting her into office every year, and consequently, she served until Mathew completed the sixth grade there.

During this time, Jeffrey saw only one or two of Mathew's soccer games, usually arriving late, and came to only one of the PTA meetings; fortunately, it was the one when the fourth grade class presented a play in honor of their fathers. She was so thankful that her son didn't have to experience being one with an absent father.

Shortly afterwards, Jeffrey demonstrated a small interest in having his son come to the office with him on a couple of Saturday mornings. Jeffrey showed him around, and they went out for ice cream afterwards, but Rosemary noticed that it wasn't a big deal to Mathew. Jeffrey was making a half-hearted attempt but couldn't seem to connect with his son. Too much time had passed. The bonding wasn't there for either of them. That was about the extent of Jeffrey's efforts to have a relationship with Mathew. After the second time, Jeffrey never offered again, and Mathew never asked to go.

For some reason, Jeffrey did go to most of the parent-teacher conferences, but he let Rosemary handle all the questions. Rosemary felt it was just an obligatory function Jeffrey needed to keep up his image. Plus, Rosemary thought Edward might have had something to do with his going at all.

Grandfather Edward saw Mathew whenever he could. He had a keen interest in everything the boy did. Edward was so proud of his grandson, and he let everyone know it. He also thought Rosemary was doing a great job raising him. Edward was proud of her involvement in the boy's activities, and he told her so. Mathew had good social skills, and for all the time his mother spent with him, he hadn't become at all spoiled. His report cards expressed his intelligence, and Edward promised himself that when the time came, his grandson would get into a good prep school and receive the best education available so he would have the opportunity of a bright and successful future. It even crossed his mind that perhaps his young grandson might one day become the new CEO of the Archer Manufacturing Company.

When the time was right, Edward did some research on private schools in their area, and he and Rosemary agreed to work together in selecting the right one. The one they liked best was the John G. Miller School, a private preparatory academy and one with a well-established reputation for turning out well-educated scholars, ready for advanced learning at the best of colleges and universities. Consequently, Mathew was enrolled at the Miller school in his seventh grade year at the age of twelve. Rosemary was delighted with the choice she and Edward had made together. Of course, it made no difference to Jeffrey, who was emotionally detached from the whole situation.

The new school did have one drawback and that was the necessity of a thirty to thirty-five minute drive each way for Rosemary on a daily basis. Edward came up with a plan. The Archer Manufacturing Company was located on the same side of the city and only ten miles from the school. He saw no reason why he and Jeffrey couldn't help with the driving. He set up a schedule for the two of them to take turns picking up Mathew a couple of afternoons a week. It would relieve

Rosemary of two return trips on those days. Jeffrey agreed, although Rosemary was sure Edward had given his son no opportunity to nix the plan. This brought Jeffrey home early one day a week, surely not to his liking. She kept hoping her husband and her son would get better acquainted during their drives, but this didn't happen. On those afternoons, the two of them traipsed into the house looking solemn and not saying much to each other. Jeffrey would then isolate himself in his office with work as soon as they got home.

Once Mathew said, "Mom, I wish Grandpa could pick me up all the time. We have such a good time together."

Rosemary felt sorry for him, "I know, Mathew. You guys have a special thing going, don't you? But he can't do it all the time. Be happy that you get to see him a lot. Not all grandsons are so lucky to see their grandfathers as much as you do."

"I know, Mom. Bennie doesn't even have one." That was Mathew's new friend. "I guess I am pretty lucky all right. I have you and Grandpa both." Then before Rosemary could respond, he had grabbed an apple from the refrigerator and was on his way to his room. How touching, Rosemary told herself—touching and sad.

Rosemary could very well have driven Mathew to school and picked him up every day for she was so used to being where he was. Now she had a little time on her hands and didn't know what to do with it. She tried writing her novel again but just couldn't get into that frame of mind. She had a weekly lunch with Mary Lou but turned down the charity lunches her mother-in-law invited her to, using Mathew as an excuse. She missed being with her son and observing his activities. He was growing up, and she was going to have to make some adjustments in her own life. She had to let him spread his wings; she knew that, but it wasn't easy for her.

❦

After relating so much to Thomas, Rosemary started to sob big body-shaking sobs.

Thomas reached over, took her hand, and squeezed it. "Oh, Rosemary, it must have been complicated for you living like that—being married and yet not being married. And trying to be both parents for your son."

Rosemary cried harder.

He held her hand tightly, afraid to move any closer, and just let her cry it out.

After a while, she lifted her head, pulled her hand away from his and went searching for a Kleenex in her pocket. He handed her his handkerchief, and she blew her nose. "My God! You must be exhausted, listening to my sad tale. I'd better go in."

Thomas didn't want her to leave and pleaded softly, "No, Rosemary. Not at all. Please finish your story. I'm interested. I told you I'm a good listener, and it'll help for you to talk it out. I promise you'll feel much better." How could he keep her there and keep her talking?

"That's a big promise," she said between her tears. She laid her head back on the seat and sighed heavily.

Thomas was delighted that she hadn't moved to open the car door, and while silence invaded the space around them once again, he sat perfectly still, willing her to go on with her story. He was almost afraid to breathe, as he let her make the decision to continue talking about her past. He watched her eyes close, and when the silence continued, he wondered perhaps if she had fallen asleep.

She lay against the seat, dredging images from her life of that unspeakable, horrible time she'd lived through. How could she begin to tell her friend about the horror of what happened next? Rosemary hadn't even been able to talk to her dad about it. He had brought it up once, but she had changed the subject. She hadn't talked about it to anyone since leaving the McCoys and Cincinnati, although the pain never left her heart. It was impossible to relate to another person the extent of her pain, and she surprised herself by sharing it with Thomas. She had to admit it felt good to lean on a friend, releasing just a little bit of the hurt by sharing it.

Thomas's body jolted, when Rosemary suddenly shuddered and blurted out, "It was horrible! There was a complete mix-up. It shouldn't have happened."

CHAPTER FIVE

I T WAS MORE THAN A COMPLETE MIX-UP. It was a catastrophe. A terrible catastrophe! It happened on a Monday, and Monday was one of three days during the week when Rosemary had to drive both to and from Mathew's school. Unfortunately, part of Rosemary's front tooth broke off that morning after she'd returned from driving her son to school. There was a dull ache radiating out from the tooth, and suspecting it would only get worse, she knew it would have to be taken care of right away. Her dentist couldn't take her until 2:00 p.m., which really put her in a bind.

She called Jeffrey but couldn't get him; he wasn't in. She didn't bother to leave a message with his secretary. Instead, she called Edward, seeking his assistance, and after juggling his schedule around a bit, he happily agreed to pick Mathew up in the afternoon for her.

Several hours later after talking to his daughter-in-law, Edward received a call from his wife. She was in a tizzy! Her car had broken down in the middle of nowhere, and she wanted him to come and rescue her. Now!

"But, Mary Ellen, I promised Rosemary I would pick up Mathew; she broke a tooth and—"

"I don't give a damn what she broke. Get Jeffrey to do it," she shouted over the phone.

"Okay! Okay!" There was nothing he could do when Mary Ellen was in one of her demanding moods. He might as well give in. You couldn't win with her. Shaking his head, he hung up and quickly dialed his son's office. Jeffrey's secretary said he left late for lunch and had an errand to do, but he told her he would be back. He was expected within the hour. She said she would be sure he received the message to pick up his son.

However, Jeffrey never returned to his office that afternoon. He'd skipped lunch in lieu of yet another rendezvous with his new love, Cindy, in her downtown apartment. He'd been seeing her on the sly for quite a while now. Usually they would meet at her apartment right after work, but something had come up two nights in a row, and he hadn't been able to pull it off. They decided to take a late lunch and meet at her place that day.

He had broken up with Carol months before because she kept making noises about his getting a divorce and them getting married. No way! He liked the way things were with Rosemary not asking for explanations while he was enjoying himself. Shortly thereafter, Carol left the company and moved out of town. From then until he found Cindy, there were several women with whom he'd spent many intimate hours. Cindy was the best. She fascinated him. Since he and Rosemary never shared any intimacy together anymore, why not get what he wanted? Cindy filled his sexual needs and listened to him when he needed to rant. Besides, she was fun to be around, even though they were pretty careful about not being seen together. Except at the club. No one there cared one way or another. Most of the members minded their own business. They had their own liaisons and didn't question each other.

On this particular afternoon, time got away from the two of them. They spent more time making love than he'd planned. They ended up spending the rest of the afternoon in each other's arms and then decided not to return to their respective jobs because of the late hour.

"I know I should be at the office, my dear, but hey, I've put in a long week already. I think I deserve a break." He kissed Cindy and then said, "Don't you agree?"

"You bet, honey. I just told my office I wasn't feeling well. I wasn't, really! I was dying to see you again. I missed you so much." She rolled over on top of him. "Jeffrey, where have you been all my life? Man, I've never met anyone like you before."

Jeffrey patted her on the behind and responded, "Why? Why am I different? Surely you've had lots of men before me."

"And none of them measured up to you, sweetie. None of them could satisfy me the way you do."

That's all Jeffrey needed to stroke his ego; he had to be the best. No one realized what low self-esteem the man had. It had always been like that, but he took great care for it not to show. Maybe it was Mary Ellen's absence in his childhood, maybe it was her high and mighty attitude, or perhaps it was his father's high expectations of him. Jeffrey was not at all a relaxed man, the tenseness in his body never completely gone, no matter what he was doing. Jeffrey worked hard to be the best, to make sure he didn't make any errors. The company would be his someday, but in the meantime, he had to jump through the hoops and make sure that everything he did was top notch. He wished his father would hurry up and retire.

Sometimes Jeffrey worried that his little forays would be discovered, but Rosemary didn't care what he did, and his personal life didn't have anything to do with the company. He continued to see other women as long as they were there.

He had been tense, even with Carol after their many years of seeing each other, but Cindy was different. Not only did she excite him also, but he was relaxed for the first time in his life. It was a totally different feeling for him.

"Well, I might as well say the same thing about you," Jeffrey said in a rousing, deep voice as he kissed her long beautiful neck. "You satisfy me, too, my darling. Okay now, let's stop with the talking. We have better things to do."

Cindy sighed. She was in love with him, had been from the first time she saw him at the club, but somehow she knew he wasn't the type of man you could just blurt that out to. She had to be sure he felt the same way, to make sure he wanted her badly enough. She wondered how she could do that. Would he ever leave his wife? She heard they didn't get along and there was no love lost between them. She was determined to have him but would give it some time, as much time as it took.

In the meantime, while Jeffrey and Cindy enjoyed themselves in her bedroom, one of the employees at the Archer plant suffered what appeared to be a heart attack. In the midst of the excitement, Jeffrey's secretary forgot about the message she'd placed on Jeffrey's desk. She thought about it when she got home, but it was so late then that she figured someone else had probably picked up the boy by that time. She didn't think any more about it.

But no one had. At 3:15 p.m., Mathew began to worry. He couldn't get his mother on the phone, and he couldn't remember either his father's or his grandfather's phone numbers at work. He'd gotten out of school thirty minutes before, and now the school building was closed. He'd already turned down a ride with a friend's mother because he fully expected his mom to drive up any minute. By the time he checked the parking lot in the back, he discovered the last staff member had already gone. Mathew had gone back into the phone booth with a missing directory located at the front of the building to once again call his mom; she still didn't answer. Perhaps this was why none of the staff saw him when they scouted the front of the building before departing. *She must be on his way,* he thought.

At three forty-five, he began to panic when his mom failed to arrive. Finally, Mathew reached a decision. He couldn't just stay where he was. He was pretty sure he knew where the bus stop was since he had seen other people waiting there when his mom drove him to school in the mornings. He had the presence of mind to call his home again before starting on his hike. Thank heavens he had money in his pocket. He left a message on the recorder informing his mother of his intentions.

He'd been in this school for only about seven weeks and had never taken a bus all the way home by himself before. And to catch one, other than the school buses, which were, of course, long gone by then, he'd have to walk close to two miles.

The school was in a remote area, a still mostly undeveloped plat of land. The property had been donated by an area pioneer and was to be used for educational purposes. His daughter built and started the school originally in the downtown area. When her father died, she moved the school to the new site. There were concrete plans for a park, a nursery school, and other educational buildings, but now, only Mathew's school was on the property, surrounded on three sides by fields sprouting withering weeds. Beyond the fields at the back part of the school grounds lay a dense forest. A narrow paved road led a half-mile or more from the school to the main highway. From there, it was a good mile or so to a small populated area of residential homes and a short strip mall off the main street where he thought he might catch a transit bus.

It was the end of October, and dusk was approaching, so Mathew hurried on his way, alone with the shadows beginning to lengthen across the road in front of him and the sun dipping behind the trees. There was a distinct autumn chill in the air. He zipped up his jacket and adjusted his backpack before starting his long trek down the road. It was a little unnerving, and after a bit, the boy began to jog in order to get there faster. His backpack and heavy coat weighed him down, and his breathing became more labored from both his physical efforts and his nervousness. He tired quickly. Suddenly his right foot rolled on a rock; he stumbled and went down on his knees. Mathew cried out but struggled to get to his feet as the pain shot through his right leg. He rested a moment, took a deep breath, and trying his best to ignore his pain, limped onward. It was now getting very dark, and he felt frightened by the quietness in the forest surrounding him. Mathew fought against the hot tears that threatened to flow any minute. He had no choice but to continue.

About the same time, just after 4:30 p.m., Rosemary rushed in the house having stopped at the butcher shop for meat. She'd been to the dentist; he'd filed her tooth down, prepared it for a new crown, and prescribed pain medicine. It had taken much longer than she had anticipated, and her mouth was still frozen from the Novocain. She wondered where Mathew and his grandfather were and was surprised that they weren't there waiting for her. They were such good buddies and probably had stopped for ice cream along the way as they did quite often. Of course, that would ruin his dinner again. She let out a sigh but smiled in spite of herself. With Jeffrey gone almost all the time, Mathew was lucky to have Edward as a father role model. Wasn't it sad, she thought to herself, that a grandfather had to take on the responsibility that should rightfully belong to a boy's father? But Edward enjoyed the role very much, and she was happy he was available to be Mathew's mentor. She felt no alarm at their absence.

At five thirty while preparing dinner, Rosemary walked past the phone in the hallway and noticed the light blinking on the recorder, indicating that messages were waiting. The first call was a message from her friend Mary Lou.

"It's me! Mary Lou! Please call me Rosemary! I have something important to talk to you about, or can we maybe meet for lunch tomorrow? Call me soon."

The recorder forwarded to the second message. She was startled to hear her son's voice. "Mom! Where are you? No one came to pick me up. It's about three thirty now, and I am going to walk in to catch a bus, you know, at that little mall we pass every day. I'll call you there to see if you're home yet. If you aren't, I guess I'll try to find the right bus to go downtown." He knew a couple of kids who did take the bus. They were dropped off from a car pool at the strip mall where they caught the bus to downtown but then had to transfer to still another bus to get home. He'd put it together in his head and figured that was probably what he would have to do, too. "If I don't get you at the bus stop, I'll call from the bus station downtown. Okay?" He was trying to be grown up about his dilemma, but Rosemary could hear the shakiness in his voice, knowing he was uncertain and frightened.

With her heart hammering in her throat, she covered her mouth and closed her eyes, trying not to scream and telling herself she had to keep calm. Mathew was old enough to take care of himself, wasn't he? He was smart and always seemed to use good judgment, but then he had no experience with taking the bus either. She realized what a big mistake it was not to have educated him about an emergency such as this. He'd been coddled and driven to and from school every day. How could he be expected to cope with this new situation? She glanced quickly at the clock and saw that it was past six o'clock now. Their home was only about fifteen minutes from downtown in good traffic, but would he get on the right bus? Would he know how to make the transfer? She had a lot of faith in her son. *But, my God, look at the time.* Did he have enough money to call her again? Where was he now? The adrenaline in her body pumped harder as each new thought played out in her mind. "He should have made that second call by now," she said aloud to herself.

As that thought entered her mind, the third message was a hang up, then the last one on the recorder played, and it was from Mathew. "Mom . . . I found the right place. This real nice guy told me to take #111 to get to the bus station downtown. He thinks #23 is the bus I need to take home from there. It's almost four thirty now. I don't know how long it will take. Maybe you can meet me downtown."

"My God," she uttered when she realized he'd called just before she came home. His final words were "I'll call again if you aren't there. Okay? Oh, the bus is here now. Gotta go!" And there were no more calls. No other messages from her son!

Rosemary already had her purse in her hand and was out the door before the recorder finished rewinding itself back to the beginning. Her first thought was that it was so dark outside. Her hand trembled as she put the key in the ignition. What had happened to Edward? He was always so reliable.

She sped through their residential area, going much faster than she should, heading to the closest access to the freeway going into the city. As she came on to the freeway, she could see traffic was at its worst, and she shivered from anxiety. Maybe Edward had an accident. Why else wouldn't he have shown up? Or maybe, just maybe, Edward had caught up with Mathew and they were now on their way home. She had better call and find out. She took the next exit from the freeway, looking for a phone booth, which was relatively easy, but she wasn't able to find the right change anywhere, either in her pockets or her purse. After dumping the entire contents of her purse on the passenger seat, she grabbed a dollar bill, ran into the 7-Eleven store to get change, and then rushed back out to the phone booth. She fumbled and dropped one coin and then used another in her hand to quickly dial the Archer residence. As she waited for the phone to be answered, her hands shook violently and perspiration popped out on her brow and under her arms. *Please, please,* she begged silently. *Let someone be there. Please let everything be okay.*

As usual, her mother-in-law's voice was very formal and snobbish. "Archer residence. Mary Ellen speaking."

"Mary Ellen? Rosemary. Edward was going to pick Mathew up for me today. He never did. Now I can't find him. Is Edward okay? And . . . what's happened?" Rosemary was close to tears with worry.

"Of course, he's fine. Here, you can talk with him yourself." She could hear Mary Ellen recapitulating what Rosemary had told her as she handed the phone to her husband.

Edward's alarmed voice came on the phone asking, "Rosemary, didn't Jeffrey pick up the boy?"

"No he didn't." She began to sob. "Was he supposed to? I thought you—"

"Mary Ellen had car trouble this afternoon. I called Jeffrey. He was out to lunch when I called him, but his secretary was going to give him the message as soon as he got back. I'm sure he would've called the school if something kept him from showing up. Rose . . . Rosemary, don't cry. Calm down now. Where are you?"

"I'm-I'm almost downtown. There was a message. Edward! Mathew . . . Mathew . . . left a message on the recorder! He . . . he was trying . . . to get home by himself on the bus."

"How?" Edward demanded. "What did he say exactly?" He, too, could feel the cloak of dark fear closing in on him.

"He said . . .," she sobbed, "he said he was going to try to get home by the bus. He gave me the bus number he would have to take to get downtown. That's where I'm headed now. Should take me only ten minutes from here, but traffic is bogged down tonight. God, Edward, it's six fifteen, and it's so damn dark outside."

"I know! I know!" Edward's voice cracked. "Listen, Rosemary, call me back the moment you get there. I'm going to call Jeffrey. See if I can find him. Maybe he's home by now."

As soon as he hung up, Edward made the call to Jeffrey and found out his son was neither at the office nor at his home. Edward didn't know what to do. He was very angry with Jeffrey and felt his hand trembling from that emotion, his mind swirling with terrible thoughts about what might have happened to his beloved grandson.

Finally, Mary Ellen suggested he call the Derby Club. She thought Jeffrey might be there. Apparently, she knew her son better than he did, Edward was thinking, as he dialed the men's club. And that's where his father finally located him.

Jeffrey and Cindy had left her apartment and walked over to the Derby Club for a drink. The club was not far from her apartment. After waiting several minutes for someone at the club to find him, Jeffrey came to the phone. Edward yelled at him, demanding, "Just where in the hell have you been? Didn't your secretary give you the message I left with her about you picking Mathew up today?"

"Well, no it wasn't my turn to . . . well . . . no . . . I-I didn't get back to the office so I-I didn't see her this afternoon," he stuttered.

"What do you mean?" His father shouted at him. "You didn't get back to the office? Where in the hell were you the whole afternoon?"

Mary Ellen grabbed his arm. "Now, Edward, settle down. Don't be so grumpy with him."

Her husband ignored her, jerking his arm away from her grasp. "Well, Jeffrey, I'm listening."

"Well . . . I went out to get—"

"Oh damn it!" Edward said, cutting Jeffrey off in mid-sentence. "We're just wasting time. I've got to get off this phone. Rosemary is going to call me back. Your son isn't home from school yet. I was going to pick him up for her, but your mom had car trouble this afternoon, so I left the message for you to get Mathew." . . . "What?" . . . "No! No one! He was taking the bus. Left her a message earlier." . . . "No, she isn't. She should be at the bus depot in downtown right now. You'd better get your ass down there. Your mother will tell her you are on your way when she calls. I'm going over to your house and wait for Mathew there. Maybe he'll show up or call."

"What's this all about?" Mary Ellen shouted when he put the phone down. "Today was Rosemary's turn to pick up Mathew. Why are you giving Jeffrey the devil?"

For the first time in his life, he angrily yelled back at his spoiled wife. "Shut up, Mary Ellen! Mathew can't be found. I told Rosemary I would pick Mathew up today, but your little emergency became priority, it seems. So don't start with me now. Just stay here by the phone. I am going to head over to their house to see if the boy shows up." Tears filled his eyes.

Mary Ellen was stunned by her husband's abusive voice, and then when he slammed the door on his way out, her body jolted, and she finally realized the seriousness of the situation. Tears sprang to her eyes when she gave her full thoughts to her beautiful, young grandson. Surely nothing bad could have happened to him.

Unfortunately, they didn't find Mathew that night. He had simply disappeared. The police talked to the bus driver on the #111 bus. He remembered Mathew as being one of only about four people to get on at the mall stop, not far from the school, and he told the authorities that the boy had been given a transfer to bus #23.

The driver of bus #23 remembered a young man fitting Mathew's description. The bus was loaded with passengers when it left the downtown station, and there had been many pickups and stops along the way; however, the driver couldn't recall the boy getting off at any point, alone or with other passengers. After further investigation, the police found one of Mathew's schoolbooks on the floor in the back of that particular coach, proving that he had at least been on it. Beyond that, there were no other clues.

Rosemary didn't know how she managed to get through that night or the next. Except for an exhausted catnap here and there, none of the family slept. The police were combing the city for Mathew, but they still had turned up nothing. Emotionally drained, the wait became longer and longer for them. None of it seemed real. They hoped against hope that someone would find him and bring him home soon. He had to be out there some place. Rosemary was sickened with dread, trying not to expect the worst, but it was difficult to look at it any other way. Each empty hour brought more hopelessness to all of them.

On the morning of the third day, Rosemary collapsed in a dead faint in her kitchen, hitting her head on the counter as she went down to the floor. The doctor, a friend of the Archers', was called to come out to the house. He stitched Rosemary's head cut and prescribed bed rest but had difficulty persuading Rosemary to take a sedative. He finally convinced her that she wasn't going to be of any help if she got sick. The doctor also promised her that the sedative was a mild one and that someone would wake her the minute they received any news. She slept for ten hours, only to wake up and find that nothing had changed.

Rosemary hadn't spoken to Jeffrey since they'd returned home from the bus station the first night Mathew came up missing. She blamed him for the nightmare they were living. Jeffrey blamed Rosemary.

Edward blamed himself. Nerves were stretched taut with raw emotions from all sides. The family was physically and mentally exhausted beyond imagination at this point. As much as anyone else, Mary Ellen was grief-stricken. Unlike her normal me-centeredness, she was quietly subdued and had very little to say, while inwardly she berated herself. She was feeling guilty and thinking that if she had just called a towing company and hadn't been so demanding of Edward, things might not have happened as they had. Overwhelming guilt, shouldered by each of them, caused the tension in the house to act like a living thing.

With no further information, the trauma became one of exquisite pain for the family. It was life changing. The TV stations did an excellent job of covering the case on the local news, and the police hoped someone would hear and come forth with a clue to give them some kind of a lead, anything that would help in their search and investigation. They also set up their telephone tracing equipment on the Archer phone, hoping for the slim possibility someone might call demanding a ransom. At least that would give them some hope that the boy was still alive.

At about 9:00 p.m. on the fourth night of Mathew's disappearance, the police did intercept a call. It was from a homeless person in a run-down area close to downtown. The man heard the information about a missing boy from others in a bar and, while walking along the street later, had discovered a boy about Mathew's age near the entrance to a dark alleyway. The boy had been hit on the back of the head with a blunt instrument; however, he was still alive. The police checked several hospitals and located the boy at one of them. He was on the critical list and fighting for his life. It was with a rush of temporary relief for everyone to think they might have found Mathew, and they prayed he would survive his injuries.

Investigators sped to the hospital after convincing the family to remain where they were for the moment. The wait was excruciating for them. About an hour later, the four of them crowded through the front door to greet the returning police. Then came the disappointment and great sadness. The boy was not Mathew. He was a runaway from another town. Another crime to be solved by the police. It was a devastating reality after a bright surge of hope. But then, hopefully, they told themselves, Mathew was still okay somewhere. For a short while, their hope was renewed but edgy. Simultaneously, they tried to keep themselves from thinking about the awful alternate. The horror of a probable kidnapping, molestation, or worse was a reality. Mathew might not be coming back. Desperately they waited, the family suffering indescribable pain, the pain of not knowing what had happened to their boy.

Finally, five long and pain filled days later, a resident from across town called when he found Mathew's notebook two blocks from his house. After an in-depth search of the area, the police also found the boy's cap and made a terrible discovery. Mathew's partially clothed body was found in the middle of a children's park. His body was hidden under some thick underbrush, very near a merry-go-round where many of the neighborhood's young children played every day. He had been molested, savagely beaten, and strangled to death with his own belt.

There's no nightmare to compare with that of losing a child, but losing one in such a violent way was unimaginable. Rosemary collapsed under the strain of her heartbreaking loss and remained under her doctor's care for weeks after the funeral, a funeral she could barely remember, so great was her pain.

Mary Ellen also took to her bed for a week, grief-stricken and worn out. And Edward? Mathew had been the light of his life. He had adored his grandson. The toll of his loss was immense, and it manifested itself in the loss of his health. A couple of weeks later, he was taken to the hospital with congestive heart failure, leaving Jeffrey in a temporary leadership role at the company. Jeffrey would act as CEO until his father recuperated. Certainly Edward's physical capacity was now reduced substantially and worrisome, but it was his spirit that was irreparable and of greater concern to his doctors and to his family.

He was still struggling almost two long months later, his strength and enthusiasm for life having ebbed away and his health in continuous jeopardy. Edward realized he could no longer stay at the helm of the company.

Jeffrey had embroiled himself in work, as usual, to avoid Rosemary, while he shuttered his own grief and guilt inside where no one could see it. Right after the holidays that came and went that year, with the Archer family barely aware of the season, Edward informed his son of his decision to name him the new CEO. After a long talk between father and son, they decided that, for the time being, Edward would remain as chairman of the board and be available for consulting, but both he and his son knew that probably wouldn't be for long.

Working was Jeffrey's great escape. Now he had a real reason for not going home until late every night. The atmosphere in his home was heavy and very depressing. He saw very little of Rosemary as she locked herself away in the bedroom. If he did see her, her pale face and gloomy eyes left no doubt of her venomous accusation for his part in Mathew's death. She didn't have to say anything. It was all there in the brief murderous looks she gave him, and if looking and thinking it was all it would take, he would certainly be lying in his grave now. Their marriage had been over long before this, but Jeffrey knew for certain this would mean a divorce, and he waited for her to make the first move.

After the funeral, Rosemary never cried again. She never let her pain surface. She wore it like a shrine. Her grief was numbing and totally consuming. She felt nothing. It was as if she were a stone in a river, her emotions washing over her and around her but not inside her.

She wasn't able even to talk with her good friend. Mary Lou stopped calling when Rosemary refused to talk to anyone at all. She continued to avoid her husband because she had absolutely nothing to say to him. And when Edward came around to visit Rosemary, she lay in her bed and turned her back on him, refusing to talk to him. It went on for weeks this way.

The new year of 1998 had begun. The weeks turned into months. Rosemary took little nourishment and lost a good deal of weight. She cared about nothing that was going on. She was unaware of the attempted assassination of a popular senator, never looked out to see the passing snowstorm, and never knew what day it was. She did not notice when spring touched the air, and she left a wedding announcement from her former college classmate, Julia, unopened, even though the name on the return address told her who had sent it.

Edward, having recuperated somewhat, along with a changed and very subdued Mary Ellen, came to see Rosemary several times during this period. They wanted her to know they supported her. For a long while, she kept refusing to see them, but they wouldn't give up trying to console her. They just couldn't reach her emotionally. Rosemary finally made a pretense of listening to her father-in-law's pleas that she should seek counseling for her grief. He was terribly worried about her. He told her he would handle all the costs and promised it would help her with her pain.

Mary Ellen was with him on one particular visit, and as she sat down on Rosemary's bed, the older woman forcefully gathered her daughter-in-law into her arms. Rosemary stiffened and tried to push her away, but Mary Ellen refused to let her. Finally, Rosemary gave in and put her head down on her mother-in-law's shoulder with a shudder. But she still didn't cry. She halfway promised her in-laws that she would think about seeking professional help, but Rosemary just couldn't make herself get up and go. She kept putting it off.

Then suddenly and surprisingly, she woke up one fine, sunny morning after having slept all the way through the night without her nightmare dreams for the first time since her ordeal began. Her heart still ached, her pain infinite, but she woke up that morning feeling alert and calm and a little stronger and knew that she must somehow, at last, begin to cope with her tragedy and go on with her life.

Rosemary looked into the mirror and couldn't believe what she saw staring back at her. Was the reflection in the mirror really herself? Dull hair, sunken eyes, and dry-looking skin, drooping from her weight loss of more than thirty-five pounds. It made her look like a scarecrow. She didn't recognize herself. It was a frightening moment of reality.

After bathing, doing something about her hair, and dabbing some makeup on her face, she changed from her robe to a pair of khaki pants, which hung on her bony frame. The big sweater she donned hung over the loose pants and gave her some bulk. Then she walked quietly down the hall and carefully and slowly opened her son's bedroom door, stepping inside. Her eyes started at one end of the room and traveled around the perimeter, looking at each item, caressing them with her eyes. How could he be gone? She inched her way to his bed, bent over and smoothed out the spread with her hands. Then she turned and gently sat down, her hands flat on each side of her, the tips of her fingers gripping the edge of the mattress. The tears came at long last, and she wept and wept and wept. She cried out loud in her pain. "God, why?

Why?" She fell back on to the bed, pulling her knees to her chest as she continued to sob.

The torrent lasted for an hour like a mighty storm, draining and pulling her sorrow from her, and finally, like a wound cleansed of infection, her soul began to mend very slowly. She lay there quietly for about fifteen minutes. Finally, she straightened her legs out and swung them over the side of the bed, bringing her body back to a sitting position. She took several deep breaths, pulled a tissue from her pocket, and blew her nose, deciding at that moment that she really wanted to go on living. For her son! Mathew would have wanted her to live her life.

With her tears dried, Rosemary returned to her bathroom and tried to repair the damage, dabbing at her eyes with a cold washcloth and then touching up her makeup. She found her car keys in the kitchen and left the house. In her car for the first time in months, she discovered it felt good to be driving again. Where was she going? Without fully realizing how she had gotten there, Rosemary found herself at her friend's doorstep. She felt a great need to talk with Mary Lou.

Her knock was answered immediately. "Rose . . . oh, my dear, Rosemary, it's so good to see you." Mary Lou stepped forward, wrapping her arms around her friend. "Come in! Come in! Oh how I've missed you. Come on, I'll make us some coffee."

After they were seated at the cozy little windowed nook in Mary Lou's kitchen, Rosemary started talking. "I'm ashamed for not calling you. You're the only true friend I've made here. I value you . . . no, don't say anything," she cautioned when she saw Mary Lou open her mouth to speak. "You must know how Mathew's death has affected my life. I just didn't want to go on living. Nothing . . . nothing made sense to me. It still doesn't. I still can't figure out how something so horrible could happen to such a young boy. But I think Mathew would want me to go on and I am trying . . ." Rosemary's hands tightened around her coffee cup as she fought the tears she felt welling up in her eyes.

For a minute, Mary Lou thought Rosemary might break the cup, her knuckles so white from the tight grip she had on it.

"I keep asking myself why this had to happen. Why wasn't Jeffrey there for his son? You know, Mary Lou, he left the office before lunch that day and never came back. His father expected him to be on the job and left him a message to pick Mathew up. He was supposed to be there for Mathew. I keep asking myself, where was he that afternoon?"

Mary Lou patted her friend's hand but kept quiet, allowing Rosemary to vent the anger and rage she was feeling. She knew there were things she must tell Rosemary, and it was difficult for her to be silent, but she waited and listened.

"Mary Lou, in order for me to go on, I have to make some changes. I'm going to sue Jeffrey for a divorce. There is no marriage; there hasn't been for a long time. Maybe there never was. I can't stand the sight of him, and I'll never stop blaming him. It was his fault," she said softly and then once again in a louder voice, "It was his fault! He was with somebody that day. I know he was. I've suspected for a long time that he and Carol were having an affair. He's been playing around for years. I knew it. I think his parents know it, too. There's never really been an explanation from any of them about that afternoon." She took in a big breath of air. "I have such contempt for Jeffrey. I do need to get out of this marriage." She put her head in her hands, elbows on the table, and her shoulders shook as she sobbed for the second time that day. Her numbness had worn off, and there was no stopping the release after all these weeks.

Mary Lou finally stood up, pulling Rosemary up into her arms and saying emphatically. "Do it! He doesn't deserve you. He *was* with someone that afternoon. You and I both know he was, but it wasn't who you think it was. I know you think it was Carol, but it was someone else." It was the reason Mary Lou had tried to reach Rosemary on the telephone the same day that Mathew disappeared. Carol was long gone. Had been for months. Mary Lou had heard about Cindy and wanted to tell her friend what she knew. She thought Jeffrey was scum and didn't want him to get away with what he was doing to his wife. "I have a friend, the wife of a co-worker of Carter's, who lives across the street from this Cindy, that Jeffrey is now seeing. She saw the two of them go into Cindy's house that afternoon, many afternoons in fact, and she watched them leave together about 5:00 p.m. Isn't that about when his father found him? It was at the Derby Club, just three blocks down the street. It's not hard to put two and two together."

Rosemary barely nodded her head. She wasn't at all surprised about Mary Lou's information. She had known he was involved. It didn't matter with whom. She just wanted to be rid of him in her life right now, and for her sanity, the quicker, the better. It was the only way she could take back her life. She wanted to be by herself. She never wanted to be hurt by a man that way again, and she promised herself she would never be.

By the time she left Mary Lou's house late that afternoon, Rosemary's burden felt lightened and her decision made. Later that evening, she collared Jeffrey and informed him that she was filing for a divorce. His response was exactly what she suspected it might be but with a surprising element. "Sure, but you aren't getting anything," he shouted menacingly. "You signed a prenuptial agreement, relinquishing everything in a divorce settlement. You know it was part of the deal to our getting married. Remember?"

She didn't remember any such thing. "Is that what it was Jeffrey?" she snarled at him. "A deal? Is that what this marriage was? A deal? And when in the hell was I supposed to have signed this deal?"

"You signed it at the hotel in Reno just before we went to get married. Don't tell me you don't remember. Easy to forget something like that after all these years, huh! Well, sorry, lady, but you signed it all right."

She looked at him for a long time, reaching back into her memory but nothing came to her. "No, I don't remember. I don't believe I did sign anything of the sort."

"Oh, but I have the papers to prove it. They are in the safe at work. You didn't think I would have married you and let you take my family's business in case something like this happened, did you? Give me some credit for being smarter than that."

"In case something like this happened? Were you planning on having other women on the side all along?"

She was sickened by the sneer plastered on his face, the tone of his voice, and the vindictiveness he displayed. What was he talking about? She didn't remember signing anything. Without further discussion, Rosemary turned and walked out the room, slamming the door behind her.

All night she thought about what Jeffrey had said to her. She thought long and hard but couldn't remember signing anything, other than the actual marriage certificate. The wedding document was in the safe deposit box, which did have her signature on it. Wasn't that all she had signed when they were getting ready to leave the hotel room? Or was it? No, that wouldn't have been signed until after the ceremony. Yet, vaguely, she did remember something. She thought about how sick she was just before they left for the short ceremony with the Justice of the Peace. In fact, she couldn't really remember much about the ceremony itself. Was it during this time that he gave her other papers to sign, which he maintained he had in his possession? It had to be. If it was true, she could be in real trouble. Would she be walking away from this marriage without a penny to her name? Could he do that to her? What would she do? It was time to find an attorney.

CHAPTER SIX

GLORI WAS HER NAME. She had a law practice that went back about ten years. Her specialty was rescuing women like Rosemary.

Another friend of Mary Lou's had gone through a rather sticky divorce the year before, and Mary Lou informed Rosemary that her friend highly recommended Glori Newton. The friend's divorce settlement had exceeded her expectations. She thought Glori was an excellent lawyer. So on that recommendation, Rosemary made an appointment to see the woman lawyer.

Glori Newton was a slim, statuesque woman with a very masculine haircut. It was cut short at the sideburns and the rest was brushed towards the back of her head. At first she seemed cool and a little on the rigid side, with a very professional stance about her. It was not long, though, before Rosemary saw through her lawyer's persona and found her to be a very warm and understanding individual. After the very first appointment, Rosemary felt Glori would do a thorough job for her and was happy she had been recommended.

That very week, the lawyer went to work for her newest client. She discovered that there had, indeed, been a prenuptial agreement signed by Rosemary. At a subsequent meeting Rosemary explained the circumstances of her wedding day to Glori, telling her how ill she had been, how she thought she'd eaten something on the plane that didn't agree with her and then, how she'd miscarried her baby. She was certain now about what Jeffrey had done to her. When she was at her weakest, he'd had her sign the prenuptial papers without telling her their real purpose.

It was hard for Rosemary to believe he'd done such a horrible thing. What a gullible person she'd been then. Her husband always had a way with words. He could be very convincing. It was ironic because he could have asked her to sign the papers, and even if she'd been completely coherent, in all likelihood, she would have done so without a second thought. Money just wasn't a big issue with her.

Glori realized that her work was cut out for her. It would be complicated to prove that Jeffrey had done all of this under false pretenses and that Rosemary wasn't aware of signing the agreement, especially with the quickie Reno wedding. All of this would be taken into consideration, and it was up to her to convince the judge of Rosemary's innocence in this matter. She took depositions from the hospital staff and gathered medical records on a quick trip to Reno where Rosemary had been a patient. Some of the staff employees were no longer there, and there wasn't much in the records she could use so she had little to go on.

Some smart detective work was needed. What could she find out about Jeffrey's liaisons with other women? It sounded like there were plenty of them, according to Rosemary. If she could find some information in that department, she could truthfully indicate what kind of a person he was and perhaps gain more sympathy for Rosemary from the court.

Glori's strategy would be to build Rosemary's case by using and dramatizing how the grieving mother, who had miscarried her baby on her wedding night, was confused and ill at the time and didn't realize what she was doing.

By this time, Jeffrey had become very hostile with Rosemary and demanded she move out of *his* house. Glori petitioned for a restraining order against Jeffrey to allow Rosemary to remain in the home until a final judgment and divorce decree were declared. She won the order, and the court issued a notice for Jeffrey to move out temporarily. He came home after having received the court papers at his office to pack his clothes and some of his belongings. As he was leaving, he turned at the front door and shouted at her, "You don't have a leg to stand on, you know. I'll be back in here in short order, and you're going to be out on your ass."

"Don't be too damn sure about that, Mr. Archer!" Rosemary yelled back at him.

He was angrier than she'd ever seen him. He shouted back, "You've made me look badly, and you aren't going to get away with this. Just wait and see!"

But she was just as angry and asked wickedly, "Will you be bringing your latest whore in to live with you?" All she got from him was a dirty look with gritted teeth before he snatched up his suitcases and slammed the front door behind him.

Rosemary trusted Glori, who had a good reputation as a lawyer, and was certain she would do everything in her power to get her a decent settlement. Her lawyer had tried some difficult cases in the past and had won good settlements for many of her clients, mostly women with marriage issues like hers. Nevertheless, Rosemary felt quite anxious about everything and waited nervously for the scheduled court date.

What would she do if she had no money? She'd have to get a job first of all or go home to Washington. That would be her last choice. She didn't want to face her father with her failures. Of course, he'd been informed of his grandson's death and had begged her to come home. His health was declining, and he wasn't able to come to her. But if she went, what would she do there? She put that thought aside for now. She would have to see this divorce through before she could make her next move, taking each day as it came, just as she had been doing for some time now.

Time seemed to drag as she waited to hear from her lawyer. The nights were still difficult to get through, missing her son as she did. She felt so alone in the darkness of the night. *If I can just get through this*, she told herself, *maybe I can get myself settled and write again.* She hoped that would be possible. She had to occupy her mind with something other than the horrible memories of how Mathew had died.

⋘⋙

It was now the middle of May. Spring was in full bloom, and the weather was getting warmer. Glori was in her office working on Rosemary's case just a week before their court date, when her secretary gave her a message that Edward Archer had called and scheduled an appointment to see her. She couldn't imagine what Jeffrey Archer's father would have to say to her. When he'd talked to her secretary, he requested that Rosemary not be present. He wanted to speak to Glori alone.

The first time Glori had made the acquaintance of the son, Jeffrey Archer, was when he was being deposed. She expected the father to be a much bigger man, strong and tall like his son, maybe balding, but one who would be somehow as imposing and as threatening as his son appeared to be. She was not prepared to see the old man who stepped into her office. He had thinning white hair and a gaunt face, wrinkled and layered from what looked like a case of losing weight too rapidly. He was stooped over, leaning heavily on his cane and breathing with difficulty as he made his way slowly to the chair in front of her desk. When he was settled, he looked straight at her, and she saw despair written in the depths of his dark and sunken eyes.

"What can I do for you today, Mr. Archer?" she asked him compassionately. Glori sensed his being there was not easy for him.

"Ms. Newton, this is not an easy task for me. I sit before you feeling very ashamed of what my son has done. I want you to know that I loved my daughter-in-law, and . . . I . . . I loved my grandchild with all my might. His horrible death has left my family in shambles, and on top of that, I find that my son, whom I also love, has not been at all faithful to his wife."

He hesitated momentarily, took a deep breath, and went on. "I'd like to be a spokesman for my son at this time and make a proposal that can settle this divorce without any more rancor. I prefer the Archer Manufacturing Company not be considered a part of the dissolution of this marriage settlement, as it is already stated in the prenuptial agreement that Rosemary did sign. I'm sure it is legal and binding anyway, and I would like to keep that part in place. I would like to offer a fair alternative to Rosemary, a proposal to settle this speedily and quietly." Edward then began coughing and couldn't seem to stop.

"Mr. Archer, are you okay? Can we get you something?" Before he could answer her, Glori had picked up the phone and rang her secretary. "Nellie, get a cold drink of water and bring it in right away please."

In seconds, Nellie was there, handing him a glass of cold water. It settled him down. "It's okay now, Nellie. Thank you." Nellie left and Edward said, "I'm sorry. Now, where was I? Oh, yes. Excluding the company, I believe half of their personal assets, half of all their investments and savings should be awarded to Rosemary, which I might add has become substantial since their marriage. In fact, we will offer her what I have just mentioned and agree to give her the house, too. That is, if she will just agree to keep the company out of this. Here are my figures on what this all amounts to." While Edward was speaking, he'd drawn paperwork from the folder he was holding. He leaned forward and, with a struggle, handed it across the desk, his hand shaking. Glori had to get up to reach for it.

"And does you son agree with this offer to resolve the suit?" she asked.

"No, he does not! But it doesn't matter. He either does it this way, or he no longer heads the company. I am still in control!" And as if to show he was in control, his voice raised a decibel higher. "He knows he has no choice in the matter. I have made this quite clear to my son." Although he tried to sound tough, his voice shook, his face saddened. "I have also made it profitable for him. If he doesn't meddle in this, I will terminate my presidency position on the board, and the company will be totally in his hands."

After reading the figures he gave her, she breathed a sigh of relief. Rosemary would be okay with this. She would be set up for life. Glori looked up from her reading, "Mr. Archer, I'm sure Rosemary will agree to this. I think you are being very fair. I will talk to her right away and let you know for sure."

She stood up, and with some difficulty, so did Edward. She reached out her hand to shake his and said, "I know this has not been easy for you, sir. Rosemary speaks very highly of you. My condolences on the loss of your grandchild."

Rosemary was dumbfounded when Glori informed her of the meeting with her father-in-law. Her heart softened when she thought of him taking a stand for her. She had always thought dearly of him. As a matter of fact, she had loved him. She was saddened to think they would probably never be natural friends again. What a loss.

So without having to fight for her rights in court, Rosemary settled her case and walked away with enough money in investments to live on for the rest of her life without having to work unless she chose to do so.

It didn't make up for the loss of her son in any way, of course. She would gladly have lived in poverty, if only she could have him back by her side. Since that could never happen, the money was a nice thing to have. And knowing that Jeffrey hadn't entirely won was quite appeasing.

The divorce was finalized in November that year. Nineteen ninety-eight had passed by in a fog for Rosemary. She was glad to put it behind her. The house sold almost immediately in December for the full $350,000 listed amount. The proceeds were invested along with the rest of her settlement. She was trying to decide what to do when her friends, the McCoys, made an offer to have Rosemary move in with them for a while. She was only too glad to accept. It would be just temporary until she could figure it all out.

The second Christmas since Mathew's death came about the time she was moving in with her friends, and Rosemary was grateful to be busy and to be with the McCoys at that mournful time.

Finally, with the dreaded holiday season over and the New Year upon them, Rosemary even attempted to find a job to fill in her time, but in the end, she found herself registering at a nearby community college. There she took some writing classes, at the same time digging out the novel she had not touched for so long.

Mary Lou and Carter enjoyed having her there, and the three of them would occasionally go out to dinner or enjoy an evening together, but usually they left her alone. They had given her a room in the back of the house that was quiet and private, had its own bathroom, and was close to an outside door, should she care to sit on the deck overlooking their pool and the green lawn that surrounded it. Her room was large enough for most of the personal items she had kept: two dressers and her desk, along with a new twin bed. Most of her furniture had been auctioned off or sold outright, some with the house, and a few remaining items were boxed and stored in the McCoys' garage for the time being.

Rosemary spent long hours, undisturbed by her friends, writing both on her novel and studying for her class, which she was enjoying so much. She couldn't say she was happy, but she was living again.

There came a time, though, when Mary Lou was concerned about how hard her friend worked, and she tried unsuccessfully, once or twice, to fix Rosemary up on a blind date with one of their good, single friends. Rosemary would have none of it. Her pain still filled her soul, and she doubted if she would ever want to date again. It certainly wasn't on her agenda.

Rosemary was fine as long as she kept herself busy. It was only during some idle moments, and especially at night as she tried to sleep, when the memory of Mathew filled her very being. It was frightening to her when, try as she might, she couldn't exactly envision what he looked like anymore. When this happened, it caused such a gigantic feeling of panic she shuddered in her bed, wanting to give up again. Desperately, her mind tried to bring him alive, as she recalled the simple dimple in one cheek, the way his naturally wavy hair lay across his forehead, and the laughter of her happy, young man. The tears would come and wash away some of the pain before she finally dropped off to sleep.

On the phone with her father regularly now, she sensed his health was going downhill rapidly. Of course, whenever she asked, he would insist he was doing just fine. She couldn't tell for sure.

In late April, Rosemary came home from school early one day, pulling the mail out of the McCoy mailbox and sorting through it as she came up the walkway. She skimmed through the short stack of envelopes to see if there was anything for her. Usually there wasn't much, maybe an occasional note from one of her brothers or a letter from her father, all of them inviting her to come for a visit. It had pulled at her heart when she had read her dad's last letter the month before, begging her to come home. It had been such a long time since she had last seen him. Without any qualms, he'd expressed his relief when he found out she had gotten her divorce. As with her brothers, there was no love lost there. Her dad knew she was safe and living with her friends for now, but she knew he still worried about her emotional health. She realized she would probably have to schedule a visit soon.

On this day, she found a letter from her friend, Julia. Rosemary had finally gotten around to writing to her, apologizing for not acknowledging her wedding invitation, and had been waiting for an answer. She put the letter in her bag and then found the second letter addressed to her. It was from Tokeland, Washington, but not from her father, and it was addressed to her in an unfamiliar hand. Feeling that it must pertain to her father though, she tore it open immediately. The letter was from her father's neighbor. The woman didn't want Rosemary to tell Matt she had written, but she was very concerned about his health and his inability to stay by himself much longer. She was afraid he wasn't eating properly or taking care of himself.

A number of months had now lapsed from the time she'd moved in with the McCoys. It was time for her to move out of their house, and it was time for her to go home and help her father. She owed him that. Once she made that decision, she could hardly wait to get there. It took her a few weeks to get her affairs in order. By June, she was on her way home.

⤜⤛

An emergency siren went off in the distance, and all of a sudden, Rosemary jerked herself back into the present, startled momentarily to find Thomas beside her. He was holding her hand, his thumb running up and down her fingers. She moved her head to look into a pair of smoldering gray-blue eyes. "Thomas, I'm sorry!" She sat up and pulled her hand back, wrapping her arms around herself. "My God, my life story."

"So, what are friends for?" When she withdrew her hand from his, he felt a loss so profound it felt as if someone had sliced his heart in two. She wasn't letting him get close to her. "Go forward, Rosemary. Don't look back," he whispered in a quiet voice, rough with emotion.

"I plan on it. No more entanglements for me. No more commitments. Ever again! I'll never let anyone like that hurt me again!" Her words were tough and flat. Each word he heard her say was a stab in his heart. He would never gain her trust. He loved her so much, and he didn't know what to do about it.

Finally, she turned to him again. "Thanks, Thomas," her voice now softened. "I really needed someone to listen. Talking it out does help a bit. There is so much resentment and anger in me."

There was a pause as he nodded and acknowledged that he understood.

Then she asked, "Now what about you? Tell me about what all those years brought you—marriage and a divorce! You've never mentioned any of it. I sense that you've been hurt badly, as well. Can you talk about it?"

For a moment, he didn't answer her. Then he said, "Well, it's what it was. It was a short-lived marriage and a divorce. That was it. There's nothing else to say. Let's save that. Maybe another time." He did not want to go into it now. He glanced at his watch. "Time for you to go in, I'm afraid, and time for me to go home." It was 12:40 a.m. He could have stayed with her forever, but they were both exhausted, physically and emotionally, and it was time for him to leave. He was determined not to give up, though.

Rosemary was thinking about how elusive Thomas was being on the subject of his marriage. He wanted her to talk about hers, but he didn't want to open up about his. She could tell he harbored pain, maybe as bad as hers. Only he'd gone forward with his life, it seemed to her. She was too tired to comment any further and agreed that it was time to go in.

Thomas got out of the car and started around to help her out, but she was already out of the car and starting up the walk. He followed her and while she was digging for her key in her purse, Thomas rested his hands on her shoulder.

"Rosemary?" She turned and he pulled her into his arms carefully. She stiffened but he just held her tenderly, and finally she relaxed slightly. "Rosemary," he said her name again. "Only you can change your life and move forward. No one can do it for you, but you can't live in the past. It will destroy you." His lips were only inches away from hers. He ached to lean over just a little further to kiss her, but he didn't dare. Suddenly his emotions got the best of him; he released her abruptly and gruffly said goodnight, quickly walking back to his car. Tears sprang to his eyes as he got behind the wheel. He, of course, didn't know that tears were spilling from Rosemary's eyes, as well, while she stood in the doorway and watched him drive away.

In the ensuing weeks, he called her, and she reluctantly went to dinner with him a couple of times, but Thomas was careful to keep his distance. Things had changed. There was obviously more tenseness between them than before. Then he ceased to call her at all.

Rosemary had only herself to blame. The last time she'd been with Thomas, she had mentioned she was planning to remodel her dad's place and wasn't going to have much time for anything else. She wanted to put in some modern conveniences and make it nicer for both of them. Apparently, he had taken that to mean she didn't have time for him. Maybe that is what she meant, but Rosemary missed him more than she thought she would. She buried herself in the plans for the cabin, covering up her loneliness to some extent.

On one occasion later in the summer when Margie and Frank came for the weekend, the three of them were unable to locate Thomas. Rosemary was quite certain Thomas knew his friends were there, for there was hardly a day he didn't travel down the Tokeland Road, and surely he would have seen the Donahans' car. In fact, Thomas often stopped at their house to make sure everything was okay when they were not around. She guessed he'd deliberately made himself unavailable. He'd been avoiding her, it was true, but to avoid his two other good friends was a surprise. It made her feel quite guilty, as if she had driven a wedge through the friendship Thomas shared with the Donahans. And Rosemary felt a terrible loss for herself. She wished that he was available so she could talk to him and enjoy the friendship they'd had, especially when he lived so close by.

Managing to put her thoughts of Thomas from her mind, Rosemary threw herself into her house project. Her time was taken up with hiring a contractor to do the bulk of the work and then supervising the job as the contractor and his assistant moved forward. She did the painting and wallpapering herself and even proudly put down the linoleum squares in the kitchen. It would be early next spring of the new millennium—the year 2000—before the project would be completed. The major work was finished by Christmas, at which time her contractor took some time off for the holidays, putting the final touches of the project on hold.

Keeping busy with small details of the remodeling, Rosemary saw the holidays pass finally, marking yet a third year without Mathew. She and her father had a quiet, uneventful turkey dinner, and she was thankful when it was over once more.

By February of the new year, two new bedrooms had been added, one down and one on top of the existing structure. The porch had been walled in and opened up to the kitchen, and new flooring installed, doubling the space. The new bathroom counters shined. Rosemary and Matt would enjoy the new windowed shower stall, which was larger than the old one. A wrap-around deck on two sides of the house was constructed so part of it faced the inlet of water in front. However, Rosemary had made sure there was a sheltered area in one corner of the covered deck, partially walled in, for those windy days that were so prevalent at the ocean.

Rosemary's father was failing steadily. She could see him deteriorating every day and was afraid he wouldn't be able to enjoy the new quarters for long. However, Matt did perk up a little into March and enjoyed being bundled up and seated periodically on the new deck in the fresh air.

By April, most everything on the house was completed except for a little work left to do on the carport. Now what would she do to occupy her time? Thomas had not called, and she couldn't bring herself to call him after the way she had acted. She was getting what she deserved. She missed his sunny nature and his willingness to listen when she needed to talk. She would have loved to talk to her dad about it, but even if he had been well enough to listen, she just couldn't talk to him about the mess she continued to make in her personal life.

There was no doubt she was lonely, and now that the remodeling was done, she discovered how alone she really was, fearing her dad's days were numbered. She needed to find something else to fill in her time, and that's when she finally dug out the novel again to work towards a completion.

In the afternoon when her father napped, Rosemary would grab her notebook and pen and go to the beach, not far from the water's edge. There she would bask in the sun when it was shining. With her back propped up against one of the large pieces of driftwood that the winter's ocean tides had brought to shore, she would write. The stacked wood sheltered her from the wind, and it felt wonderful to be back at her writing, filling in the long, lonely days.

At first, her thoughts flowed easily, and she busily and intently wrote them into her notebook, reforming her story as she took a different path. Then she came to a place where she was stuck for the lack of some research needed after changing an earlier idea. She would have to go to the Aberdeen library, about a half-hour's drive, to find out more about the country of Ireland where her main character was living at the time. In the meantime, Rosemary was trying her hand at writing some short stories and working out other interesting plots she had stored in her mind.

People she knew, or more likely people her father knew, waved to her on their way by or stopped and chatted as they hiked along the shoreline. She would suggest they stop to visit with her father in the afternoons. "Call me in the morning, and I'll tell you whether it seems to be a good day for him," she would say, and a few did come by. Her father loved the visits.

It was a quiet life with few intrusions, and she settled into her new life, enjoying the sense of freedom and the ownership of her time, even though she missed seeing peers of her own and mostly feeling the loss of her friendship with Thomas. He had not come around yet, and it was getting close to May already. The estrangement bothered her, but she didn't feel brave enough to call him. She'd waited too long. She was just too afraid of the intimacy she was certain he wanted from her.

The weather became warmer except for a few days of heavy rain. On most days when the weather permitted, Rosemary sat in her little retreat on the beach where she wrote and meditated about her life. She tried to ascertain where she was going with it.

⬙

Several times as Rosemary was staring off into space, she noticed a man and his dog further down the beach. The man threw sticks out into the water for the dog to retrieve. They seemed to be enjoying their little game so much. A man and his dog, it is often written, are inseparable, she remembered. Where did she read that? She'd had a pet once. Why had they never gotten a pet for Mathew? Mathew loved animals. Then she would think about her son and shed a few tears; once again, her pain at the forefront of her emotions.

Rosemary enjoyed watching the stranger and the dog on more than one day. The observation gave her a new idea for a story. She wondered about the stranger's life. Who was he? Where did he live? Was he married? Did he have children?

The man and the dog showed up on the beach on a regular basis, and Rosemary found herself looking forward to seeing the pair off in the distance every day. They were out there almost every afternoon at about one o'clock. She made sure her timing was right, but one day she was unable to go at her customary time due to her father's needs. She didn't get out to her secluded spot until about one thirty. They weren't there. She had missed them.

Still on another day when the weather was wet and very cool, she'd come back, drenched from her morning jog and decided not to go out again that day. She thought about them, however, and assumed the pair would also stay indoors where it was warm and cozy. She didn't know the reason why she was so disappointed whenever she missed seeing them. She didn't know them, and the man meant nothing to her, but it was just the joy of seeing the man and his dog together that warmed her heart.

She used her emotions about them as a theme in the short story she was writing. Her creative juices were flowing again, the tenseness departing. Writing always gave her more confidence in herself, and how she needed that.

Letters came from her friend, Mary Lou McCoy, often long chatty letters, which she so looked forward to reading. In the last letter, Mary Lou had written, in part:

> You probably don't give a hoot but thought I'd pass on the information anyway. Your ex has remarried, and no, it wasn't with Cindy. It was this friend of his mother's. Gaile Moyan! Don't know if you ever met the woman or not. She's in our women's group, and I can't stand her. She's Miss-Know-It-All. She and her ex-hubby got a quickie divorce, and then she latched on to Jeffrey. Think she's at least ten years older. I understand Mary Ellen isn't very happy about it either. Actually your ex

mother-in-law hasn't made too many appearances since you left, and I haven't seen Edward out anywhere either, the reason, of course, being his health. I don't think he gets around well.

But Jeffrey sure does. He's taken over where his parents left off, running the show. Just between you and me, I think he married Moyan for her name and money (and likewise she probably married him for his—ha!), and I think he's still seeing Cindy on the side. Guess she wasn't good enough for him to marry but okay for trips to the bedroom. How in the world does the skunk work all that out? There now, is all my trashy news, though I am sure you couldn't care less.

Miss you, honey. Hope your dad is holding his own! And you, how are you doing?

"Right on," Rosemary said aloud, "I couldn't care less about Jeffrey." However, she felt sorrow for the Archers, even Mary Ellen. After all, they lost a grandchild, and she understood how badly that affected them. Look at Edward's failing health! The only one it hadn't seemed to affect much, it seemed to her, was Jeffrey. *What a jerk he was. Thank God, he's out of my life,* she thought.

Rosemary finished reading her friend's letter, folded it, and put it away in her bag. As she was settling herself into her little nest of driftwood, she caught a glimpse of the man and his dog playing on the beach again. She hadn't seen them for several days, and it made her smile to herself as she watched them frolicking together, the man throwing a stick and the dog tirelessly chasing it.

⚭

The weather was extremely warm all that week, and on Friday, after finishing some small chores for her father and tucking him in for his nap, Rosemary couldn't wait to get out in the sunshine. She made sure she was out on the beach by one o'clock. However, the man and his dog were nowhere to be seen. How long had it been since she'd first spied the two of them having such fun? It had become almost a daily activity for her to watch them. She stared at the spot where she usually saw them for quite a while, but when they still didn't appear, she shook off her disappointment, pulled out her writing pad and pen, and began to concentrate.

She still hadn't made the trip to the library to look up the information she needed for her novel. Maybe she could get a neighbor to look in on her father while she made a quick trip into Aberdeen next week. She was in her final chapter now and proud of what she'd accomplished. Some day she would buy herself a computer, maybe a laptop, so she could do her research online. Even with a computer, she would probably handwrite outdoors in the fresh air.

Rosemary scribbled a big question mark in the margin of one page and began to record a new thought. She stopped and read one of the paragraphs over to herself. Something was wrong with it. It wasn't expressing what she wanted to say, and she couldn't figure out the problem.

Very intent on what she was doing and deep into her thoughts, Rosemary wasn't even aware of the sounds coming from a group of kids playing off in the distance or the droning of a boat engine as it cruised into the harbor. So, of course, she didn't hear the man approaching her either. She was startled when she heard a deep male voice say, "Hello there! Oops! Sorry, didn't mean to startle you. Curiosity got the best of me, and I had to come over here and find out what it is you're doing." The tall stranger was grinning down at her.

Rosemary looked into the deepest, greenest eyes she'd ever seen. Set against his naturally dark skin, his smile was dazzling. Italian? Indian? Whatever! He was undoubtedly the most handsome man she'd ever seen. Jeffrey had been good-looking, but this guy was beautiful.

"Hello." She returned his smile.

"The name's Gile Hammond." He bent over and offered his hand.

"Rosemary Archer." She shook his hand but was glad he spoke next because she suddenly felt very tongue-tied. Her heart was racing, and she felt her cheeks color. She silently reprimanded herself for acting like a teenager.

"I see you every day down at this end of the beach," he said. "One minute I see you standing; then I see you sitting down. Wondered if you were just sunbathing. Then I noticed you were never in your bathing suit. Of course, it hasn't been all that warm yet." He lowered his voice and said, "Much to my disappointment! No bathing suit, you understand!" There was that grin again, and he wiggled his eyebrows up and down at her and laughed.

At first, she didn't know what to say. But then she suddenly guessed who he was and realized he was teasing her, so she laughed with him. "You're the guy with the dog." She looked around for the dog. "Where is he, by the way? I would have guessed you never went any place without your dog."

"So you've been watching us, too." Again, Gile grinned. "No, the dog isn't mine. He belongs to the neighbors, but he thinks he has to show me the way to the beach every day, and then he wants to play. You see I like animals, and anyone who likes dogs has to be a nice guy. Right?"

She nodded her head. "Right!" She was slightly disappointed that the dog wasn't his. They seemed like such an attached pair. What a nice man to play with someone else's animal, though.

"What is it you're doing?" He pointed down at the pad and the pen in her hand.

"Well," Rosemary made a face, "I'm in the throes of trying to finish a novel I am writing." She was embarrassed to say it as if she wasn't good enough. I've always loved to write. Well, I-I am trying to write, anyway!" Was she stuttering? "It's rather my very favorite thing to do, but this novel is something else," she said shyly. "Don't know how successful it will be, but I am enjoying the exercise."

Gile seemed surprised and told her, "Imagine that, Rosemary. I, too, am a writer. In fact, I've been here since January writing my third novel. Renting a little cottage up the road. I hope to have the book ready for the publishers in a few weeks or so."

Rosemary's mouth dropped open. She was in complete awe of the fact that she was talking to a real author. "Oh, my gosh. You've published two other books? Oh! Tell me the titles. I'd like to read them!"

"Yes, I've been lucky to find a publisher for my books. The titles? Well, let's see. My first novel was *High Grass, Long Road*, which took me a long five years to complete, as I got started late in my writing. I guess I was about twenty-seven when I finally got going. The first time is always the most difficult, and I certainly had a lot of rewrites to do. Let me tell you, it was an exercise in patience. It was published about nine years ago. Got an agent finally who did a good job for me. Promoted me well! Be sure you do that when you're ready."

Rosemary was nodding, taking in his advice, as he continued to talk about his writing.

"Anyway, I took some time off, then was bitten by the bug again and decided to write my second one in 1994. I always go to live on location while I write and do a lot of research of the area where my stories take place. This has worked quite well for me."

"So that means you are on location now and situating your new novel here in little old Tokeland. Is that right?"

"That's right. It's a beautiful place for a story, don't you think?"

"Oh, yes, no doubt about it. How about that second book? What's the title? I'd like to read both of them."

"That was published a few years ago. Went a little faster than the first book. It takes place in recent years in the South, and I spent six months in Atlanta, Georgia, four months in San Francisco, and a little time in South Beach, Florida, too, before I finished it."

"And the title?" Rosemary asked again.

"It's called *Burden of the Heart*. I'm afraid I don't have a copy of it at the cottage, but I do have one of the first book, which you are welcome to have."

"That would be perfect," she said, delighted at his offer.

"Mind if I sit down for a minute?"

"Of course not," she said a bit nervously. Not only was she acting like a teenager, she also was feeling like one. There wasn't a whole lot of room in her little carved-out spot in the surrounding driftwood, but she scooted all her writing materials as far to one side as possible in order to make room for him to sit down next to her. He squeezed in beside her, the length of one leg lying snuggly against hers. She felt the warmth of his body through their clothes and felt that warmth travel through to her own.

"Nice and cozy, isn't it?" He wiggled around to find a better fit, bumping against her hip in the process. "Not bad at all. Like having a tree house when you were a kid. Private and personal. Thank you for inviting me in," Gile remarked, grinning at her again.

Well, no, he'd done the inviting, but that was okay with Rosemary. She was beginning to feel comfortable with him. She admitted she rather liked him there. It had been a long time since she'd responded to a man like this. "You're welcome," she said as she grinned back at him.

Their conversation lasted nearly two hours. They talked mostly about their common interest in writing and a little about their backgrounds, though she held back on hers. Mentally she calculated his age, deciding from the hints he'd given her that he was near her age, maybe a couple of years older. Gile was very personable, and it was quite easy to talk to him.

She felt herself succumb to his charms, while at the same time trying, but not quite succeeding, to drown out the internal alarms going off in her head. *Watch yourself, Rosemary, old girl,* she cautioned silently. *No more hurt! No more pain! Focus on what you are doing,* she kept telling herself.

The time passed quickly, and her new friend finally excused himself. "Hey, I've got to get going. Rosemary. What a delightful afternoon it's been. I would like to stay and talk for a lot longer, but I have work to do. Gotta get at it!" Gile stood up, offered his hand to help her up, and said, "Let's do this again some time."

"Yes, I've enjoyed it, too. Thanks for stopping by." As he walked away, Rosemary wondered what had happened to the time; it had disappeared so soon, and she had enjoyed herself immensely. It was wonderful to have someone around who had the same interests, plus he seemed like such a nice man. He was so engaging in his conversation.

Her happy thoughts suddenly took a nosedive when she glanced at her watch and saw the time. She hadn't checked on her father. Quickly, she gathered her all her writing gear and made a mad dash for the house.

CHAPTER SEVEN

ALMOST EVERY AFTERNOON, Gile came by to see Rosemary. He would be out on the beach with the dog, wave to her, and then show up at her spot shortly afterwards. Although she tried to stop herself, her attraction to him intensified. And even though he was so sweet with her and they had so much in common, she thought, she kept cautioning herself. With no contact from Thomas during most of last year and only a few phone calls all winter from Margie and Frank, Rosemary realized just how much she needed the company of friends in her life. She'd discovered how wonderful it was to converse with someone her age again; consequently, she wasn't listening very closely to her internal voice.

For some reason, she never mentioned any of her visits with Gile to her father. She never admitted to herself that it was because he might not approve. She told herself she was enjoying herself too much, didn't want to analyze her feelings or have anyone analyze them for her either, at least for the moment.

There was deep disappointment when Gile didn't show up one afternoon. It made her realize how much she looked forward to their discussions and the comradeship they shared. Furthermore, he never made an appearance for several more days, and it worried her. Rosemary knew the little cottage he was renting but had never ventured over there. She did not want to seem too forward in their newly established friendship, but she ached to see him and hoped he wasn't backing away from her. Until now, visiting him hadn't been necessary since he'd always come her way. Finally, she decided it wouldn't hurt to go over to his place and make sure nothing was wrong.

Her father was doing fairly well on this day and taking his usual daily nap, so Rosemary jaunted down the beach, finding the path leading to the little road, which ran in front of his rented cottage, nestled back in the trees. Neglected flowerpots sprawled at random on a tiny deck, empty, except for a couple of dead weeds. A bright red door marked the entry, and a sign above it said, "Joe and Mary's Getaway Cottage." She saw a blue car, a newer model Thunderbird, parked in front and presumed it was Gile's. She hesitated a moment, wondering if she should be there, but then she courageously knocked on his door. He opened it almost immediately.

"Ah, are you busy?" she asked him meekly. "If so, I'll leave you alone. Just wanted to make sure everything was okay." *What a jerk I am*, she thought. *He doesn't owe me any explanations. Just what am I doing here?*

"I have been, but no . . . come in. It's nice to see you. Just gonna have me a cup of hot chocolate. Want some?"

Rosemary breathed a sigh of relief. She tried to read him, but apparently it didn't bother him that she'd come by to see him without an invitation. "Thanks, Gile. I'd love some." As she stepped inside, she asked, "Are you getting to the end of your book?" His computer was up and running, and the printer held a stack of printed papers on its output tray.

"No, I ran into a snag. Haven't been out on my daily trek because I've been trying to work it out a bit. Shane—you know my dog friend—comes over and scratches at the door and leaves very disappointed without me." Then he laughed and asked, "Why? Have you missed me?"

"Well, I . . . yes! I missed our little chats. I'm very interested in your writing." *And I'm interested in you*, she admitted to herself. "By the way, had to take my father to the doctor the other morning, and while I waited, I started your book and am about halfway through it. I'm really enjoying it, Gile. It's very good. I'll have to buy a copy of the second one soon."

"Um, I wish I had a copy for you so you wouldn't have to buy it, but I . . . don't." He was standing very close to her. She could feel the warmth of his body transferring to hers.

"Here's your chocolate. Want marshmallows? As far as I'm concerned, it isn't hot chocolate without the marshmallows."

"Oh, yes! Love them!"

He put three or four of them in each cup and handed her one.

Like the little girl she used to be, Rosemary poked at the fluffy white marshmallows, pushing them into the hot, brown liquid, then pulled her finger out, and put it into her mouth, sucking off the sticky stuff. She did this several times unaware of what she was doing as she talked to him. "Um, this is—"

Right in the middle of what she was saying, Gile reached down, took her arm by the wrist, and casually brought her sticky finger up and into his mouth, sucking the chocolate and marshmallow from it. "Um, good is right!" Slowly he backed Rosemary up to the sink, pressing against her. She caught her breath from the unexpected motion, and an exciting, warm sensation riveted through her entire body, leaving her physically weakened. He lowered her hand and took the mug from her other hand, placing it on the counter behind her. Then he cupped her chin, pulling it towards his mouth. It was a sweet, breathless, testing kiss. It was a wonderful kiss.

Was this what she'd come for? She didn't draw away, although warning bells were going off in her head, and an inner voice was telling her to stop. *Don't do this, Rosemary! You don't really know this man. You'll be hurt again!* But she couldn't stop it. She wanted more.

Gile whispered her name, and she could feel his warm chocolate breath as his face stayed close to hers. "One of the reasons I haven't been over to see you is I couldn't stand to see you without doing this. I've wanted you since the very moment I saw you way over at the other end of the beach." He kissed her once again, a deep, tongue-thrusting kiss this time. Bending over her neck, he kissed it; then moving her shirt to one side, his lips found the soft spot on her shoulder. She tingled all over, a sweet, aching pain sweeping through her body. "Ah, Rosemary, you sweet, sweet girl—the only person in the world who understands the work I do."

"Gile, . . . I—"

"Shh, doll. Just let me taste you. I'm so glad you came to me; I've been dreaming about you every night." He had her shirt unbuttoned, then his hand was on her breast, and he bent to suckle her. It drove her over the edge. Before she could protest, she found herself being carried to his bed, swept away by a passion she didn't know she had.

Gile finished undressing her, his hands manipulating every inch of her body until she couldn't think. She wanted him so much she was hardly aware that he'd taken time to put on a condom for protection, but when she did realize it, she was grateful to him for remembering. When he made love to her, he did it slowly, making her body arch with desire. Just when she didn't think she could stand it any longer, he entered her, and she spun into space. It had never been this way with Jeffrey. She hadn't known it could be this way.

Later when she came out of his bathroom, flushed with the telltale sign of one who had just enjoyed good sex, she felt guilty and elated at the same time. Her mother hadn't brought her up to just jump into a stranger's bed at the snap of a finger, but then isn't that what she had done with Jeffrey? Why was she doing this again? *Damn it anyway*, she said to herself, *I'm no saint, and I'm already thirty-eight years old. I've never experienced anything like this.* After all, it was her life! She didn't have to answer to anyone.

Gile shooed her out of the door then, saying he had to get back to work, as there were deadlines to meet. She understood and popped up on her tiptoes, giving him a quick kiss before opening the door to leave. "Bye! I'll leave you to your work now. See you later," she said with a sad smile.

"Come back tomorrow at the same time, Rosemary, and we'll have more hot chocolate." His voice was low and sexy as he wiggled his eyebrows up and down, an expression she was used to seeing him do by now. He gave her a wink as he shut the door.

The implications of his last words didn't escape her, and she flushed a little in embarrassment. The further away she got from him, the more she chided herself. *No, Rosemary, don't go running back like a lovesick teenager tomorrow. Let him come to you! Just go out on the beach and wait for him to come to you.*

But the next day after she told herself she wouldn't go, her will power disintegrated, and she headed in the direction of his cabin. She couldn't help herself. He was so beautiful, so charming, and so sweet in his lovemaking. She'd never been treated like this before. He made her feel wanted and loved, and she was so hungry for that.

Of course, Gile Hammond was no fool. He knew how attracted to him Rosemary was, and he had deliberately skipped his pattern of going to the beach. Somehow, he knew she would come looking for him if he didn't go to her. To prove his point, she had come willingly. He knew she would be there the next day, and so she was. Like a spider with its web, he had spread his net and took full advantage of her vulnerability. And yet, he thought she was a wonderful person, a person he could become very involved with if his situation ever changed.

Rosemary appeared at his door fresh as a daisy. One look at her, and he felt his passion rise. With his charming smile, he invited her in for hot chocolate and much more.

The sex was better than ever. Rosemary was certain now that she was falling in love with this magnificent man. He was wonderful! Gile was so masculine yet so tender in his loving. Jeffrey had taken more than he'd given; but she was blindsided into thinking this was different. Rosemary did not see any comparison, as she was feeling the completeness of being a woman for the first time in her life. She was so full of herself, so full of him. New energy was flowing from her very core, making her feel like a brand-new person with emotions she'd not felt since being a young college student—confidence, vigor, and yes, even doubt, but alive. Really alive!

Afterwards, as they lay catching their breath, she turned to him, touched his face, and said, "Gile, you're wonderful. Where have you been all my life? You make me feel so happy and alive," she whispered to him.

"You are *so* alive, my dear." His hands stroked her. "You have a gorgeous body, Rosemary," he whispered seductively. She did make him feel alive for the first time, too. "I find it impossible to keep my hands off you." It was true! Gile had never thought he could feel so much for any woman, but he did, and he had to smother those feelings. If only things could be different. If only he were free. But no, he had planned his path. He must follow it.

She kissed him again, wanting to stay here beside him forever. They discussed their books for a little while. He wanted to know how hers was coming along. Not very well actually. In addition to caring for her father, spending time thinking about and being with Gile was taking up her writing time. She didn't tell him that, though, and right now she didn't care.

After the second hour and more lovemaking, he patted her bottom and pushed her towards the edge of the bed. "Come on, Lady Beautiful, off you go. I have to go back to work. That's how I make my living, remember?"

She got up reluctantly. "Okay! Okay! I have to check on my dad, anyway. Say, why don't you come over for dinner one night and meet him? He's a very nice old man. You'll like him." It was an instant decision; it was time for the two men in her life to meet. It was a huge disappointment when Gile told her he couldn't.

"Oh, I can't. Thanks, Rosemary, but I'm really under the gun." He put his index finger on the tip of her nose. "You've been taking precious minutes away from me the last couple of days, you know, not that I'm complaining, you understand." He kissed her on the forehead.

"Oh, by the way, I'll be gone for a few days. Going to see my publicist," he said as he gave her a quick kiss on the mouth.

Rosemary twisted in his arms and looked up at him. "Just a few days?" She suddenly had a sense of panic.

"I'll be back soon," Gile said soothingly. "Leave tomorrow, back on Monday. I'll see you on the afternoon I get back. Meet me here. Okay, love?" He was going to miss her a lot. He'd never felt quite this way about anyone before. Could he change things? Could he fit her into his life? He didn't know. He only knew she was becoming special to him.

For the next few days, time dragged for Rosemary. She kept herself busy, tended to her father's needs, prodding him to come with her to the grocery store and to pick up the mail, even taking him to lunch in Westport one day. His legs gave him problems, but he managed; she was sure it was healthy for him to be out and about.

Missing Gile as she did, she could hardly wait for her father to take his usual nap on Monday, the day Gile said he would be back. Shortly after two o'clock, she hurried down the road to his cottage

She'd barely knocked on the door when he opened it and pulled her inside, immediately walking her backwards towards the bed. With no preliminaries this time, he laid her on the bed and began undressing her, getting her ready for sex with his lips and hands roaming every-where. She put up no resistance. "I thought the time would never pass. I missed you, sweet lady. You take my breath away, do you know that?" He kissed her until she was breathless. "Your turn, sweetheart! I want you to undress me now." She was hot with passion and felt like a wanton woman as she did his bidding until he said, "Hurry! Hurry!" and began to help her. The next thing she knew he joined them together, taking her almost roughly, but she was lost in her own passion and matched him stroke for stroke until the world exploded around them.

"Gile," she cried out, "I missed you so much. I love you." There, she had said the words. She waited for him to say them back, wanted him to say the words to her, too, but he didn't.

"You are sweet and adorable," were the words he whispered, as he proceeded to make love to her again. He was insatiable on this day. "Sweet and adorable and so full of exciting passion."

⚮

Things seemed to settle into a routine as the little affair continued for a couple more weeks. Gile never seemed to go to the beach anymore or to come to see her, as he had before, and always waited for her to show up at his cottage. Rosemary wasn't certain she was doing the right thing. He never said those words she wanted to hear, but she missed him too much when they weren't together and continued with the affair.

July turned to August. Every day she found time to run over to his house, and every day they ended up in bed making love. There wasn't time for anything else. She tried to understand how hard he was work-ing to complete his book but began to wonder about some of his excuses when the lovemaking was over. Yet she couldn't wait to see him; she couldn't get enough of him.

One day in August, her father, nauseated and weak, wasn't able to get out of bed. She was unable to spend any time with Gile on that day, her first priority being her father. She tried several times to call him, but his line was always busy. Maybe the computer was online, or he wasn't answering because he was working. She couldn't leave her father, even considered taking him to the hospital after his vomiting continued for hours. He slept for a while, and then she managed to get some chicken soup down him. That seemed to do the trick, and she finally relaxed.

After her emergency was over, Rosemary tried calling Gile again towards evening, but the line was still busy. She couldn't leave her dad now. Oh well, she would see him tomorrow and explain; he'd understand. Wouldn't he? She was exhausted by early evening and fell into bed.

The next day, Rosemary's father was better, weakened but able to get out of bed for his breakfast. She was grateful for that. At naptime, she took off for Gile's.

He was very upset with her. "And where were you? I waited and waited. Don't do this to me, Rosemary. Don't leave me hanging. I expected you. I wanted you here." He gripped her shoulders and froze her with his angry eyes. He seemed different. So obsessive!

Rosemary tried to explain about her father, but it didn't seem to simmer him down any. Rosemary was shocked, and she felt confused and hurt by the incident. She'd never seen this side of him. She wanted to leave, scared out of her wits.

Then Gile's tirade was over like a flash, as if it hadn't happened. He took her into his arms with no apology whatsoever. As he carried her to the bed, she almost forgot about the anger he'd directed at her just moments before. Temporarily, he made her forget about it by loving her and whispering sweet, adoring things to her as usual.

She couldn't stay long, and when it was time for her to leave, he seemed distracted. As she kissed him and said goodbye, his smile seemed forced, and he appeared sad and lost. Something was wrong. She wanted to stay and comfort him, find out what was troubling him. She reached her arms out, but he grabbed them before they went up around his neck.

"Oh no, lovely one, I've got to get back to work." It was the same thing he said every day. "I'll see you later." He gave her a peck on the forehead and then gently turned her towards the door. Walking home slowly, she realized she didn't like what was happening. What was going on with Gile?

⌐∞⌐

Labor Day was only a week away. Margie came to the coast to spend her first weekend since the October before. She called Rosemary as soon as she had her car unloaded. "Hi, girlfriend. Finally made it. Been so anxious to get down here. How're you doing? How's your dad faring?"

"Great to have you here. I'm good, Margie. Dad's holding on right now, but the last few months have been up and down for him. The very warm weather we had all month seemed to perk him up. But he's always feeling tired. When he's feeling up to snuff, I bundle him up and get him out for a bit each day. The fresh air helps him sleep at night, and he still takes a daily nap. A couple of weeks ago, he had an intestinal thing. That didn't help much. Every day is different. I never know for sure what to expect. Right now, he's okay. You'll have to come over and see him. He'd enjoy that; he always likes company."

"I will. Thank God, you're here with him. I am sure you've been the best medicine for him, Rosemary."

Then Margie changed the subject. "Frank's coming day after tomorrow. Can we get together for dinner if your father is feeling well enough for you to get away? We'll call Thomas and make it a foursome. How's that sound?"

Rosemary froze! Margie must assume that she and Thomas were still seeing each other. It had been months since she had seen Margie. Actually, she and Thomas had lost complete touch with each other this last year.

She wasn't sure she wanted to tell her best friend about Gile; yet she needed to let her know since Thomas wasn't in the picture anymore. "Uh, Margie, Thomas and I haven't seen each other in quite a while." She didn't mention how long it had been. "I saw him driving past a few times, and he was with another woman each time, the same woman, in fact, so I think he is seeing someone. And Margie, I am, too."

"You're seeing someone? Who?" Margie was so surprised she didn't even let Rosemary answer before she exclaimed, "Wow! Things sure do happen fast sometimes. I would have bet money that you and Thomas were going to get together. I always thought you were made for each other. Guess I was wrong, huh? Well, tell me about your guy."

Rosemary still wasn't sure about sharing her wonderful secret with anyone, not even her best friend. She was afraid if she did, her telling would burst her wonderful bubble of happiness. But she had now opened up the door, and she couldn't think of a way to close it. "Well, he's a writer by the name of Gile Hammond, and he is living here in Tokeland while he works on his third novel, which is almost finished."

Margie was impressed. "Say now! How interesting! I'd love to read his books. Why don't you give me the titles so I can order them?"

"Uh, *The Price We Pay* is the one he is working on at the moment. I've barely started his first one, *High Grass, Long Road*, but haven't had a chance to purchase the second one yet. That would be *Burden of the Heart*.

Thanks. I'll order them right away. So ask him to come with you to dinner. We'd love to meet this new man in your life. My! A writer!"

Rosemary would love so much for Gile to do something with her, like go to dinner at the Donahans' house. It would be such fun, and she would like to show him off. The four of them would have a great time. Frank was intelligent and easy to like. So far, however, Rosemary and Gile's togetherness was limited to her short visits, and most of them were in his bed. Why did she suddenly let herself face that reality? And she was almost certain he wouldn't go to that dinner with her. He always used his writing as a reason, or was it really just an excuse? She suddenly felt uncertain about everything. Well, maybe she'd just test the waters and ask him to go with her and see what he said.

"Okay, I'll ask him," Rosemary told her friend.

That afternoon, she took her usual walk up to Gile's cottage. Right away, she saw that his car was gone. There was no Gile. Perhaps he'd gone to buy groceries, although she knew he did this every Thursday, the day he'd set aside for all his errands during the week. She walked on to the beach and sat on a log for thirty minutes, then jogged back to see if he had returned, but he was still not there. Arriving back home, she waited an hour and tried calling; there was no answer.

Rosemary didn't sleep well that night, worried and wondering where Gile was. The next morning on a Saturday, she tried calling again but received no response.

❦

"Where's your friend?" Margie asked Rosemary on Saturday night when she found her standing on the front steps alone.

"He's on a short trip to see his agent. Sorry, he couldn't come. Maybe another time."

Margie looked at Rosemary rather strangely. It was so unlike Rosemary not to let her know earlier that her friend would not be at dinner. She thought it was a little on the rude side, but she let her feelings slide and welcomed Rosemary into the house.

Does she know I'm lying? Rosemary wondered. She had no idea where Gile had gone, of course, but she wanted to spare herself the embarrassment of admitting it. In fact, the fear in her heart was shaking her to the core. Her instinct told her he wasn't coming back. Why did she feel that way? He wouldn't do that to her, would he? Just leave and not explain or say goodbye! It was true he'd never said the words "I love you" that she'd wanted desperately to hear, but she was so certain that he had strong feelings for her, and they had so much in common. Isn't that what he'd told her? Or did they? Just because he was a writer and she was trying to be one, did that tie them together?

She tried to enjoy the evening, an evening Rosemary would much rather have spent at home. If she hadn't come, she knew there would have been too many questions. Margie and Frank were the usual good hosts. They were both witty and humorous as always. Generally, Rosemary was in stitches from laughing when she was with them, but tonight it was an effort to concentrate and to respond to their cheerfulness.

She had called her father during the early part of the evening before he went to bed, and he was fine, but by nine o'clock, she used him as her excuse, refusing a ride home from Frank, deciding a good old walk was what she needed.

❧

When the Donahans left on Tuesday morning for Seattle after their short stay, Margie knew something was amiss with Rosemary but was unable to get her to talk about it. She was being very evasive. Margie was betting that it had something to do with the new man in her life.

At home, Rosemary had no sign of Gile. No call. Nothing. There most definitely was something wrong. Two weeks passed, leaving Rosemary nervous and on edge. The weather was still warm for

September, known by many as an Indian summer, though it did get quite cool at night, and you could certainly feel autumn in the air.

Towards the end of September, her father became gravely ill again. Rosemary was feeling quite despondent over the way her life was going and her father's, too. Would things never turn out right for her?

Her father woke up the next morning, gasping for air. Rosemary frantically called 911. Before anyone could get there, her father stopped breathing. She attempted CPR, and when the aid car finally arrived, Matt had a slight pulse. After stabilizing him, the medics rushed him to Grays Harbor Community Hospital in Aberdeen, a good thirty-minute run. Rosemary followed them in her car, frightened that this might mean the end for her father. She thought of her son, bringing back her despair, the grief and sorrow, and her depression. Rosemary felt it all. She didn't want to lose another member of her family. Whom would she have then? Gile? She didn't think so now. Her hope of ever seeing him again had diminished with each day that passed. The last week had been so difficult.

At the hospital, Rosemary sat for an hour and a half, waiting for someone to give her information about her father. All she knew was they were working on him. When the physician finally came to find her, she was informed that they had pulled him through the present crisis, and he was in a guarded but satisfactory condition for the time being. They were going to keep him for several days before deciding whether he could go back home or whether he needed the services of a nursing home.

A little while later, Rosemary was in the car, driving back to the beach to pick up a change in clothes and a toothbrush for herself. When she got home, she tried calling Gile once again. Still, there was no answer. While packing, she remembered Gile's book and stuffed it into her overnight bag. She had read the first part and was anxious to finish it. Quickly placing some apples and a couple of cans of soda pop in a bag, she grabbed up everything and threw it all into the car. She took one second to drive past Gile's rented cottage, even though she knew she would find no one there, and then she returned to Aberdeen.

While keeping vigil at the hospital, Rosemary finished reading Gile's first book. It had been a very good read and wonderfully written.

Gile was very clever in keeping his readers on edge and wanting to know more about the story.

It was a story of a young writer named Brad who had pulled himself up from the slums of Chicago. A very wealthy woman, declining in health, hired Brad, who was trying hard to save money to go back to college, to paint her beautiful, large country home. The woman's husband had left her well off. She liked this young man very much and spent a lot of time talking with him, inviting him in for coffee and then for dinner, while he worked on her house. He wanted to go to college and become a writer he told her. She wanted to help him, and when he finished the painting project, she had a proposition ready for him.

The woman's heart-broken daughter was moving back home to live after she had been jilted by her fiancé. The woman wanted to see her only child settled and taken care of before she died. The older woman had MS, had suffered a long time, and the disease was getting worse. She knew she didn't have a lot of time.

After offering Brad a nice drink, she told him her daughter was very shy and had little confidence in herself. She'd gone to college for a couple of years and then surprised her mother by becoming engaged. Shortly after the engagement, the relationship folded. The daughter refused to go back to school and was very depressed. She told Brad that the girl would just come home, mope, and destroy herself unless she did something to prevent it.

She reminded him that he had told her he wanted to finish college, and she wanted to help him financially. "I can make that happen for you," she informed him.

Her proposal shocked Brad at first. If he would court the woman's daughter and marry her, the woman promised to provide him with his education and would stipulate in her will that he be given a very hearty annual stipend for as long as he and her daughter remained together in the marriage. But the daughter must never know of their agreement, and if he ever left the marriage, divorce or otherwise, he would receive only the balance of that year and no more money after that. If he stayed with the daughter, the stipend would be increased sufficiently every couple of years. And if her daughter died, through sickness or accidentally, while they were married, he would inherit everything that was left in the trust. Brad couldn't resist. He wanted to finish school, and he'd never had enough money to do that. He loved to write. He wanted the education and hoped to complete the novel he'd already started.

Brad took a couple of days to think about it, and in the end, he made a contract with the woman without ever having met the daughter. When he did, he was appalled. The daughter was quite homely, badly scarred on one side of her face from an accident early in life. She was shy and uninteresting, probably because of the scarring. He was not attracted to her in any way, but for the sake of money, Brad put on a good act and wooed her. Eventually he married her, making a bargain with the Devil for his new life.

Rosemary thought Gile's story was very intriguing. It took place in Chicago where Gile said he'd lived while working on the book. She didn't learn much from the book jacket about "her" author. It said he was thirty-two years old at the time of the publication and that he lived in the area where his writing took place. Yes, that added up to what little he'd revealed to her. He had a dog, named Kip, but the write-up did not mention any family, like a wife or children. It was strange he'd never mentioned the dog, since they had discussed animals and how much he liked them. She'd never asked, of course, but she'd hoped he wasn't married, not that it made any difference now.

Exhausted, she fell asleep on the hospital couch in the waiting room and was surprised when one of the nurses woke her in the morning. Her father was doing okay but was still a very sick man. His heart was failing him. Matt was asleep when they finally allowed her to go in briefly to check on him. She stayed a few minutes watching him sleep and then decided she would return later. Maybe he would be awake then.

In the meantime, she drove her car the few miles back to Aberdeen's shopping area to get a couple of personal items before checking out the motels, where she would spend a night and maybe subsequent nights. While she was at the small Aberdeen Mall, Rosemary passed a bookstore. On an impulse, she went in and discovered Gile's second book, *Burden of the Heart*, on the shelf. She wanted to read it, and she seldom got to town, so she grabbed it up. She'd start it tonight to keep her mind occupied while waiting.

Upon her return, her father was awake, and although he was terribly weak, he finally had a little color in his face and he rewarded his daughter with a smile. "Hi, baby! This old man appreciates having you around, you know."

"I know, Dad. I'm glad I can be here. Now, your order for the day is to get well so I can take you back home with me soon. Right?" He nodded his head. Then she saw his eyes close, and after waiting a few minutes to make sure he was asleep, she left the room. Rosemary knew he wouldn't be going home for a while. She was certain of that.

She called the Simpson Motel, located close by, made an overnight reservation for herself, and then waited around the hospital for a couple more hours until her father was once again awake. She wanted a short visit with him before leaving for the night. It was close to six o'clock when she kissed him goodnight and went to check herself into the motel. Once there, Rosemary refreshed her makeup and then walked to a restaurant nearby. She wasn't terribly hungry, but she thought she needed to put something in her stomach, not having eaten at all that day.

Rosemary had just finished her chef's salad and was waiting for her bill when a familiar male voice said, "Hello." Looking up, she was startled to find Thomas standing beside her table. His usual, sunny smile was absent as he said, "Surprised to find you in town. Everything okay?"

"Oh, Thomas, it's so good to see you. My dad is in the hospital. I'm spending the night here in a motel to see if things improve for him. He's not doing very well."

"I'm really sorry to hear that, Rosemary; he's a great man in my book."

She thanked him for his words and noticed how tired and withdrawn he seemed. His sparkle was missing, and he looked so sad. Her heart went out to him. What was wrong? He had been one of her best friends. She had to control herself from reaching out to comfort him—she had hurt him and didn't feel she had a right to do that anymore.

The thought had barely entered her mind when a woman, apparently now his companion, came from the restroom and found him talking to Rosemary. Thomas took the woman's hand in his, introduced her as Marie, and then almost abruptly said they had to leave. "Please give your father my regards. I hope he will be back on his feet soon."

"Thank you, Thomas. I'll tell him that. Nice meeting you, Marie."

Rosemary was feeling miserable when she watched them walk off. He was such a nice man. She'd held him at bay because she didn't want to get involved, and that was with a person she knew and trusted. Look at what she'd done! She'd had an affair with a stranger, and he'd left her without so as much as a goodbye. What an idiot she was.

Back in her room, Rosemary couldn't wait to get into the shower. Afterward, feeling refreshed and a little stronger emotionally, she put on her bathrobe and stretched out on the bed. Rosemary was tired but feeling restless. She thought about Thomas and hoped he was happy with his friend who seemed very nice. She thought of Jeffrey and hoped he wasn't happy, that in some way, he was paying for what he'd done. She thought of her son and missed him with an aching heart as always. Then she thought about Gile, wondering where he was and why he hadn't let her know he was going away. It was then that she remembered her purchase, got off the bed, and searched through her bag for the book.

She planned on reading only a few pages before turning out the light, but once she started it, she couldn't put the book down. After several pages into the story, Rosemary realized the story was a continuation of Gile's first book.

Brad had married the woman's daughter at the end of the first book to seal the agreement he and the old woman had made. A contract had been drawn up and a year had passed since their marriage. At the beginning of *Burden of the Heart*, the old woman succumbs. Brad has no feeling whatsoever for the woman he has so callously married for money. He receives fifty thousand dollars every year from her mother's estate, and in nine years, the payment will increase to one hundred thousand dollars according to the contract. This is fine with him. He takes advanced writing classes at the university and continues to write. Brad did well with his first novel; he is now writing his second one. He has plenty of money. He travels. He keeps in touch with his wife just to let her know he is around, and when he's home, he dutifully makes love to her, lets her believe he has missed her.

His wife, a very meek woman, is intimidated by his personality, by his handsomeness, and by his intelligence. She has grown to love him, but she knows she isn't good-looking and feels she's lucky to be married to a man like him so she makes do with her life, keeps herself trim and neat and breathlessly waits for him to make his brief appearances from time to time. His work is so important, and she can't bother him with her complaints.

The wife is entirely unaware of Brad's contract with her mother and not fully aware of how rich she is. The mother verbally informed her daughter she would be taken care of after her death, that all financial matters would be handled by her lawyer, and that she would never lack for anything. The unethical lawyer handling the case received quite a sum of money so has been far from truthful with the daughter after her mother's demise. Her husband is now in control of her life. She'd never amount to anything, but she'd never have to worry about anything either. With the money he receives in the deal, the lawyer easily can keep the big secret locked in a box.

Rosemary couldn't put the book down. Gile's writing was superb, and she became so involved in the story, she couldn't put the book down. However, she felt badly for the wife. The poor woman, having to put up with someone so heartless!

It was getting so late Rosemary finally had to give up reading. She fell soundly asleep as soon as she turned off the lamp. And then she dreamed of the character, Brad. He was trying to treat Rosemary like his wife, and of course, she was resisting. In the dream the man began to look like Jeffrey; then his features changed, and he was Gile. He became very angry. He scowled, then growled like an animal, and came rushing towards her, his arm raised to strike.

RING!

The sound of the phone ringing made her jerk awake, her heart pounding. It took her a few seconds to realize she wasn't in her own bed, but alone at the motel. Then it came to her. It was the hospital. They were the only ones who knew she was here. Her hand trembled as she answered the incessant ringing. *Please God*, she uttered silently, *don't let it be bad news.*

"Hel-hello."

"Hello. Rosemary Archer, please."

"This is she," her voice croaked.

"This is Natalie. I am a nurse at the hospital. Your father has taken a turn for the worse. You should plan on returning to the hospital now."

By the time Rosemary was able to get there, her beloved father was gone. She was numb. He couldn't be gone just like that! She felt completely disoriented. They let her in to see him for a minute before removing his body from the room. She stood over him, shaking her head and finally leaning over and kissing him softly on his still warm cheek.

Some fifteen minutes later, Rosemary followed the gurney a little way down the hall as they rolled him away. She stopped and stood in the doorway of the waiting room, her mind blank, not knowing what to do next. She wished she had a friend or a family member with her. Anyone. It was so difficult to be alone at a time like this.

Her father's doctor found her standing there, and he put his hand on her shoulder speaking quietly. "Are you okay? Do you have someone who can come and be with you or to drive you home?" He was very kind and sympathetic.

Rosemary shook her head. "No, I'll be okay. I'm fine," she said dully.

After talking with the physician, Rosemary walked slowly down the main hallway to a bank of telephones. The hospital would take care of calling the undertaker at the mortuary, and she would have to go there a little later during business hours to take care of the necessary paperwork. But first, she had to notify her brothers. Taking out her personal phone book, she located Daniel's phone number. She was closest to him. He could call their brother, David. She fought her exhaustion as she picked up the phone receiver, and she was reminded of the other times when she'd lost the family members she'd loved so, her son and her mother.

As she waited for her brother to answer his phone, she said aloud, "Dad, I'll miss you so much. Take care of Mathew for me, and Mom, too."

When Daniel answered the phone on the third ring, she barely held back her tears as she gave him the sad news about their father.

CHAPTER EIGHT

D ANIEL WITH HIS WIFE AND DAVID flew into Seattle on the same day. Their planes arrived only two hours apart. David was the first to set down, and he waited for Daniel's flight to land a little later.

When Rosemary's brothers arrived, the tears she had been holding back finally came. They comforted her while she sobbed in their arms. It was a nice surprise to see Mimi. She wished her other sister-in-law, Jean, and her nephews could have been there to complete the family circle, but she was overjoyed to see her brothers once again and to have their loving support.

They had a whole day before the funeral and two days after to visit. Rosemary felt as if she was really getting acquainted with them for the first time in her life. She had been so young when each of her brothers had left home. Without interference from Jeffrey this time, they had a much more relaxing time catching up. Although the brothers mourned their father's death, they both realized that their sister's sorrow was much greater than theirs. It had a deeper impact due to the terrible loss she had already suffered by the unbelievable death of her son.

During their time together, the siblings recalled many incidents when their father was there for them while they were growing up, and they especially remembered all the times Matt was out in the community helping others in some way, big or small. He had been a good man.

On September 25, the Presbyterian church, where Rosemary's parents had been members since the early days of their marriage, was packed with people for Matt's memorial. It was the same church where Margie, Thomas, and she had attended Sunday school together in their youth, where their close friendships first began and continued through their high school years. The three beach rats!

Matt and Louise's church attendance was off and on during Louise's long illness. After her death and through the long months of mourning, Matt's faith seemed to stall, but eventually he did return, that is, until his health became a factor and he could no longer drive his car.

Once Rosemary came home, the two of them managed to attend church on most Sundays. It was so good to be back at the church again, helping her contend with the loss of her son, but after a period, it became too difficult for her father to go anywhere. They stopped attending.

Many people from the small local areas of Grayland, Westport, Aberdeen, Hoquiam, and Raymond—all neighboring towns where Matt had been raised and had raised his family—filled the pews of the church. In fact, Rosemary and her brothers were overwhelmed and amazed by the huge crowd. Many were younger than Matt, so their presence left little doubt as to the respect a great many people had for their father.

The young pastor, James Bosc, was not long out of the seminary and was well liked, although he'd served them for only little more than a year. Rosemary had always enjoyed conversing with him after church on the Sundays when they were there, and she had even considered asking for counseling for herself but had never taken that first step.

The congregation grew quiet as Pastor Bosc stepped to the pulpit. He spoke warmly, welcoming everyone, and then paused a few seconds before saying, "What if we feel we have no hope? Then we must rely on our faith! And what is faith? It is the deliberate confidence in the character of our God whether we understand it or not. For you see, without that hope, there are only two choices, faith or despair. Matt Reegan chose faith. Reading from Isaiah 40:31, Scripture says, 'Those who hope in the Lord will renew their strength. They will soar on wings like eagles.'

"I did not know Matt Reegan very long, but after meeting with his family and knowing some of his dear friends, I know he was a man of integrity, respected and well-loved in this beach community surrounding us. He embodied what Jesus taught us about love by his care and concern for those who needed help.

"There is understandable grief by all of you at this moment, knowing you will not see him again in this world. That only makes you human. But we also know that he has gone home to his Creator, where he no longer suffers. He has earned his rest. Let us now bow our heads in prayer."

When Pastor Bosc's prayer ended, a gentleman approached the pulpit, introduced himself as Jack Jefferson, a friend of Matt's. "Rosemary Archer, Matt's daughter, requested that I read a eulogy she wrote for her father." Slipping on his glasses, he began to read:

> My dad was our dad, and he belonged to me and to my brothers, but I realize he belonged to others, as well. I am certain that there are those who will tell stories that, because of Matt Reegan, they would not be here today if he had not stretched out his helping hand during their desperate need.
>
> He was the kindest, gentlest, and most loving man I've ever known. I was so very fortunate to be his daughter. He was always my biggest fan, always encouraging me to try new things, to spread my horizons. He gave me enormous confidence when I was growing up and helped me to learn about our world. He and my mother made many sacrifices for their children, sacrifices that can never be repaid.
>
> Help me to pass on his legacy of love and concern for those in this world, as best we can.
>
> If there were more Matt Reegans in our world, there would be no one wanting and no hate from one human to another. He may be gone from our visual aspect, but he left very large footprints on this earth.
>
> My dad's faith was very strong, so I know where he resides right now, in peace and love with his Lord. God only knows how I will miss him, his smile, his great attitude, and all-abiding love for mankind. Rest in peace, my loving father. You will never be forgotten.

There were not many dry eyes in the crowd, including Rosemary's and her family. When Jack Jefferson returned to his seat, the pastor asked if there was anyone else in the congregation who wished to speak on behalf of Matt. There were a few older men, even some younger ones who had worked with Matt, and they spoke out about his humor and love for his fellow man. As she was wiping her eyes, Rosemary heard a familiar voice speak from the middle of the room. She turned to look. It was Thomas!

"I would just like to say that when I worked with Matt Reegan, I never thought of him as being a generation older than myself. He could work with the best. In fact, it was difficult sometimes to keep up with him. He always treated me like his equal. Matt was always helping someone who was financially strapped, perhaps someone losing a job, especially if it was a family and children were involved. I fished with him, too. He would often give his whole catch to someone who needed the food. He was a very giving person. I had great respect and love for this man, and I'm much richer for having known him."

Oh, Thomas, Rosemary thought to herself. *How sweet you are. I think you knew him as well as I did.* Overcome with emotion, fresh tears spilled down her face. She wiped them away with the tissue she gripped in her hand. Daniel put his arm around her shoulder and pulled her close to him, and David, seated on the other side of her, took her hand in his. Her brothers' strength calmed her. Thank God they were there for her.

As the service came to an end, Rosemary thought how glad she was about her decision to come home and reconnect with her father before he died. Rosemary knew she would be a lost person after her brothers departed. And she would be lonely without Gile, too, for she had given up on ever seeing her lover again. There were times when she was so angry with him and other times when she told herself it was her own damn fault. How could she have thought he cared? She'd come to the realization he cared only about using and hurting her. What else could she think? Well, he'd certainly succeeded, hadn't he?

Marie had come to the service with Thomas. From the distance across the floor, Rosemary thought Thomas looked healthy, but she couldn't be sure. At least he looked better than when she had seen him the week before. Maybe he'd just had a bad day. As she circled the fellowship hall thanking people for coming, she could feel Thomas watching her from across the room. It made her uneasy. He must be very angry with her, she decided. How she wished they were still friends. She certainly could use a friend beside her now. Margie had been ill and, much to Rosemary's great disappointment, couldn't make it to the memorial. It would have been nice to have her there to lean on, too.

Rosemary joined her brothers and Mimi, who were talking with a friend of their father's, just as the food, prepared by the women of the church, was ready to be served. The four of them waited until a long line had formed and then headed for the back of the line.

Thomas came up beside her. His hand reached out to touch her shoulder, but before contact could be made, he dropped it back to his side. As he spoke, she turned around to talk to him, while her family moved on in the food line without her. When Thomas spoke, his voice lacked luster, but perhaps it was the occasion that made him sound different. Now that he was closer to her, she noticed the sadness etched into his eyes. Her heart went out to him.

"I just wanted to say again how very sorry I am for your loss, Rosemary. I know how hard it is to lose your parents."

"Thank you very much. Those were some beautiful things you said about my father. I really appreciated them."

"He was a good man." Then Thomas turned and signaled to Marie across the room that he'd be right there.

"Well, I've got to go. Nice to see you again."

Rosemary didn't want him to leave. She wanted to talk with him, win his friendship back. "Aren't you going to stay and eat?"

"Ah, no, Marie and I have another commitment. Take care of yourself." Abruptly, as he'd done at the restaurant, he walked away from her. Rosemary felt a sense of unexplained loss when he left her side. The connection between them had been fragile before, and now it felt permanently severed. She had truly lost a good friend. More tears came to her eyes. What a sad, sad day for her.

⸎

Before her brothers departed, they urged Rosemary to visit them, but it wasn't something she could think about then. She still had things to sort

out. Her life had turned upside down once again, and she needed time
and space to get her feet back on the ground.

After they left, to keep herself busy, Rosemary returned to her
writing, and after a while, she finally gave herself a respite, taking a
short trip to Seattle to do some shopping in mid-November, not for
Christmas gifts but for herself. She thought some new clothes might
give her a lift. She needed something. Rosemary stayed over a couple
of nights with Margie and Frank in their beautiful home on the water,
and that was a welcome change. Even though it was freezing outside,
she loved looking out at the crisp, sparkling waters of Puget Sound,
sitting by the warmth of a roaring fire, and enjoying the chats with her
friends while sipping a glass of wine. Rosemary had a wonderful time,
but it didn't help the awful loneliness that caught up with her when
she returned to the ocean.

In the car on her return trip to Tokeland, the memories of Gile
interrupted Rosemary's thoughts, even though she tried to brush them
aside. It was then that she remembered she had never finished his second book. She would do that tonight. That would get her mind off
other things. Had he published the third one yet, she wondered.

Later, after unpacking and getting settled in for the evening, she
picked up the book and began to read where she'd left off weeks ago.

Brad had moved to San Francisco with his "contracted wife."
There he finished his education, earning his degree in journalism and
English. He was almost finished with his second novel and was on a
six-week stay in Florida to research his book. While he was there, he
met his neighbor, a cute little blonde by the name of Katie. Katie's
husband was in the navy, gone for months at a time. In between the
times he worked on his book, Brad charmed the poor, lonely woman
and finally seduced her. In the end, Brad left his little blonde and
went back to his wife because of his greed for money. Rosemary felt
sorry for Brad. He was pathetic. His whole life was all about money.
Nothing else seemed to have any significance in his life. And his wife
was a pathetic creature, too, letting him walk all over her. *What a dis-
mal life that poor woman led*, Rosemary thought.

It was early in the morning when she finished the book. The end
of the novel left her crying, and she grabbed a tissue and blew her nose.

Nonchalantly, she flipped the book over to look at Gile's picture on the book jacket. He was so beautiful with that dark skin and his spectacular smile. She ached at the memories and began sobbing uncontrollably. Following a ten-minute siege of crying, she finally dried her eyes, blew her nose again, and got up to put the book back in her bag. It was then that the inside flap of the jacket came open. There was a short bio on him. She read:

About the Author

Gile Hammond is the author of *High Grass, Long Road* and this, his second novel, *Burden of the Heart*. He is presently writing his third novel, entitled *The Price We Pay*. Gile has been married to his wife, Nelly, since 1987. Kip, his golden Lab, is his close companion when he is not traveling, which is frequently. Doing extensive research on the background for his books—details of the area, history, and local events where his stories occur—he has made it a habit to live in these locations until he has completed the telling of them.

Rosemary was stunned. She was crying again. Married! He was married after all! He was married when he was here with her! *Oh, my God, what a dunce I was. How could I have been such a naïve fool the second time around? First Jeffrey and now Gile!* Her naïveté made her feel worthless and used.

It was a very restless and sleepless night for her. She kept waking up, each time crying out into the darkness, "Why? Why did you do this to me, Gile?" At one point, she got out of bed, very angry, so angry she picked up the book and threw it across the room, "You're a contemptible jerk! Damn you, Gile Hammond. Damn you!"

Rosemary finally fell into a deep sleep for only a couple of hours before the phone rang about 8:00 a.m., bringing her awake from another dream. The terrifying dream had substituted Gile for Brad from the story, and as he was reaching out to her with a calm and endearing grin, she was backing away from him in fear. The grin, no longer endearing, changed to a sneer. He had the nightmarish mouth of an animal, its fangs showing. She was so frightened! Just as he reached for her, someone rang her doorbell. But it wasn't the doorbell. No, it was the alarm, and she reached to shut it off, but it kept on ringing, and then she finally realized it was the phone ringing.

"Hey," Margie shouted over the phone when Rosemary finally answered. "How are you, stranger?"

"Margie!" Her heart was still pounding from the dream. "Gosh, it's so darn good to hear your voice. Are you here in Tokeland?" How she hoped her friend was here, just down the road. She needed to talk to someone before she went crazy, although she didn't quite know how she was going to tell her friend what she'd discovered to make herself feel such shame.

"No. Wish I were. It's been a rat race here, but right after you left us, I began to long for the beach again. Need to come down soon and get recharged. Very soon! Just had to call and tell you I read the latest book by your friend, Gile Hammond. Never did read the first two. And hey, girl, it's pretty steamy. What an imagination he has. Really held me entranced. I finished it in just two nights. That's really something for me. Suppose you've read them all?"

"Uh, no . . . I haven't read that last one." Rosemary imagined the same information about the author was on the third book, as well. Had her friend looked at the date and read how long he'd been married? If so, she wasn't saying anything. Margie probably was just curious to see if Rosemary knew that little tidbit. Who wouldn't be?

"He's one good looking man from his picture. Are you still seeing him?"

What could Rosemary say? She couldn't tell her the truth. She just couldn't. There was a brief pause before she answered, "Not really. He travels a lot. Haven't seen him in a while."

Rosemary quickly changed the subject to something a little safer. "And I've been real busy with the house and studying the gardening books. Want to put in a little garden in the spring."

"Sounds like you're keeping yourself occupied. Speaking of books, are you still writing on yours?"

"Have been lately. I just need to do some final editing. It's been hard to get back into a routine since losing Dad. I will, though. I really would like to finish it." Then Rosemary changed topics again. "When are you coming to Tokeland? The weather hasn't been bad lately. Some drizzle but not much hard rain!" She was hoping for Margie's promised visit. Soon the holidays would be upon them, and as usual, it was to be a sad and challenging time for Rosemary.

"Not sure," Margie answered. "With construction, it depends on the weather, but I will let you know next week for sure.

Well, got to go, girl. You better run out and get that book. It'll warm your bed. The sex scenes are torrid."

Rosemary hung up the phone carefully and then shouted out loud, "To hell with you, Gile! I don't need your damn book to warm my bed."

But during her next trip to Aberdeen a week later, she purposely went into the bookstore to find the third book. She couldn't stop herself. She told herself that since she had read the first two, she might as well read the last one, as well.

After dinner and with some trepidation and after muttering another curse at Gile, Rosemary began to read his third book. It was not a surprise to find that the book was the final story of a trilogy about Brad.

Brad had again gone home for a short period, taking care of his obligations, before saying goodbye to his poor wife again. The man was searching, not only for the background of the final version of his story but also for something beyond that.

It was the first time Rosemary felt sorry for Brad. In the earlier books, he was such a dishonest person, and to treat his wife as he did soured Rosemary, but now she thought he was beginning to realize that he was missing a real purpose to his life.

Brad moved to the Pacific Coast temporarily.

She read about his move and the things that happened along the way, his settling into his latest pad at the ocean, becoming very involved in this character, Brad, who had even caused her bad dreams. After reading most of the first chapter, she felt as if she'd read the book before. Then all of a sudden something hit her. She read on and began to hyperventilate. She continued to read Gile's next words.

He watched her jogging along the water. She didn't
see him, but later in the afternoon, he watched from
the open as she sat herself down on the sand in the sun,
amongst the driftwood brought in by past winter storms.

Brad's neighbor's big old dog followed him every
afternoon, and it made him think of his own dog in
San Francisco. Brad missed his canine friend, who was
now twelve years old. The dog wouldn't be around for
many more years. Soon Brad would finish his book
and go home once again. He threw a few sticks for the
yellow Lab to chase and noticed that the woman was
still there at the other end of the beach, and for some
reason, he felt she was watching him and the dog play,
even as he observed her.

As she read, Rosemary's hands began to tremble. She could hardly
hold the book. She couldn't believe what she was reading. Her heart
was pounding, and her whole body began to shake. She knew what was
coming next. It was difficult to read any further, but she had to go on.
Why had it taken her so long to comprehend what was this all about?
She brought the book back up from her lap and read the next words.

Brad was determined to meet the woman, curious
to know if she lived there permanently as a few owners
did, or was she vacationing? Maybe she had a summer
home here. He was also looking for a new character for
his latest book, and this is how he found his characters.
He lived the story he created while he researched it. It
made it more realistic for him.

One day, he decided to brave it, and instead of
going to the beach as usual, he walked down along the
highway and then turned toward the beach where he
found her location. The woman appeared to be close
to his age, and she was concentrating on writing something in the notebook she held on her lap. She never

heard him approach. He spoke softly so as not to spook her. "Hello there!"

She jerked at his words, but then she smiled at him.

"Sorry," Brad said. "Didn't mean to startle you. But curiosity got the best of me, and I had to come over here and find out what it is you are doing."

She had a nice smile, and he liked the looks of her. When Brad introduced himself, she seemed very friendly, and they hit it off immediately as he had hoped they would. He was known for his charm, and he poured in on. Brad knew where this was going to lead. He could sense right away that she was ripe for company, probably very lonely. This was the one! He wanted this woman, and he would have her one way or another. It was just a matter of time. Her name was Roseanne, the name as lovely as she was.

The two talked for about an hour and a half. She was trying to be a writer, too, and he sensed Roseanne was intelligent and would probably do an excellent job. Yes, there was no question about her intelligence, but she was a very lonely woman, a woman who needed someone to love her. He knew, though, that she held part of herself back and that she was a little nervous about him. He attempted to draw her out, trying to give her a feeling of self-confidence. He talked about her book, giving her pointers and assurance she was doing well in her undertaking. Brad noted how her eyes lit up if she was excited about something. He really liked what he saw.

Brad began to walk down to her private writing spot every day, enjoying their daily conversations, patiently waiting but wanting more. He detected that Roseanne had an abundance of buried passion within her, a passion that had never come to fruition, and he would like to be the one to discover it.

Rosemary put the book down and drew a gasping breath, still not believing what she was reading. Drawing air deep into her lungs, she closed her eyes, squeezing them tightly, holding back her tears. Although she was completely shocked and devastated by the enormity of Gile's betrayal, she took control of herself after a few minutes. She was disheartened but unbelieving for the moment and picked up the book and proceeded to read a bit more.

Several weeks later, after meeting with Roseanne almost every day, Brad decided to experiment. He didn't show up at their regular spot for a few days. He'd told her where he was living—the cottage at the end of one of the beach roads. Sure enough, Roseanne arrived there, wondering about his absence. He invited her in and found her to be a willing and able partner, and she was really something. It was a wonderful experience for Brad. He'd never felt like that with anyone in is life. If only things were different for him. He felt there was something very special about her, but his life was already mapped out. Sadly, he realized there was no way to fit her into it.

By now, Rosemary's tears streamed down her face until she couldn't see the words anymore. She wiped away her tears, but new ones replaced those that she'd shed. There was no mistaking it. Gile was Brad! Or Brad was Gile, however one looked at it. And this was about her! He had even used a slight variation of her name. How callous was that? She had been set up, and he had used her trust and their affair as the story for his third book. Rosemary had been an experience. Just an experiment for him!

"Oh God," Rosemary cried aloud, "I feel so terrible. How did this happen?" She felt like she was dying a slow death, and the pain made her double up; it hurt so badly. How could this have happened to her again? She was stupid to trust anyone.

Rosemary didn't bother getting out of bed the next day. She lay curled in a little ball, crying periodically and then falling into a deeply troubled sleep with violent, recurring nightmares waking her up, her heart hammering. Awake, she would cry until she was exhausted, then sleep would come once more, along with the terrible dreams, and they would wake her up as before. The vicious cycle continued. She thought she was going to put her life back together again, and instead, it had fallen totally apart. Rosemary felt as if she had crashed into a brick wall.

She was so despondent that it was two days later before she forced herself to get out of bed. She hadn't eaten a thing during that time. She looked into the mirror and hated what she saw. She detested what she had become—a zombie, like after her son's death.

Rosemary was the wife of a marriage that had failed before it became a marriage, a mother who had lost her baby through neglect before he had a chance at life, and a woman who always let her others use her. On top of it, she had lost the father she so loved, and now the man she had loved had betrayed her in the worst way. Gile was a user—a user of women. And she'd become his prey. How ashamed she felt! Should she move somewhere else? Make a fresh start? But where would she go? Where could she run? Where could she hide? She'd be running from something she would never be able to escape. Rosemary had hit the bottom. It couldn't get any worse.

Stumbling to the shower, Rosemary washed her hair, put a little makeup on her white, ghost-like face, and then fixed herself a bowl of soup, the first thing of substance she'd had in two days and was surprised that it tasted so good. She'd only taken a few spoonfuls when there was a knock at the door.

Her first thought was that maybe it was Gile returning. If it was, Rosemary promised herself she would claw his face to shreds. Her anger gripped her like a vice. However, instead of getting up, she sat without moving. Whoever was there could just go away! Then she heard a woman's voice call out her name.

"Rosemary, are you home?"

There was an element of panic in the tone of the voice, which made Rosemary finally rush to open the door. The woman standing in front of her looked vaguely familiar. "Yes, can I help you?"

"I'm Marie Mallory," she said, and Rosemary quickly discerned that the woman was Thomas's lady friend. Marie was trying not to cry, and she blurted out, "We met briefly before. T-Thomas has been hurt in an accident at the cannery." She was out of breath. "They took him to the hospital. He's pretty badly crushed. Something heavy tipped over on him, I think. I don't know . . . if . . . if he's going to make it." The tears were now flowing.

Rosemary stared in horror as she listened to Marie's story, crying out, "Oh no." Not another nightmare! This couldn't be!

"I can see . . . see part of the cannery from my place, and when I . . . I heard the sirens and went out to look, I could see they had stopped at the cannery." Breathlessly, she went on, "I rushed over there. Got there about the time the medics were putting Thomas in the ambulance. He was unconscious. His foreman, Mark—I think that's his name—was there. He told me that before Thomas lost consciousness, he asked for you, Rosemary, but Mark didn't know who you were. I said I would come—"

Before Marie could complete her last sentence, Rosemary had backed into the house and grabbed her jacket out of the coat closet near the door, along with her purse and car keys. "They went into Aberdeen, didn't they?" Rosemary asked. Sometimes the injured were taken to Olympia to a bigger hospital, another forty-five minutes away from Aberdeen. She wanted to make sure.

"Yes," Marie answered, "Aberdeen!"

"I'm going to drive in. Would you like to go with me?"

"No," Marie answered. "You ride with me. My car's already warmed and ready."

Rosemary didn't argue. Her mind was boggled with all that had happened, and she probably shouldn't be driving anyway. They rushed to Marie's car. Nothing was said for several miles as Rosemary silently said a prayer for God to spare Thomas's life. Marie finally broke the silence, "Rosemary, you know he's in love with you, don't you?"

Surprised, Rosemary turned and looked at Marie with a puzzled frown. "But I thought you and he . . ." Her mind was racing. *Oh no, Thomas! Oh, my God!* Recognition came at last! Thomas had always shown his love in his own way. She kept imagining they were just good friends, that he really didn't love her, that he just thought he did. Rosemary hadn't wanted to get involved except to be his friend. Hadn't she told him she didn't want to be involved with any man? That was her excuse. But look how she had gotten involved with that scoundrel, Gile Hammond. How two-faced could she be? And now one of her best friends might be dying after she'd abandoned him. Rosemary's heart ached. What had she passed up? A chance for happiness with a man who loved her for herself, who wouldn't have used her as she had been used too many times before. *Oh, Thomas*, she screamed silently. *I'm so sorry. Please, dear God, don't let him die*, she prayed again and again.

Rain was coming down in torrents, the wipers barely keeping the windows clear. The weather matched the solemnity of their situation. The rain slowed them down, and Rosemary had the urge to push Marie to drive faster.

Marie spoke again. "Rosemary, Thomas told me he has loved you forever, but you never reciprocated and that you don't have those same feelings for him. In spite of it, he treasured your friendship and has regretted not having you in his life in any way he could." Rosemary was very much aware of the other woman's love for Thomas, too, as she listened to what she was saying. "We tried to make a go of it, but Thomas was honest with me about his feelings a long time ago. We kept our relationship on a friendship basis only." She turned her head to look at Rosemary for a brief moment and then turned back to her driving, saying quietly, "You know, of course, you're passing up a very good thing, don't you? He's the nicest guy I've ever known."

"Yes . . . he certainly is," Rosemary sobbed out her words. "I haven't been a very good friend at all. I –I-thank you, Marie, for telling me all this. I've had some real losses in recent times, and I don't think I could stand it if something happens to Thomas, too. He IS a good man . . . so sweet and so real!" The tears came and the sobs gushed from her.

Marie reached over and patted her arm and handed her a Kleenex from her pocket as they neared the hospital. Both women dreaded the real possibility of bad news waiting for them, but they hurried into the emergency waiting room to find out where Thomas had been taken and the extent of his injuries.

It took the medical team a couple of hours to stabilize Thomas. Once the doctors were sure he was strong enough to go through surgery, they began to put him back together again. It was several more hours before the women were given any information on his status.

The wait was unbearable, and Rosemary was grateful to have someone there with her this time. She remembered how lonely it had been for her when her father had died. Until now, she always seemed to be by herself.

Finally, Dr. Lewis appeared, still in his surgery gown.

"Are you the ladies waiting to hear about Thomas Henderson?"

"Yes," they both answered as they stood up.

The doctor put a hand on each of their shoulders, their three bodies forming a small circle. "To be honest, Thomas is fighting for his life. That large container of fish at the cannery probably weighed close to five hundred pounds. It slid forward crushing him against the wall and pinned him there for some time. His coworkers had to find equipment that was heavy enough to free him. In the process, an artery was punctured, and he lost a tremendous amount of blood. We have had to give him five pints of blood so far. He's lucky to just be alive. So considering everything, Thomas came through surgery better than I'd hoped, which is a good sign, of course, but only time will tell what his recovery might look like. His right leg was partially severed. We've reattached it, but I have no idea just how successful we were, and I won't know for days. He may very well lose the leg in spite of our attempts. A specialist from Seattle will be here tomorrow to take a look at him."

Crying silently, Rosemary shed uncontrolled tears from already red and swollen eyes, while Marie sobbed audibly into the wadded up tissue she held in her hand. At least he was alive, they were both thinking. So far, Rosemary's prayers had been answered.

The doctor waited for a moment until both women could get control of themselves and then continued, "He has many broken bones in the right arm, both in the forearm and the wrist, and in the right shoulder, some of which have not been set yet. We will be doing that tomorrow as soon as the worst of his body trauma is settled. The left leg has multiple fractures but smaller ones. A shoulder ligament on the left side was stretched pretty badly. What I worry about most is the right leg. It's the one that we put back together again. I don't know what use he will have of it. Infections are also a big enemy in dealing with this serious situation. It's a "wait and see" issue. We will do the best we can. The least of it will be more surgery and many weeks of therapy. You need to know that it will be a long haul."

Marie asked quietly, "Is he awake?"

"He's been in recovery for about forty minutes now," the doctor told her. "Let's wait another twenty minutes or so; then one of you can go in for five minutes. That's all. I don't want him excited."

"Thank you, Doctor," Rosemary said as Dr. Lewis reached out and patted them both on the arm before taking his leave.

Rosemary and Marie threw their arms around each other, hugging and weeping with relief that their friend was at least alive. When the nurse came to get one of them, Marie nudged Rosemary forward. She hesitated, but Marie insisted, "Go on. Go to him, Rosemary."

Thomas was a mass of wires, bandages, and tubes, looking thin and pale against the white sheets of his bed.

Rosemary leaned over him, whispering his name, "Thomas, are you awake?"

No response.

Then she whispered his name again, and the one eye that wasn't swollen shut opened for a split second. She thought she saw a little smile on his face but couldn't be sure. She didn't know if he had recognized her or not. He didn't open his eye again.

An hour or so later, Rosemary rode back to Tokeland with Marie, but it was only to get her own car and pack another overnight bag. She'd book herself into the same Aberdeen motel where she had stayed before.

However, Rosemary wanted to be there when Thomas was awake and conscious, so before she did anything else, she drove straight to the hospital. There was a wait of about thirty minutes, as the nurses were working on him, before she was allowed to step into the room for a few minutes.

Thomas had been in and out of consciousness since she'd been gone, due in most part to the sedation and pain medicine they were giving him, but he opened his one good eye when she said his name; this time she knew he recognized her. He tried to smile, but it was barely perceptible. In a moment, he was unconscious again. Rosemary sat down in the chair next to the bed. Not expecting anything but to just observe him sleeping, she jerked, when some minutes later, she heard him speak. Rosemary had to lean forward to make his words audible. Her eyes misted when she heard the words. "I love you, Rosemary."

"I . . . I love you, too, Thomas."

Then he went out like a light.

Rosemary had much thinking to do. It was getting late. Only two people were sitting in the waiting room. She tucked herself into a corner behind a tall magazine rack and meditated. How had she messed up her life so thoroughly? Seeing Thomas lying there made her realize how precious he was to her. But did she deserve another chance with him? Did she deserve another chance with anyone ever again? He loved her. She still couldn't believe that fact. How could anyone love her? Was she even lovable? And did she love him? It had never occurred to her before. He'd always been, well, just Thomas. On the other hand, he was much more than that. He'd always been such a gentle soul, someone she'd always depended on, and he'd been so supportive and protective of her. How many activities in school had he taken her to? Who took her to the prom when the boy she planned to go with went with someone else? Who always made sure she got home?

She remembered their school days. Thomas was always there to pick up the pieces when things went awry. She'd taken him for granted all these years, thought of him only as a brother, and had never looked beyond that until now. And all this time, he loved her. Really loved her! Why hadn't he told her that before? Even more than that, why hadn't she seen it? Even now when she'd come home, he'd let her cry on his shoulder, and still he never said anything to her about his true feelings.

She turned her thoughts to God and prayed he would forgive her for all the mistakes she'd made and how messed up she'd made her life. All right, dear Lord, she prayed, if Thomas still wanted her, she would be his. She realized she loved this gentle and wonderful man. And she would care for him and try to make him happy. Would he still want her? She felt a moment of fear. Maybe he would change his mind when he found out what she really was like. No doubt, she would have to tell him about Gile. That would not be easy, but they had to start with no secrets. Rosemary would have to be up-front about everything in her life. She could do no less. That would be the test. He might not love her so much after that.

Rosemary stayed only a couple of nights at the motel, but in the ensuing weeks, she made hospital trips every other day to see Thomas.

The Christmas holiday came without her being much aware of the day. She spent Christmas morning feeding Thomas his breakfast.

Soon the year 2001 would arrive. Would it be a new start for her and Thomas? She didn't know but planned to take it one day at a time. It was slow going for him the first two weeks after the accident; however, his recovery seemed to pick up speed. The doctors and the medical staff were more than pleased with his progress.

Rosemary's presence was a great aid to Thomas's recuperation. He was always elated to see her when she appeared at his door. He would reach for her hand and try to smile as she kissed him on the forehead. In addition to all the other breaks and contusions, they had discovered a small fracture in his jaw and it was taking some time to heal. She would do most of the talking and even brought her novel along to read to him. He enjoyed that and delighted in listening to her voice as she read.

Halfway into January, Rosemary came down with the flu and wasn't able to see Thomas for almost a week. During that time, she discovered how much she missed him and how her recent problems no longer seemed that important. He was her life now. He was all she cared about.

When Rosemary was able to make the trip once again and entered his room, she found him propped up in a chair. "Hello, beautiful," Thomas said with a gleam in his eye. "Look! I'm going to live!" He extended his good arm towards her, signaling for her to step closer. "I promised myself a reward the first time I got off my back. It will be up to you if I get to collect." He gave Rosemary his boy-smile.

"Yeah! How's that?" She grinned back at him as she moved towards the chair.

"Come here, bend over, and plant a kiss right here." He pointed to his mouth.

"Won't that hurt your jaw?"

"I'll be the judge of that. If it hurts, I'll say ouch!"

And so she did, and he didn't even grimace. It was a sweet, gentle kiss, and she felt such tenderness for him. The kiss lasted and lasted as his left arm, the only part of himself he could use at all, tightened around her. She was surprised when she felt her body respond to his touch, and a wave of passion flowed through her. There was a desire she didn't know she'd felt for him. It filled her with a kind of awe. Rosemary pulled back, her face flushed, her breathing coming in gulps. "Ah, Thomas, we'd better stop while we can."

He'd felt her response as their lips touched, and the knowledge glittered brightly within him. She loved him, too! "Heck, why do we have to stop? Just lift me up on the bed, and we can finish what we started, eh?" Then he laughed as she shook her head and wrinkled her nose at him.

"I don't think so. Not here, Thomas! Not here, I'm afraid." Rosemary held her hands alongside his face and gazed into his eyes.

"No, my sweet," he said in a heavy voice. "Not here! Not yet! But there'll be a time in the near future. It's all I dream of. I want you, and I make no excuses. If you'll have a guy with a gimpy leg, he'd like you to marry him."

"Oh, Thomas! I . . . we'll talk about it. I . . . I have some things to tell you about first, some things that may make you change your mind."

He shook his head. "Whatever you have to tell me won't change anything for me. I promise you that. I love you, no matter what it is, and I'll be waiting for an answer to my proposal. And I'll expect it just as soon as I get out of here."

Just then, the nurse appeared to take him to therapy and their conversation ended.

⌒∞⌒

Eight weeks after the accident, Thomas was released from the hospital, although as he put it, he had a "gimpy" leg. That would still require therapy three times a week. Rosemary brought him to her house to care for him until he could get around a little better. She planned to drive him in for his therapy sessions, too. She was determined to do everything possible to help him until he could do it himself.

Thomas was able to get around fairly well by using crutches but tired easily, having lost so much strength while lying in the hospital. Rosemary planned for him to have her bedroom. The bed was firmer and more comfortable than her father's bed. She had already adjusted the closets, putting her clothes in her father's old room, and she had gone to Thomas's house, gathering up much of his wardrobe and the personal items from a list she had requested from him earlier.

Upon arriving at her house, Rosemary helped Thomas to the bed, taking his jacket from him and hanging it up. He needed her help to get his right leg up on the mattress. While she was doing that, he reached up with his good arm and pulled her down beside him.

"Be careful, Thomas. You'll hurt yourself," she cried as both his arms, one with the cast just removed, went around her tightly.

"I'll be careful. I just want you close to me. I want to feel your body snuggled against mine. For now, that's enough." He sighed deeply as she hugged him back and then spoke again, "I wouldn't have made it without you, Rosemary. You gave me the only reason to want to live. I thought I'd lost you. When I opened my eyes and saw you there, I knew I would survive. I had to." He pulled her closer and buried his face into the side of her head. "I love you," he whispered. "I've always loved you. Do you know that?"

"I know it now." Rosemary's voice was shaking with raw emotion. She had to tell him now—about her affair and the way she had handled herself. It would be difficult, but she had to do it now. "We have to talk, Thomas. I did a terrible thing, and you need to know about it or we cannot—"

Thomas cut off her words as he tilted her head up to look into her eyes. "Rosemary, you don't have to tell me anything. Besides, I know all about that bastard Hammond. I told you nothing that's happened in the past makes one iota of a difference in how I feel about you. It's not what you did. It's what that damn jerk did to you. I think I could kill him with my bare hands if I had the chance."

Rosemary was utterly stunned. She couldn't believe he knew about Gile. "How . . . how did you know?" She whispered the words, her head bowing in embarrassment, her eyes closing so she wouldn't have to look at him.

He put his hands under her chin and raised her head up again, making it impossible for her to keep her eyes closed against his scrutiny. Again, he looked squarely into her eyes and emphasized each word. "I . . . love . . . you . . . Rosemary. Remember that, will you? Margie told me about the man. She put it together. It was her concern for you. You know—the three musketeers thing! We stick together, right?" Then he kissed her soundly and wrapped his arms around her. They lay like that for some time, her body and her mind finally at peace for the first time in a long, long while.

Thomas observed her silently, admiring her long, beautiful lashes, which lay fanned out below her closed eyes. Some of the lines of sorrow and pain had smoothed out on her still beautiful skin. Poor Rosemary, he thought. She'd been so full of anxiety. So much had happened to her. She'd finally surrendered and was now relaxed in his arms; in fact, he was pretty sure she had fallen asleep. He felt peaceful at last, too. Rosemary was his finally. He had what he'd always wanted. The love of his life. "She's all mine," he whispered quietly to himself.

CHAPTER NINE

THOMAS'S PROFESSIONAL THERAPY ended eventually, but he still had exercises to keep up with every day and periodical visits to see his doctor. He suffered pain in his right leg constantly, but with medication, it was minimized, and he was doing quite well.

Rosemary shared his bed from the first night they were together in her home. She was afraid she would roll over and hurt him, but he insisted she be there. They would hold each other throughout the night. He dreamed of making love to her but physically didn't think he should try until one night in May after a scheduled appointment with his doctor.

That night in bed, he pulled her into his arms and began to kiss her in a very different way. She sensed something had changed, but before she could ask, she was overcome with desire and let herself succumb to his passion and to hers. Unable to wait, Thomas pulled her over on top of him.

"Thomas! You'll hurt your leg. Be careful," Rosemary admonished him.

"I'm sick and tired of being careful. The doctor said it was okay. Just keep your leg there. Don't move it. Oh, Rosemary, you beautiful lady! I love you. I love you. This has been my dream." The position was rather awkward but doable. His endearing words of love filled Rosemary's soul. He kissed her eyelids, her nose, her chin, and her throat while unbuttoning her nightgown and then claiming her breasts with his mouth. In moments they were carried to the heights of their passion as they joined to make Thomas's dream come true, and now Rosemary's, too.

After wasting half of their lives separated from each other, Rosemary finally felt safe and secure in the knowledge of being truly loved. It wasn't just the passion; it was also the tenderness in which he loved her. One body, one mind, and one soul! It was a spiritual love she knew God would sanctify. How could he not? Thomas was and had always been her soul mate.

Physically spent and relaxed in Thomas's arms, Rosemary thought for a moment—just a brief moment—about Gile. Why had she thought she enjoyed sex with that man? Gile's had been a selfish and greedy sex. Thomas was gentle; his love and passion were for her, not just himself. He was absolutely and totally the most wonderful thing that had ever come into her life. Thank God, she hadn't lost him! Tears of joy and happiness trailed down Rosemary's face. Thomas reached over and brushed them away.

"Are you okay?"

"Oh yes. I just love you so much, Thomas. I didn't know it, but I always have."

In a quiet voice," he said, "I always hoped you did." He kissed her on the cheek, tasting her salted tears. "Rosemary, love, we're getting married as soon as possible. No arguments! We've waited long enough."

She smiled, nodding in agreement.

Now," he said soberly, "let's clear the deck. You told me all about your life. Now, I think I'd better do the same."

Rosemary had often wanted to ask him about the part of his life he had never shared with her. She never mentioned it after the one time she had broached it in the car. She was surprised that he was now willing to talk about it. She didn't say anything but waited expectantly.

Thomas stared at the ceiling. Slowly he began to talk. "In 1980 when Margie told me you were leaving for college, I meant to move to Seattle right away, but after you were gone, I got on one of the fishing boats that first summer and stuck around for almost two years before I finally packed up. During that time, I saw Margie only a couple of times. She was working for Dr. Malcolm in Westport, and when she was off on weekends, I was out on the fishing boat. But we did have dinner together shortly before I departed. That night she told me you were leaving college early to get married. I thought my life had ended. Up until then, I guess I thought you might still come home. The news devastated me."

Rosemary's eyes filled with more tears. She silently squeezed her tears back, waiting for him to go on with his story.

⊸❦⊷

Rosemary and Margie had given Thomas a lot of support with their friendship; he didn't know what he would have done without them. The information about Rosemary's marriage sank in, and he gave up the slight hope of ever seeing her again. Being an only child made it more difficult to pull away, but he definitely needed a change in his life. If he didn't do something with his life now, he feared he'd rot it away.

So Thomas moved to the Seattle area in October 1982. He invited his father to come along and share an apartment with him, but his father declined. He had his friends and his routine pretty well established in the little bedroom community of Grayland. He promised his son he would get along fine. Just go and get on with your life, he told him. Thomas hated to leave his dad. They had formed a loving and close relationship since the passing of his mother in his early teens.

In Seattle, Thomas took a job with Elliott's Portrait Studio. Photography had been a special interest of his in school, but he'd learned only some of the basics and had never been able to afford the right equipment to carry on with it. However, what knowledge he'd gleaned from school was enough to secure his new position with Elliott's in the Green Lake area of the city. There was so much more to learn than his high school photography classes were able to teach him. The studio specialized in portraits, and he discovered the techniques for photo lighting, the intricate settings of the different camera equipment, and variable backdrops to use for getting the best results, both in the studio and outdoors.

The studio was exceptionally busy during the months between February and April with high school senior pictures and then in the fall with school yearbooks soon after school began. That's when they also took their cameras and equipment to many of the elementary schools in the area for individual school pictures and returned to the same schools for class pictures in the spring. Summer months brought wedding contracts to them in good measure. They worked many Saturdays to keep up with all the work during those busy times. It was what Thomas liked, to keep busy. It left less time for him to think about Rosemary, his lost love. The nights were the worst. She never faded from his memory. He would always miss her.

Whenever he could, he made a point of driving to the coast to visit with his father. The older man seemed to be getting along rather well, but it still made Thomas feel guilty each time he returned to Seattle.

He worked at Elliott's for four years, learning every aspect of the business. Being a fast learner, he became quite an expert in the art of photography. When the manager resigned in 1986 to move to Chicago in order to care for his sick mother, Thomas was given the management spot. By that time, the owners had opened another store in Lynnwood, twenty minutes or so away, a little north of Seattle. There were now ten employees between the two stores.

Thomas was engrossed in updating the appointment book with some changes at the studio one day. He heard his next client come in the door but didn't immediately raise his head, intent on finishing his records. The woman coughed softly to remind him she was there, and he turned to tell her it would be just a minute. He looked up to see a young, beautiful Asian woman standing in front of him.

Her name was Kim Chen. She was poised and mature for someone who looked so young, he thought. He was to learn later that she wasn't as young as she appeared, as was true with many young Asian women; in fact, she was a few years older than Thomas. He would discover that she was second generation Chinese but very definitely all-American and a very confident young woman. Kim was having her portrait done as a gift to her parents for their anniversary and additional shots for her professional portfolio, as well.

"Oh, Miss Chen! Sorry, I was engrossed in my work here. We can get started in just a couple of minutes. Why don't you take that dressing room over there to make any adjustments you'd like to your hair and makeup? I'll set up everything and be with you in a few minutes."

"Thank you. I'll do that." She stepped quickly into the small room with her satchel and the clothes she carried on a hanger and closed the door.

Thomas was thinking what a beauty she was as he dropped the background drape behind the garden bench he would use, having selected a park setting. He strategically placed a bowl of flowers at one end of the bench about the same time the phone rang. He answered the call just as Kim came out of the dressing room. She'd changed into a low-cut, off-the-shoulder, black dress, which even though she was small breasted, showed enough cleavage to make a sexual statement. He couldn't keep his eyes off her as he tried to complete the call. He found himself very attracted to her, something that hadn't happened to him in a long time. He motioned her to the bench and finished his call.

She was a dream to photograph. It didn't seem to matter which way the camera pointed at her or which way she turned; her features were soft, her skin glowing, and her smile enticing. After he'd taken a half-dozen shots, he said, "I think these will be very good. You are very photogenic, Miss Chen. Let's just try a few more so you'll have plenty of proofs for your selection."

"Thank you," she said to his compliment. "I'd like to change into something a little more formal and business-like so I can add them to my portfolio if we have the time."

"Of course. My next client isn't due for fifteen minutes or so."

Kim returned to the dressing room. Thomas took a big breath. He was excited, excited about a woman for the first time since Rosemary. He wondered if she would go out with him if he asked her for a dinner date. He wasn't sure he had the nerve to ask. She might think he was being too forward. Maybe he'd wait until she came in for the proofs.

Thomas had plenty of time to take more shots of her in a sweater and a tailored, green jacket, the coloring of which contrasted beautifully with her pale, soft skin. She was so pretty he kept shooting and stopped only when his next client arrived. He'd used several rolls of film on her. "These should be ready by next week, let's say around Wednesday. When would you like to pick them up?"

She opened her date book. "I have several interviews next week, but it looks like I could make in on Thursday. Thursday morning sometime?"

Now he checked his appointment book again. "Thursday morning is pretty booked up until eleven fifteen. Will that work?"

"I'll be here. Thank you very much, Mr. Henderson."

"Thomas," he said and smiled at her as he reached his hand out to shake hers. "It's been a pleasure working with you, Ms. Chen. See you next week."

"Please call me Kim." She smiled back at him.

They released their handshake, but her eyes held his for a moment, a secret lurking behind the gleam they held. Thomas was mesmerized with her dark eyes.

He thought about Kim all week and anticipated her return with great hopefulness. He was going to ask her out. What was the worst thing she could do? She could only say no.

With his heart in his throat, he asked her for a date when she returned the next week, never dreaming she would make herself available, and when she said yes, he was completely astonished. He really had prepared for her refusal. After all, she didn't know him at all. He was delighted, of course, and they set the date and time before she left the store. Thomas wore a silly grin on his face for the rest of the day. He looked forward to the prospect of having a new person in his life.

On Saturday night, he took Kim to a new restaurant on Lake Union. They had a window seat in a pretty setting next to a boat marina. It was a pleasant evening with them sharing background tidbits of their lives while making the meal last several hours. There was dancing in a room beyond, and after their meal, they even took a few turns around the dance floor. Kim danced well, much better than Thomas did, but he enjoyed holding her in his arms. He didn't know what perfume she wore, but the scent was enticing, and she let him hold her close. He could hear his heart pounding in his ears. His body felt hard and an unexpected and fiery desire swept through him. He'd been with a few women but never one he desired so much. That is, except for Rosemary who, of course, had been inaccessible and who for the moment was completely forgotten. This was just what he needed.

They spent much of their time together after that. Eventually Kim allowed Thomas to take her to bed, and they began to camp out in each other's apartments. They enjoyed being together, and with both of them having busy jobs, they made an effort to have at least one day and evening a weekend for each other; sometimes they even managed a whole weekend.

Kim had a wonderful position as a buyer and decorator for a large furniture store in downtown Seattle. Many of the clients were well-to-do and could afford an expert interior designer like Kim for their homes. She was excellent at what she did, and she suddenly was in great demand. Her client list grew as her happy customers referenced other important people to the company. She also assisted new start-up companies with the designing and setup up of newly established offices, and the word spread quickly to other companies about her polished talent and the feeling she created in the environments using color, contrast, and space. Her promotion with the company grew in leaps and bounds.

Thomas was as happy as he could remember being since moving to Seattle four years before. He didn't realize until he met Kim just how lonely he was. It was very nice to have someone who cared about him. Nineteen eighty-six was ending nicely for him, that is, until his father became ill with a liver dysfunction. Thomas was obligated to make several fast trips to the beach. Each time his father seemed better when he left, only to become worse again. Several anxious weeks passed as Thomas numbly made trips back and forth before finally having to put his father in an Aberdeen nursing home where someone could care for him. His father was there for only three days before dying.

Thomas took a week off to settle his father's affairs. There was a will leaving everything to him, of course, but there wasn't much in the way of an inheritance. However, by the time his father's small house and the little boat were sold—the one Thomas had used so often–and the bank accounts closed, Thomas would realize a moderate nest egg, which he banked in his Seattle account.

It was a depressing week, and Thomas felt not a small amount of guilt for the short visits made to see his father and surely not as many after meeting Kim. Before she came on the scene, he had routinely telephoned his father every week, but in recent times, even that he had let slide by too often.

After the small funeral service and the week completed, Thomas felt tired and sluggish, his energy level completely depleted by the time he returned to Seattle. Needing a boost to his spirits, he was so anxious to see Kim again. He'd truly missed her company.

It was late afternoon on Friday when he arrived back in town, just enough time to shower, change clothes, and meet her for dinner. Right after receiving their drinks, Thomas was dumbfounded when Kim said to him, "I have something to tell you." She smiled and raised her glass in a salute. "I received a job offer from the Larry E. Lawton Furniture and Design Company in Los Angeles a couple of days ago. I'm so excited. I couldn't wait to tell you."

Thomas just stared at her and didn't say a word. His one thought was that he was going to lose her, too.

"Honey, did you hear what I said? That's one of the biggest companies in the business on the West Coast. My salary will double, and they'll move me without cost. This is my chance—big time!"

"Is this the polite way to brush me off?" He said it half-seriously and half-jokingly.

"Oh, Thomas! I want you to go with me. There will be photography studios all over the place. It will be easy for you to find another one. Please, please say you'll go."

Kim was a woman who was aggressive in her challenging work, in their lovemaking, and in moving forward in life. Thomas certainly didn't want to be the one to stop her from what appeared to be a wonderful opportunity, nor did he want to let her go. Besides, he had plenty of money in the bank at the moment. He could take his time finding a new job. A change would probably be good for him now that he didn't have to worry about his father.

He told Kim he wanted to think about it, but by the time they arrived back at his apartment, he had already talked himself into the idea and agreed to make the transition to Los Angeles with her. She rewarded Thomas by throwing her arms around him and drawing him into his bedroom. Her excitement over the move infected him, and suddenly he was looking forward to the change and new opportunities waiting for both of them. *It's a good decision*, he thought, as he wrapped himself around Kim's warm and loving body.

It was very near Christmas when Thomas formally proposed marriage to Kim. It was something they hadn't talked about seriously yet, but he thought it was the perfect time to bring it up. He presented her with a glittering diamond engagement ring. She accepted, and that made them officially engaged.

Two days after the New Year of 1987, they made their move. Most of their furniture, both his and hers, was trucked ahead of them to storage, while they took a week to enjoy their trip south, stopping along the way to see the sights. Thomas had never been south before and enjoyed the scenery and new terrain. He and Kim had a wonderful, relaxing trip. The weather was warmer than usual in Los Angeles, and the two of them enjoyed the respite from the usual Seattle drizzle of January, now behind them.

They did find time to get married right after their arrival in California, and Thomas used a good part of his inheritance money to purchase a rather nice condominium close to downtown. It was convenient for Kim since her place of business and her office were not far away, if not so convenient for him. He located a job with a photography studio in Pasadena. The recommendation given by Elliott's had been exceptional, and because of it, he was given the job opening immediately. He would be there only three months before he became manager of the studio.

Kim's job was as exciting as she had dreamed. In short order, she became the store's top representative for the design and furnishing of new office spaces all around Los Angeles County and sometimes beyond. She loved her new job but was terribly busy, putting in long hours. In fact, the couple actually did not see each other much during the week as both their jobs required late hours much of the time.

⁂

Thomas's body became stiff from lying flat on his back, and it began to pain him. He shifted a little to his left side, and as he turned, he rolled Rosemary partially over his body. He kissed her tenderly, drinking in her sweetness. It was difficult for him to talk about Kim when he had his only love beside him. He would never get enough of her. Thomas couldn't quite believe she was his, and the knowledge that she loved him as well put him in heaven. He settled himself down and struggled for his next words, speaking quietly. His eyes were closed, and Rosemary watched him, wondering what the rest of his story was and waited patiently for him to go on.

"I don't know what happened to us. Things just seemed to change in a few months. Maybe we'd been there about six months by this time. I knew something was wrong, but I was helpless to find a solution to our problems. The most important thing was we just didn't spend any quality time together."

"Were you both still working long hours?" Rosemary asked him.

"Yes, I had some extra hours to work, but she worked all the time, and I began to feel she didn't care anymore."

❧

Making time to be together became an important yet elusive goal in their new life style. Thomas didn't like how little time they had together. Their sexual life was almost nil and then practically by appointment only. He tried getting home a little earlier on certain days, but she was never there anyway. He was asleep many nights when she finally arrived home. At one point, an entire week went by before he actually talked with Kim, and then it was for only a couple of hours on Sunday morning. During most of that time, she went back and forth to the bathroom, doing her hair and her face. She was a woman who spent an extraordinary amount of time exercising her body, doing her makeup, and maintaining her weight. She had an exceptionally high energy level, and Thomas always found it difficult to keep up with her.

It was not difficult to see their relationship was becoming quite fragile and they were traveling down a rocky road. Thomas was uncomfortable and worried about the pitfalls lying ahead of them if they didn't do something about the situation soon.

The large condo complex housed mostly young people like themselves, but Thomas and Kim had little chance to meet their neighbors. There was a swimming pool and an exercise room on the premises, and Thomas did try to take advantage of their availability whenever he could, mostly on the weekends. Occasionally during the week, he would manage to escape his job early and swim in the pool while he waited for his wife to come home.

A young man about his age, Nat Cahill, lived in the apartment next to them. He was single and into photography, too, only he worked for a LA magazine publishing company. Thomas met Cahill one afternoon at the pool, and when he discovered they shared an interest in photography, he made a point of being at the pool whenever he thought Cahill might be there. He felt fortunate to meet someone who had a common interest with him. He began to look forward to talking with his new friend whenever possible because at that point, he hated to admit, his life seemed very empty.

During one of their conversations, Thomas was surprised to discover this newfound friend had already met his wife. Apparently they had met at the pool, also. Thomas was somewhat confused. He didn't think Kim had ever visited the pool, certainly not at any time with him. And when did she get that chance? She was always gone. However, he wasn't one to look for trouble, and he trusted her, didn't he? Just to be sure, he mentioned it to her on the telephone when she called from work. "I met our neighbor Cahill a couple weeks ago. I wasn't aware that you knew him, but I understand you've met him, too."

"Oh, you mean Nat."

"Yes, Nat. I get the opportunity to talk with him out at the pool quite a bit. When did you meet him?" Thomas tried not to sound suspicious, but he needed to know, wanting very much for her to tell him there was nothing to worry about.

"Oh, I met him at the pool, too, same as you did, honey. Nice guy, isn't he? Guess he likes photography, just as you do. Isn't that nice?"

"Yes . . . yes, I guess . . .," he answered, but he wanted to know more. "I didn't think you ever went to the pool. I wasn't aware you were ever at home during the day. I didn't think you had that much extra time."

Nonchalantly, she had a ready answer for him. "Not much, but I manage to sneak in some R&R once in a while. If I land the company a big job, I figure they can just give me a little down time, like a couple of afternoons off here and there."

He heard himself asking silently why she didn't use some of that down time for them.

Someone said something to her in the background, and he heard her muffled reply as she covered the phone with her hand. In a moment, she was back on the phone and said, "Gotta go, Thomas. They need me. See you later. Bye." And the phone went dead.

Thomas sat with the phone in his hand for a couple of minutes while mulling over their conversation. He'd always trusted Kim; she was a busy bee, but she would never be unfaithful, would she? Finally, he told himself he was being foolish, and he pushed the matter from his mind, refusing to think about the incident anymore.

An alarm sounded in Thomas's brain when Kim called him from work one evening and told him she'd invited their neighbor Nat and a friend of his for dinner the next Saturday evening. Then before he could comment, she had to hang up again. Was it possible that Nat was more than a mere acquaintance? Why else would she be inviting him to dinner? Well, he was bringing a date along, wasn't he? So what was wrong with the invitation? Nothing, he convinced himself and tried again to push those negative thoughts from his mind.

Nat showed up for dinner with an Asian friend. But she wasn't Chinese like Kim. Thomas figured she was Japanese since her name was Yoko something-or-other. He hadn't caught her last name when they were introduced. She spoke very little English. Nat seemed to know a little of her language and translated as best as he could. She smiled a lot and laughed when the rest of them did. Thomas thought Nat must be bedding her. It didn't seem that there could be much more to their relationship. She was a beauty all right with long black hair, silky and shining. She had small delicate features and was very petite in size, with the exception of a rather large bosom for someone so small and which was unusual for her race.

It was a strange dinner party. Kim and Nat did most of the talking. Thomas was beginning to see another side to his neighbor. He seemed controlling and manipulated the conversation to his interests, expecting the others to listen to his stories but seemingly uninterested in what the others had to say. Thomas didn't think they had as much in common as he originally thought.

After dinner, Yoko excused herself and left to use the bathroom. To Thomas's surprise, Kim suddenly picked up her wine glass and toasted her husband. "Happy birthday, darling!" Thomas had forgotten that his birthday was only a couple of days off. His mind had been on other things, other worries. "Have I got a surprise for you," she exclaimed. He felt a pleasant sensation flow through him, grateful that she'd remembered the occasion when lately he'd begun to have his doubts about their future together.

Then suddenly Kim stood up, reached for the light switch on the wall, turning it to the off position. The room was thrown into darkness, except for the candles still burning in the center of the table. Thomas could see the door to the kitchen open as the light was still on in there. From somewhere, romantic music began playing. Then Yoko appeared in a red kimono, not the slacks and sweater she'd had on when she'd left the room. She was dancing slowly toward him, twirling and twisting, her hips undulating sexually as she untied her wrap. It dropped to the floor as she stood in front of him. He could hear Kim and Nat chortle as Yoko reached behind her back and began to untie her skimpy bra top, leaning over Thomas's red face. She managed to brush her chest against him.

Thomas was completely and totally embarrassed and laughing nervously, without humor. He growled, "What is this?" He looked over at Kim for an explanation. She was laughing loudly. Nat was busy snapping pictures with his camera and joined her in the laughter. Yoko had her top off now, spread her legs, and sat down on his lap facing him as she pulled him to her bare breasts.

Thomas froze! He didn't know what to do. His embarrassment turned to anger. He wanted this charade to end. Yoko took his hands and placed them on her breasts, but he pushed her off and stood up. She almost fell off his lap but caught her balance and stood, not knowing for sure what to do next. She looked over at Nat and Kim and shrugged her shoulders. Thomas's face was red with rage.

"Okay, enough is enough! The fun's over!"

Yoko was now stepping out of her skimpy panties, trying to complete her seduction. She was completely nude. Smiling, she took his hand and tried again to entice him.

This time, Thomas angrily withdrew his hand and walked around the table, away from the woman, shouting, "Kim, dammit, I asked you what this is."

"Oh come on, Thomas! Don't be such a prude. It's a joke! We hired her. That's what she does. It's just a birthday present."

It was no joke to him, and he didn't like the gift. He wanted them all out of there. "Yeah, well let's call it a night, huh? Nat, take your so-called friend and get the hell out of here. Now!"

He watched Nat and Kim subtly grin at each other. It took a lot to make Thomas angry, but he was angrier than he had ever been before, and her attitude infuriated him even more. He stood with his hands on his hips, clenching his teeth, ready to physically strike out at someone. Under Thomas's steely stare, Nat shrugged his shoulders, picked up his camera and gear, and shoved it all into its case. Yoko had quickly covered herself with her kimono, gone into the bathroom to retrieve her other clothes, and the two of them departed.

The minute the door closed behind them, Thomas grasped his wife's arm. "What on earth . . . do you . . .," but he couldn't find the words to finish his thoughts. He shook his head violently, trying to shake away the immense rage, which completely filled him. Before he allowed himself to say any more, he quickly turned away from his wife and headed for the door. His hands were still clenched into fists. He needed to cool down. The door slammed behind him.

Thomas slept in the guestroom that night. The next day, he came home from work, and after a great deal of thinking, he hoped to talk things over with Kim. He wanted her to explain why she'd done this to him. It had been so humiliating. It was obvious they needed to do some real repair work on their marriage, but he wasn't sure he could ever forget what had happened. However, he had to try. Maybe they could get some counseling. Would she go with him? Would it do any good? Things couldn't go on as they were now, that was for certain.

He changed his clothes and, then from force of habit, looked for something in the refrigerator to have for dinner, not that he had much of an appetite. When he closed the refrigerator door, he saw Kim's note hanging from a magnet.

Sorry, honey. We gave it a good try, but it doesn't seem to be working. I am filing for a divorce today. My lawyer will be in contact with you. Thought you should know I am pregnant but haven't decided yet whether to carry it to full term. I'm not the mother type. Don't you agree? I am moving in with Nat since I have no place to go at the moment. Don't worry. We are moving to a new area so you won't have to run into us accidentally. I hope you'll be fair about this. I'll need support if I have this baby.

Thomas was completely devastated. He crumpled the note in his hand and threw it across the room. Fair? What did she mean? He'd had a nice little savings account coming into the marriage with what he'd saved, even before Kim became a part of his life, plus his dad's money. In fact, he and Kim had planned on selling the condo to buy a house soon. And the baby—was it his? Had she been seeing Nat behind his back for a long time? He remembered the discussion about the pool. Had they been rendezvousing here in their own condo during the day? Perhaps in his own bed! Was it Nat's child? There were so many questions Thomas wanted answered. And how could she even talk about aborting a child, no matter whose it was? He had not known she could be so callous.

Once Thomas tried to get in touch with her, but she refused to talk to him directly. When her lawyer sent a letter listing the assets Kim was requesting, Thomas was appalled, and he decided it was time to get himself a lawyer, too. Kim wanted the condo (for the baby), half of their assets, and child support of one thousand dollars a month when the baby was born. Was her salary even going to be taken into consideration?

When he saw the support amount listed, his immediate thought was it must mean she was going to allow the baby to live, and for that he was grateful, even though he wasn't sure whose child it was. Actually, he would have no problem supporting the child if it was his.

Then came the picture! In the mail! A gross picture of him and Yoko! That is, if Yoko was her real name. It was really a grotesque picture of the girl straddled on his lap, naked, except for the brief panties adorning her rear end. Actually, it almost appeared that she had none on at all. Her breasts were squashed up against his chest. His head was thrown back as if in ecstasy, when in fact, he remembered how disgusted he had been with the whole sordid scenario. A note was attached. His eyes darted to the one line note.

Not a pretty picture, is it? Kim.

Thomas looked at the picture again. It had been cropped, and there was no way to tell where it was taken. It would appear to be a sexual liaison to any viewer, and he was certain that Kim would try to use it in that way. She'd turned out to be just a greedy money grabber. And Nat was the type to support her in this endeavor.

In the future, Thomas would not be able to remember anything about the next few weeks of his life. He came home in the evening bone-tired, full of anxiety and despair. He could not help the depression he was feeling; he didn't care what happened to him. Thomas just plain gave in. He had no fight left. He just wanted the whole thing finished. In the end, he settled it all with her, giving her the condo and half of the money in their accounts. Apparently, she'd given up on the request for support as that issue was dropped once she'd gotten the other assets. Maybe that was because it wasn't his child and she was afraid he'd be able to prove it. As soon as things were settled, Thomas immediately gave his notice at the studio.

In a few days, he walked out of her life without knowing whether the child Kim was carrying was his or not. He packed his car with some of his personal items, his clothes, and not many good memories and headed north. Although he didn't know where he was going when he started out, the car pointed its nose toward the coast of Washington, back to his beginnings.

Thomas picked up a part-time job as a photographer for the small weekly newspaper in Westport and some work at the cannery when he could. He had enough from the bank account to make a sizeable down payment on the tiny house he purchased and settled in for a simple life. There wasn't a day he didn't wonder about the unborn child, but at least the quietness and solitude of this little corner of the world gave him some peace of mind.

In January 1989, a coworker of Thomas' from LA, familiar with their break-up, sent a short note saying that Kim's baby was born and that it was a boy. That was the only information he would receive.

When Thomas finished his story his head was tucked into his chest, his eyes tightly closed. He didn't look up at her, but Rosemary felt the moistness of his tears as she hugged him to her. "He would be going on thirteen now, I think," he said in a faraway voice." She pulled him even closer and rubbed his back as she hugged him. His voice broke when he remarked, "I would give anything to know if he was mine, even though I know I'd probably never have the opportunity to see him. It's just something I think about all the time."

"I know your pain, Thomas. It brings back the pain of losing my child. At least I know. You don't."

"Rosemary, thank God I have you. You fill the hole that was in my soul for so long. I love you so much."

CHAPTER TEN

THOMAS AND ROSEMARY WERE MARRIED that year in early November 2001. Both of them did their best to put their pasts behind them and move forward in their new life together. Of course, no one was happier for them than the third musketeer and their lifelong friend, Margie. She and Frank were their only witnesses at the brief courthouse marriage in the small town of Montesano, the Grays Harbor county seat, about an hour from home.

When the ceremony was over, as they came down the steps of the courthouse, Margie let out a scream of joy. She couldn't believe they'd finally done it. "This is so wonderful," she yelled. "I knew this would happen eventually, but you guys sure did take your time. I don't think I've ever been so happy. Well, maybe I was when I married this guy." She laughed as she took her husband's arm and smiled at him. "My three best friends," she remarked, including her husband in the circle. "We have to celebrate this momentous moment. Come on! Dinner's on us, and we have a reservation at the Country Club Restaurant in twenty minutes."

It was a great evening and Rosemary had stars in her eyes as she and Thomas drove home, after dropping the two good friends off at their beach place. Thomas was driving a little now, and he took his right hand from the steering wheel and placed in on his wife's knee, giving her a little squeeze. "Happy?"

"Oh yes," she said as she leaned her head into his shoulder and placed her hand over his. "I pray my bubble doesn't burst. I don't deserve to be this happy."

"I beg to differ with you. We both deserve it, Mrs. Henderson. Okay?"

"Okay, Mr. Henderson. We do!"

They were living in Rosemary's house, having sold Thomas's a month or so before. She still used the upper bedroom for her hide-away to write and to have her quiet moments alone. She had always required those quiet times in her life where she could focus on her thoughts, even now as she thoroughly enjoyed spending every day and night with the man she loved so much. Thomas was very understanding and gave her all the space she needed.

Until recently, she'd let her novel lie on the shelf again. Now it was very close to completion. Driving Thomas to therapy three days a week for such a long time had been time-consuming, and she'd put everything else aside. Now that he had finally completed his hospital therapy and was following his therapist's instructions to do the routine exercises at home, she had much more time.

The second bedroom on the main floor doubled nicely as an exercise and therapy room for Thomas. She didn't know until he'd moved in with her that Thomas still earned part of his income from doing local portraits and photos for the local, weekly beach newspaper. He hadn't given up his photography when he'd moved back to the coast. Rosemary turned the room's closet into a makeshift dark room for him, although it was now becoming more of a hobby than a job. Thomas might be able to contribute photos now and then, but he wouldn't be able to work full time again. He had an obvious limp, the bad leg now more than a half-inch shorter than before. It would never be otherwise. With all the muscle and nerve damage the accident caused, he would always use a cane. At least he had not lost the leg.

Rosemary finally purchased a computer and spent some time learning how to operate it. She could see how it was going to make her writing so much easier and faster. Once in a great while, when she was by herself typing intently away, she thought briefly of Gile, not of the love she thought she'd felt for him but of her disbelief at how he'd treated her. The anger she'd felt for so long was now replaced with her gratefulness for having Thomas in her life. All she felt for Gile was sorrow. He would never know what it was to really love someone, never have what she had for herself. He was only a speck in her memory.

Unhappy memories with Jeffrey faded away. Her wretched life with him had been put to bed. Although memories of her son touched her heart often, he, too, remained in days gone by, in another lifetime. Almost everything regarding Cincinnati was buried and gone, with the exception of her friends, the McCoys, with whom she still communicated periodically. They were so happy for Rosemary and were talking about making a trip to Washington to visit them. Rosemary looked forward to that.

Focusing her energy on caring for her husband—her soul mate and her best friend—and writing were all she cared about. Rosemary wanted to think about only her future, hers and Thomas's. She still couldn't believe she'd wasted all those years when Thomas was right there under her nose. She felt blessed to be with him. The bonding of their relationship became stronger day by day.

Her book was completed, except for a few details, and she already had an outline for a second one. She was contented and fulfilled. Her happiness with Thomas was the epitome of her perfect dreams. She was enjoying her life every single day. She wished her dad could know how happy she was. Maybe he did.

Several months of unbridled happiness followed. They continued to look eagerly forward to the years ahead of them. The future was bright. Thomas received Social Security disability benefits, and although his interest in photography waned, he did pursue what became an avid interest in reading and took time to critique Rosemary's book as she finally brought it into finished form. She'd successfully contacted a literary agent and was going to meet with him in a few weeks.

After their marriage, Rosemary and Thomas became more involved in the community. They took part in the Fire Fly Parade, an annual event in Grayland, with Thomas as one of the parade judges. Later in the year, they joined friends of Thomas's from the cannery for Thanksgiving. During the Christmas season, they drove around the bay to the little town of Raymond to enjoy the Christmas Parade of Lights, an annual event there. And they once again enjoyed attending church services at the Presbyterian church. Thomas became a deacon, and Rosemary was involved in several activities and events in the life of the church. Life was good.

Then they spent their second Christmas together, the first time as husband and wife. Comfortable in front of the fireplace, they toasted their love with a glass of champagne and opened their gifts to each other. Thomas gave Rosemary a brass and oak nameplate for her desk, inscribed with her name: "Rosemary Henderson, Author." She gave him tour pamphlets to consider a trip to France if she was fortune enough to get her book published. And they discussed a future trip to visit her brothers. She longed to see them again, and she wanted them to know Thomas and love him as she did. There were several other presents to open, but Thomas and Rosemary let them wait for morning while they made love on the floor in front of the fire.

Anytime Frank and Margie were able to come from Seattle, the four of them would have dinner together, sometimes at the Donahans', other times at Rosemary and Thomas's house, or they would go to a restaurant, more than likely the Tokeland Hotel Restaurant dining room nearby. It didn't matter. Wherever it was, they had a great time. It was wonderful for the three musketeers to be back together again.

Thomas adored his Rosemary and considered himself a very lucky man. The accident was a very bad thing to have happened to him, but because of it, he had her back. In fact, they were so happy both of them sometimes feared there would be a burst in their bubble.

⊱✦⊰

It was already March, with spring weather showing up for a couple of days, making them want more as the rainy ones came back. The crocuses and tulips began popping up, and the birds sang their sweet songs each morning as they constructed their nests outside the Hendersons' bedroom window.

Like everyone else, Rosemary and Thomas were glad the winter cold was losing its grip, and they were looking forward to warmer spring weather and an upcoming trip to Seattle to see Frank and Margie. The four of them were planning to see the Irish performance of "The River Dance" at the Fifth Avenue Theater. The dancers had been a tremendous hit on both television and on stage a few years before and were making a return engagement with a fresh group of dancers in the troupe. Rosemary expected she and Margie would also take time to do some shopping while they were there. She could use a new pair of jeans and some good walking shoes.

Rosemary came back from a short trip to the tiny grocery store in Grayland and a quick stop at the hardware store to purchase some replacement hardware for the old screen door. She had stopped at the post office, too, and was excited about finding some travel brochures she'd ordered in their box. They'd been talking about an extensive trip somewhere soon. They had not decided whether it would be a cruise or just a visit to another country, maybe France.

She entered the house loaded down with her purchases and humming her favorite song, anxious to look at the brochures with her husband. Rosemary opened the door and stopped suddenly, almost dropping her bags of groceries. Thomas was sitting on the edge of his chair, doubled over and sobbing his heart out. His face was pale and crumpled. Her first thought was that he had physically hurt himself, and her heart stopped. She quickly set her burdens on the floor and rushed to his side in alarm. Falling to her knees in front of him and grabbing his shoulders in her hands, she exclaimed, "My God, Thomas, what is it?"

He tried to tell her what was wrong, but he didn't make much sense through his heartbreaking sobs. Finally, she heard the word "letter" and looking down where he pointed to the floor, she caught a glimpse of the sheet of white paper, halfway hidden beneath the couch next to his chair. A business card lay nearby. She picked both of them up and began to read the letter.

Thomas,

I did a terrible disservice to you fourteen years ago, and though I'm sorry, I don't expect forgiveness. I had our son, and he's a fine young man I named Mathew. To tell you the truth, I wasn't sure he was yours or Nat's. Nat offered to have his blood matched, and it didn't, and he left me shortly afterwards. I am sure he would have, even had Matt been his. I found out later what a sorry excuse of a man he was. I thought he was exciting

and our life—yours and mine—seemed so dull. I was
still trying to grasp the golden ring in my life. I never
found it. I hope you did.

Rosemary paused, looking briefly at her husband's bowed head,
making sure he was okay, and then continued reading the letter.

Matt and I lived okay the first couple of years, but
I squandered your money, as well as mine (you were so
generous) and I (this is difficult to admit) got mixed
up with a guy dealing drugs. I had to sell the condo, of
course. I lost my career, too, and couldn't find another
decent job. I just drifted, my life was the pits, but I did
love our child. He always had food and a caretaker when
I wasn't there. I want you to know that. I found out I
was HIV positive when Matt was ten. It set me straight
but too late. My mother took us in, and as you can see
by the return address, we live in Indiana with her now.

   After a couple of years, I managed to find a job,
but it was not enough to live on our own. Mom and I
don't get along very well. She's old and cranky with Matt
most of the time. I guess I can't blame her. I try to help
around the house as much as I can so she doesn't have
to be so burdened. I owe her what's left of my life, and
that isn't for long.

   That's why I am writing to you. I had an investi-
gator look for you because I wasn't sure where you had
moved. I guessed right when he discovered you were
back on the coast of Washington.

   Thomas, I am dying of AIDS and have very little
time left. I know Mom cannot care for our son after I
am gone. Poor Mathew! I didn't provide him with a very
nice life as an infant, but I really have tried to change
that. In spite of my being a rotten parent, he really is a
nice boy. He needs to be with you, his birth father. Can

you find it in your heart to take him in? I've told him all about you.

He understands what's going to happen to me, and he's agreed to come to you if you'll have him. I would die so much easier knowing he has a chance to grow up normally. So I am pleading with you to take him. He deserves so much.

You do not have to deal with me directly. Joe Stanton, my attorney's representative, will hand-deliver this to you to make sure you get it and will leave his phone number for you to call after you've had a chance to think about it. I know I've probably blind-sided you, but please don't take too long. If you can't see it in your heart to do this, I must have time to look at other options, though at the moment I see none.

Thanks from the bottom of my wretched heart. You are and have always been the nicest of men.

Sincerely,

Kim

By the time she finished reading, Rosemary was crying. She dropped the letter on the floor beside her and put her arms around her husband, hugging him close. "Oh, sweetheart! My heart breaks for you." They cried together for a few minutes, hugging and comforting each other. It was quiet for a while before Thomas found his voice and began to speak.

"Rosemary, in my heart of hearts, I've always felt it was a great possibility, and I worried so about it over the years." Thomas was still white-faced and grim and couldn't seem to look at Rosemary. "This man . . . this man just appeared at our door. It . . . was such . . . a bombshell! Honey, what am I going to do?" Thomas looked up at her finally. His frightened face implored her for an answer to this dilemma, even while he questioned himself. How could he possibly ask Rosemary to take on a child neither of them knew? How could they take on a boy in his early teens, usually the hardest years to raise a child?

Thomas Henderson underestimated his new wife and closest friend. Within a space of a second, she grabbed his hands and said, "What will *you* do? You mean what will *we* do, and right now *WE* are going to call this number and make travel arrangements for him immediately. Of course, we'll take him."

The color began to flow back into his pale face then. Thomas loved Rosemary more in that moment than anyone could love another person. He smiled at her through eyes brimming with tears. He reached for her and pulled her up from the floor and onto his good leg, hugging her tenderly to his chest and laying his cheek against hers, giving a silent prayer for this wonderful woman.

"Are you sure? This could be a big job. It'll change everything for us."

"Then we'll do it together, Thomas, and it can't change how much we love each other." He kissed her. She pulled back, locking his eyes with hers and said, "Do you realize your son is only a little older than my son was when he died? And, Thomas, he has the very same name. Mathew! It's a good omen, don't you think?"

"That's right! I didn't even think about that. Yes, it's a good sign. Rosemary! Honey! What would I do without you? I love you so much."

"I love you, too. Now let me up. We have plans to make."

⚬⚭⚬

Rosemary took a last look at the upstairs room, which she had redone in less than a week, painted in a crisp red, white and blue. It was all ready for their new son. The walls were purposely left free of pictures or any other ornaments. She wanted Mathew to pick out his own accessories, maybe a new spread for the bed. Maybe he would even bring some things along with him. If he wanted a different color on the walls, they would repaint them. His mother had already sent several boxes of stuff that lay unopened and waiting for him to follow.

Her computer, desk, file cabinet, and other writing materials were now stuffed into the "therapy" room, or the "everything room," as it would later be called. There wasn't much space left over, but they would manage okay.

Rosemary still couldn't believe she'd have another Mathew and another chance to have a son, a ready-made son but still a son. She promised herself she would try with all her heart to make it work for the three of them. She and Thomas had a lot of love to give him. Oh, there would be a period of adjustment, she was sure, but she was ready and up to the task, willing to do whatever was required. In fact, she was eager to begin.

The refrigerator was full of food, and his room was ready. Rosemary met her husband at the door. Thomas already had his coat on, and he hugged her before she reached into the coat closet for hers.

"Our life is going to change a great deal now. You know that, and it's too late to back out," he said to her very seriously. "You okay with this, honey?"

"You bet! Now, Dad, let's get this show on the road. It wouldn't do to be late getting to the airport, would it?"

"You're absolutely right. I'd just like to give you one big kiss, though, before you become a mother." And he did.

She grinned at him and wiped her lipstick marks from his mouth with a Kleenex from her pocket before she turned and opened the door.

⌘

They had brought Mathew home with them, and adjustments certainly had been made by all of them, but things had gone very smoothly so far. Their new life with Mathew was working out very well.

⌘

Rosemary took her sandwich and coffee into the "everything" room. It was a little cramped with her writing materials and computer, along with Thomas's exercise machine and photography equipment, but she hadn't regretted for one moment giving up her large beautiful studio above to Mathew.

He'd loved the room and thought it was cool that he had such a great view of the beach. Mathew was delighted to be with them, but he dragged his feet when it was time to register at the school. It wasn't long, however, before he became friends with a couple of nice boys in the area, who were now at the house a good deal of the time. Finally, he settled into school life, making the necessary adjustments as he encountered each new change.

Rosemary sat down with the intention of typing while she had the chance, but after turning on the computer, she sat staring out the window. She loved to look at the beach, although her view wasn't as extensive as it had been from upstairs. The window was open a little, and she felt the cool night air penetrate the room. Moving over to the coat tree where her sweater was hanging, she could hear the awesome sound of the surf across the bay. It was one of her favorite sounds. It always provided a calming type of medicine that cleansed her soul whenever she had a problem or wanted to meditate. She was meditating now about her family.

It was almost seven o'clock on a nice May evening. Dusk was creeping in. There was a tiny bit of red in the sunset to the west—just a line of it across the sky. Rosemary hoped it would be another nice day tomorrow, Saturday. Maybe she could entice Mathew to join her in a morning jog again as he had done the weekend before. He was almost as tall as she was, and they were compatible in their jogging steps. It had been most enjoyable. She could feel the beginnings of a bond between them, but she was careful to ease into it and concentrated on not pushing too hard.

She thought of Mathew and Thomas, saying another little prayer of thanksgiving to God for all the love she had in her life. The last month and a half had been the best she'd ever known. At first, Mathew was a bit shy with her and seemed to do better with his father.

Mathew's mother died shortly after he came to them, less than two weeks later. The boy cried when they told him. Overcome with sadness for the young boy, Rosemary put her arms gently around him, even though she was afraid he might pull away. To her surprise, he clung to her, and she tightened her hold and enfolded him into her arms. Holding back her own tears, Rosemary comforted him by stroking his back and telling him everything would be okay, that she and his father loved him.

Since then, she and Mathew moved on to becoming friends. He was a dream son, so respectful of her and his father. He had many of his father's traits, was kind and loving and seemed to fit right into their lives with little trouble.

He and Thomas were out now at an Ocosta High School Father's Night in Westport. They'd been gone since about five thirty, so she expected them home soon. She knew they were having a good time together.

Rosemary pulled her eyes away from the beach scene outside, which was now mostly in the shadows as the sun dipped below the horizon, and she glanced down at the desk where her book stood. *Making Dreams Come True*—her very own published book! She never tired of looking at it. Rosemary still couldn't believe it was published and was receiving raving reviews. Of course, her agent was as delighted as she was. She was even given an advance on her second book, the one she was working on now. Yes, she had finally done it! She picked the book up, turned it over, and looked closely at herself pictured with Thomas and Mathew on the book jacket. Mathew had arrived soon enough to be included. They looked so nice as a family. Rosemary felt so proud.

She was trying to work on her new novel now and had the best of intentions of getting involved in the third chapter while her family was gone. *Better get at it.* Rosemary twisted in her chair and placed her hands on the keyboard. She opened up her book file with a stroke, and as it popped up on the screen, she heard them drive in.

The car doors slammed; the front door opened.

"We're home," Thomas called out. She could hear his cane tapping across the entry.

"Hi, guys," she shouted back. "I'm in here at the computer."

She heard Mathew going up the steps to his own room as Thomas came into the room to greet her. He leaned over and gave her a kiss.

She smiled at him. "Have a good time?"

"Of course, but I missed you."

Isn't he just so sweet, she thought.

"Get anything done without us in your hair?"

"Nope. Meant to. Just been sitting here daydreaming and being lazy."

"Good, you need some relaxing time," he said as he stripped off his hooded sweatshirt and left the room again.

Rosemary typed a sentence or two, heard Mathew come back downstairs, and then listened to the two of them in the kitchen, doors shutting, dishes clinking. Thomas said something to Mathew, which wasn't audible to Rosemary's ears. Mathew laughed and said, "Sure, Dad!"

"Oh, the hell with it," Rosemary mumbled to herself, hitting the key to save her file and then turning the computer off with a click. She left the study and entered the kitchen. Thomas was waiting by the stove for the teakettle of water to get hot. Cups and packets of hot chocolate mix were spread out on the counter. Mathew was seated at the table.

"Hey, Mom," Mathew said, "want to join us for hot chocolate and marshmallows?"

She was stunned to hear him call her Mom for the first time. Her heart burst with joy at hearing her new title. She grinned at him and wrinkled her nose. "No thanks. Can't stand the stuff." She hadn't been able to drink hot chocolate without remembering Gile. He flashed through her mind for the briefest moment again. Why did she always think of him during her happiest moments? Maybe it was because she knew how lucky she was. *I have other things to do with my time besides thinking of that man,* she thought to herself and tossed him from her thoughts.

Rosemary sat down next to Mathew and draped her arm loosely across the boy's shoulder. He leaned slightly into her. No, Gile Hammond wasn't worth thinking about. She had burned all his books and declared him dead. She had better and bigger things to do with her time. There was a husband to love and a son to raise.

She tightened her arm around Mathew and pulled him closer to her. He turned his head and smiled at her.

EPILOGUE

THE HUGE MANSION OF A HOUSE WAS perched on the hillside above, alone with no other houses in sight. Its large and imposing gate with its fancy grillwork shut out the world at the bottom of the long, steep driveway, which led to the top of the hill. An eight-foot iron fence skirted the property, in some places hidden by trees or hedges, protecting against all unwanted guests. Actually, there were no wanted guests here either; no one ever visited.

Inside, the marble floors in the massive foyer and the hardwood floors throughout the place gleamed in the sunlight filtering through the half-shuttered windows. Although most of the large rooms were not lived in by anyone, everything in every room was in its place with not a speck of dust to be found anywhere. The two maids kept everything immaculate on a daily basis.

Expensive and renowned art pieces, including paintings on the walls and sculptures on small occasional tables, were visible in every nook and cranny. Rich and valuable area rugs were used extensively in every room, most of them purchased and shipped directly from Persia by a professional broker.

There was a servant's apartment on the premises, in the back, and the cook, who lived there, was available to serve her employer at any given moment. With time off for the moment, she was napping.

If visitors had entered the house on this day, they would have found only a tomb-like stillness, no voices, no music, no sounds at all. The house would have appeared to be vacant and empty, but in the huge library in the corner in a chair, sat a man. He sat immobile as if frozen, holding a drink balanced on his right knee, staring straight ahead, his eyes fixed on a wall but seeing nothing.

His mind was working, though his thoughts were grave, graver than death. He was despondent and a little drunk from his third glass of brandy. Finally, after a long length of time, he lifted the glass to his mouth, drained the last of the liquor from it, and slowly pushed himself up to his feet. Moving unsteadily towards the door, he jumped when he suddenly saw his image reflected in a huge mirror hanging next to the archway of the door. It was a stranger who appeared there. If one looked closely enough, one might have found a trace of his once handsome face, but he was no longer young looking; in fact, he had aged way beyond his years in the almost three years since he'd gone to see her. His sideburns once dark were now whitened, and the rest of his hair sprinkled with gray. Deep, dark circles of puffy skin sagged under his sad and tired eyes. The life had literally gone out of him.

Gile Hammond had everything, and yet he had nothing. His wife had been very ill when he'd returned from Washington State, and although she'd had the best of care, she'd passed away within weeks of his return. Gile felt some guilt from his treatment of her, but he had never loved her, and it wasn't long before she disappeared from his thoughts. All he could think about was the money he was going to inherit. There was a lot of it, more than he realized, not that he needed it that much. His books had been on the bestseller lists for a long time.

Actually, there was so much that he didn't know what to do with it all. He was a very rich man. At first, it had been wonderful, an answer to his dreams. All he ever wanted was to be rich, to never have to worry about what anything cost, allowing him to do anything he wanted or go anyplace he desired without constraints.

He refused to be poor again or to live as his mother had in a dirty hovel of a house. Gile wouldn't ever be poor again. Never!

His writings had all been successful, and he had thought about doing another book, but he never did. Although in fiction form, he'd told his life story in three books, there was no more to tell. What else would he write about? He certainly wouldn't tell about his early childhood. That was locked up inside him, there to stay. It had been too awful—his father's beatings, his mother's abandonment. There had never been anyone for him to love or have it returned.

It was only after his third book was published that Gile realized just how much he missed Rosemary and what a void there was in his life without her. He'd enjoyed her so much, their conversations and their lovemaking. In fact, he realized he'd been in love with her, and his heart ached for his loss, a loss of his own making.

To make matters even worse, his beloved and aged dog passed away several short weeks after his wife, and he suddenly found himself completely and terrifyingly alone.

He decided to take a few trips. Gile traveled around Europe for a month, went on a safari in Africa, and took a few weeks to lie in the sun in Hawaii. He had his mansion built while he was gone, and for a time upon his return, he enjoyed the beauty and magnificence of his lovely home. But with time on his hands and idleness his enemy, he began to think of Rosemary more and more. How much he missed her. How badly he had treated her. No matter where he went on his travels, no matter what he was doing, he thought about her and yearned to see her again, to make love to her once again, to feel her body melt into his as it had once done.

He finally made a trip back to the Washington coast, hoping to make amends. Would she ever forgive him for leaving the way he had—without a word? If she had read his last book, and he was sure she had, would she forgive him for that? He was used to getting what he wanted, and now money could buy him everything, almost everything—it wouldn't buy Rosemary back. Just maybe she would talk to him. Just maybe she would accept his sincere apologies and his love for her. If she did, he would make up for all his ill treatment of her. He'd make everything right again. He'd give her anything she wanted, take her any place she wished to go, and they would be so happy together.

It had been only about a year and a half since Gile had left for Washington. He'd been as excited as a kid when he had arrived at the beach again, hopeful that things would go well. The morning after checking in at the old Tokeland Hotel, Gile downed only a quick cup of coffee before hiking down the road towards Rosemary's house. It was a warm April day, and without thinking, he walked right to her favorite writing place where a new stack of disarrayed driftwood had accumulated since the previous winter. He was hoping she would be there or maybe walking out on the beach. Gile looked around but saw no one. He knew he was crazy for thinking she'd still be doing the same thing as if no time had passed at all. As he came back past her house, he could see the place had been remodeled. Maybe she'd sold it and moved away. He didn't have the courage to knock at the door, so he returned to the hotel room, not knowing what to do. Should he stay? Should he leave?

Later in the day after having a bite of lunch and doing a great deal of thinking, Gile gathered up his courage and took another walk towards Rosemary's house. One more look. This time, he watched from across the road as a car turned into her driveway. He squinted and saw that it was she in the driver's seat. There was also a man in the passenger seat beside her. As they stepped out of the car, Gile could see that the man struggled to stand up and then used a cane as he moved on towards the house. Rosemary pulled a bag of groceries from the back seat, then rushed to catch up with him, and assisted him up the steps to the front door. He said something to her, and the two of them laughed together. Gile's heart sank. Who was he? A brother, maybe, or just a friend! *Not likely*, he thought. Then he saw the man pull Rosemary into his arms and kiss her with a familiarity that burst his heart. That's when he knew for sure. He'd lost her, as he deserved to do. He packed up immediately, leaving for home that same afternoon, and for all purposes, his life defeated and over.

The last year and a half had been very painful and very lonely, and Gile no longer wanted to live, his millions not important to him anymore. He had learned that money had its price. But for his greed, he could have had Rosemary. He could have had her love if only . . .

Now he struggled up the stairs and stumbled his way into his bedroom. He was numbed with alcohol and slumped to the bed. Gile sat there for a long time and finally picked up the glass of water and the vial of capsules on the bedside stand. The cap was already off the container. They were ready for him. He sat for a few more minutes, not moving, with the vial in one hand, the glass in the other. Numbly he made the final decision, tipping the vial to his mouth, swallowing the contents, and washing the capsules down his throat with the water.

Gile stretched out on the bed with tears sliding down the sides of his face, closing his eyes. He envisioned Rosemary life-like by his side and could actually feel the warmth of her body against his through his drugged mind. She was there! Rosemary was there, leaning into him, her smile directed at him as her mouth came to meet his. Oh so sweet! Gile put his arms around her, and a calming peace enveloped him.

ACKNOWLEDGMENTS

I WOULD LIKE TO GIVE SINCERE THANKS to my editor, Julie Scandora; to my friend, Sheryn Hara, owner of Book Publishers Network; to her staff, who were involved in the completion of this book; and to my partner, Maine, for his support through this process. Without them and all their help, my dream and the many hours spent working on this novel would never have come to fruition. I also want my family, especially my three sisters—Vivian, Joyce, and Jane, and my friends to know how much I have appreciated their ongoing encouragement regarding my writing endeavors.

ABOUT THE AUTHOR

ROSETTA SMITH grew up in Hoquiam, on the west coast of Washington State. Although marriage took her to the Seattle area, where she and her late husband raised their two daughters, Washington's Pacific coast remained securely in her soul.

Rosemary takes place in Tokeland, Washington, about forty minutes from Hoquiam and an area most familiar to Rosetta. She spent many vacations there with her family and, later, at the summer home of her in-laws. Eventually, she became co-owner of that house, one that held more memories than she can possibly count, and inspired Rosetta to create the background for the book.

Long since retired from working at Seattle Country Day School, Rosetta now lives with her partner, who also lost his spouse. They reside in Bothell, Washington, during the summer and, for five months of the year, enjoy the sun and warmth in Indio, California.

CPSIA information can be obtained
at www.ICGtesting.com
Printed in the USA
FSHW020932011218
54163FS